SOMEONE ELSE

VICTORIA R. BENSON

SOMEONE ELSE

Visit
BLACKDRESSBOOKS.COM
to preview other books authored by Victoria R. Benson:
Captured / Claimed / Concealed
Diamond Cliffs
Indie Songs
Just for Now
Perfect Timing
Reversed Roles

ISBN: 978-1-7325443-6-9

Black Dress Books

DEDICATION:

To all who have loved and lost.

Keep living.

Let change complete its work in you.

Chapter 1

"I'm a freak! No doubt."

You're not a freak. You're... eccentric. Don't be so hard on yourself.

"The fact that I'm sitting here talking to myself is a pretty good sign that I'm a freak."

Just because you have a vivid imagination and you just happen to have no one to talk to at the moment does not make you a freak. If you are that concerned, go find someone to talk to.

"Where am I supposed to find other humans similar to myself?"

Ugh! Try to be normal! There are more than seven billion people on this planet. Certainly at least one of them is like you.

"Gross! I change my mind. Why on earth would I want to hang out with someone who is like me?"

Harmony Hope! Get up and get out of the library! Start by hanging out in places where you can have conversations with people. Try that.

"Okay, so I get up from my comfy spot on the floor way over here in the corner of the Witches, Wizards, and Wanderers section, I pack my books, and I go...?"

"You could go fifty feet that'a way and sit in the coffee shop." The back of a head belonging to a male human spoke softly whilst pointing to his right. "At least then you and the friend you are talking to on your phone could have a conversation without you having to awkwardly whisper and mumble every word."

Harmony gasped, "How much of that did you hear?"

"I heard all of the chatter but only the last few of the actual words. Just trying to help." He walked away.

Harmony sat. Humiliated. She studied the back of the man's head until he turned at the end of the aisle and disappeared. She slid her stretched out feet up toward her torso, gripped her hands around her shins, and placed her forehead gently on her kneecaps. By doing this, she bumped her baseball hat off and it tumbled clumsily down her back. Her messy braids were dangling and itching her cheeks. Silent tears fell. "What is wrong with me?" she whispered to herself.

Nothing is wrong with you. You've lost and now you're lost. Get up. Let's face this.

With that, she was determined to not allow her pity party to last any more than a few final moments. She'd been the sole guest at this gathering for seven months now and she was slowly building up a resistance. Harmony reached behind her and grasped her cap. She pulled it tightly back down onto her head and shifted it low to hide her puffy eyes. This Saturday night had been much like every other since she had moved to this godforsaken town six months earlier. What had she been thinking?

Before standing, resting her head gently on the wall, Harmony imagined what her family was doing tonight three thousand miles away. They'd all be gathered together in a tiny house that sits in an old neighborhood in the heart of the south. They'd be playing board games and card games: cousins, parents, grandparents, siblings, aunts, uncles. They would have had a hodgepodge of all the leftovers in Grandma's refrigerator in anticipation of the big Sunday meal she'd have prepared for them after church services tomorrow.

Sunday dinner is what the meal is called back home when it's eaten in the afternoon. Supper is the meal that is eaten at night. Way out in the west, the word supper doesn't seem to exist. You have lunch during the day and dinner at night time. That was merely one adjustment she had to accept now that she was living west of the continental divide.

Harmony wiped another tear. She worked on convincing herself that she's there for a reason, though she's still not sure of that reason.

A smile came to her shadowed face when she thought about him... then another tear... then a forced smile. He'd say, "Have you lost your mind?! What were you thinking moving so far from home? You need them!" Of course maybe, just maybe, now he might actually say, "I see your future and even without me, it's beautiful. Keep going. There's hope. Please keep going."

Tears now rained down. Harmony wiped her face and then nose with the back of her plaid flannel sleeve. She looked around to see if anyone was lurking nearby. Seeing no one, she whispered, "I'm here because of you. I'm here, in this state, because it reminded me of you, different from anything I'd ever experienced. But, even though I was trying to escape from the memories of you, I think I brought them with me."

An audible encouragement escaped her lips, "'Get up!' Evan would say to me."

Harmony drooped her head. She crisscrossed her legs in front of her and played with her fingernails. Pulling her sleeve over her hand, she wiped her face hopefully for the last time this evening. One of the straps of her overalls had fallen to her elbow, so she secured it back onto her shoulder and fumbled with the metal buttons. "Get up, Harmony," she commanded herself.

New books in hand resting on her hip, backpack flung over one shoulder, feet planted, spine straight, chin up; she walked forward. This week was officially over. Harmony proceeded to the front desk. She scanned each of her books, then pulled the ticket from the kiosk. After neatly stacking them all in her pack biggest to smallest, she pushed her way out the revolving library door.

He watched her unlock her bike and ride away. With meticulous focus, the young man had been peering through an empty slot on the bookshelf one row over captivated by the strange young woman in the corner. He had watched her drop

4

her forehead to her knees, then wipe her eyes and pull her cap down low enough to almost cover them. During those moments, her body language made it clear that she was contemplating something that filled her with grief. When she dropped her head against the wall, he believed she was building courage to move. The only thing that kept him from attempting to console her as he watched her cry was the simple fact that he did not know this girl and she would probably think he was an imposing freak. He smiled when she finally regained her strength. His eyes didn't leave her as she checked out her stack of books. She had gotten five. *I think I'll come back next Saturday to see if she gets five more,* he thought to himself. *Wait, does that make me a stalker?*

He shrugged.

The early autumn night air was chilled, more than chilled, down right cold as Harmony rode home. To keep her mind off of her misery, she lost herself in more thoughts of home, both past and present. Harmony had run far and fast from her former life. Her parents were shaken and terrified for her, but they knew to support her decision and let her go. They told her they understood that she's an adult and only she can repair the damage she feels inside.

Every day had been the same for her since she moved to Idaho. She woke up in her tiny studio apartment in the historic district of town. She went to work in the mornings and attended classes in the evenings. Harmony always studied first, then read a book until bedtime. On Saturdays, she shopped at the fresh market, followed that with hiking or biking, and she concluded each Saturday by checking out new books from the library. Without any close friends to speak of yet, Harmony's only entertainment was *self-motivating* speeches she offered to herself. No matter how encouraging she tried to be, she still felt nothing but out of sorts and lonely.

A girl raised in the south amongst countless relatives, neighbors and friends, Harmony hadn't known loneliness before now. A beauty, a truly breath-taking beauty, Harmony Hope was raised to always look her best, try her best and be her best. There was no obscure pressure on her, it was just a way of life. When you've been given gifts, talents, wits, strengths, or even beauty, you show gratitude and you use those gifts to help others. Harmony was always helpful and she had always shown up prepared to be and give every task her all. That existence got her noticed by just the right guy and it was also the reason she was once again facing life alone.

Shaking thoughts of him out of her head, Harmony tried to remember her ride home and she tried to remember letting herself into her apartment.

"I have got to get out of my head more. I am daydreaming my life away."

Harmony placed her backpack on her table and she glanced at her current work in progress that was already hanging on her wall. Her canvas had the beginnings of a nighttime scene with a brilliant, glowing, full moon. She was still deciding if this moon was lighting the mountains or the ocean, which she longed to hear at the moment.

Harmony gently touched the textures that had been created by the application of the oil paints. So many people think paintings are to be ogled, studied, evaluated, but she liked the feel of the ridges, the swirls, and the pointed peaks that were created by all of the brush strokes that worked together to create a piece. This new, unfinished, mystery scene made her smile.

"Maybe I'm only a freak *sometimes*."

Chapter 2

"Wake up, wake up! Wake up, wake up!" A cartooned mousy voice chirped at her from her phone sitting on her bedside table.

Harmony couldn't believe she had slept late enough for her alarm to go off. She wasn't aware of what time she had fallen asleep reading one of her new books. The book that lay on the pillow next to her was about a princess who had caught the eye of a young wizard. Harmony had a nasty habit of figuring out story lines before finishing entire novels. She was guessing the wizard was disguising his old creepy self behind an attractive facade. She just hadn't decided how the young princess was going to handle the situation. Would she love him for his looks or for his heart? *Weird?* "I'll finish you but you better not disappoint." She spoke to the novel.

Shuffling her bare feet to the shower, Harmony was craving her morning kick start. However, she knew if she had her coffee first, she would grab her book, sit down on her sofa, and never make it to church. One thing she had been raised to do was attend church on Sundays, unless she was honestly ill and Jesus knows the truth. Harmony knows her truth too, and that is, she likes church. She had always loved the congregating of neighbors and family members on Sundays. It's one short hour of her entire week. One hour. It's replenishing. And now, it is sometimes the only thing that gives her the energy to face the following one hundred and sixty-eight hours of the week.

Stepping into the hot spray, sadness oozed out of her pores. Scrubbing her hair and inhaling the sweet aroma of her shampoo awakened her. The gentle exfoliation of the long night from her skin refreshed her senses. Shower complete, she emerged a new woman. Her body, that felt as if it had turned fifty over night, was once again an energized, healthy, twenty-one year old sculptured creation.

Timers have to be the best inventions ever.

Harmony's coffee had made itself, so she wrapped up and fixed her next rejuvenating necessity. With cup in hand, Harmony proceeded to get ready for church.

In the south, church is a big deal. It's part of people's lives and the culture. Out here in the west, church goers are hit or miss. There's no prayer at the sporting events. There's no prayer in the schools. Religion is sporadic. Outdoor activities seem to be the norm, which suits her just fine too.

Harmony Hope dressed… in a dress… a nice one. Then she dried and curled her hair. Finally, she applied makeup as if she were going to a special event, an event like church. Relishing the way her shower uplifts her spirits, and basically snuggling up to her cup of coffee, the lonely hermit felt renewed and ready to emerge to face another week. Legs out stretched from her shell, off she went.

Harmony parked on a narrow side street, gathered her necessities and confidently strode to morning service. Upon entering the building, Harmony found her favorite spot midway down the aisle. The corner seat on the end of the pew was both cozy and functional. Since she was only five feet, four inches tall, she needed an aisle seat or she couldn't see over the heads of the people who sat in front of her. Her preference was to be able to see the pastor; she felt maintaining focus went hand in hand with frequent eye contact.

Although Harmony was living in a decent sized city, she had found a little neighborhood assembly that met in an old, wooden building. This aged church was on a protected registry due to its history. She felt lucky to have found this group because it was a young congregation. Most of the attendees were college students and people in their twenties and thirties. Her boss had mentioned that his son was a member there before he graduated from college and moved to California. He thought Harmony would fit in and find a group of friends there.

Her employer had been mostly correct and Harmony did feel like she fit in. It was the making friends part of the equation that still had not come to fruition. Although, she was fairly certain she had only herself to blame. Casual conversations with people she met were easy for her, but as soon as anyone, male or female, asked her to join them in anything social, she got nervous and made excuses as to why she wasn't available. Harmony was deeply afraid that she just wouldn't be very good company to anyone.

The music began. It filled her. Watching the band forced a smile that could not be contained. Joy began to tingle within her. Her view was blocked. *Seriously?* The back of a head with broad shoulders had slid in front of her. Harmony looked at the girl beside her and raised her eyebrows. The shoulder shrug that accompanied the enlarged eyes instigated a quiet giggle from the female neighbor. Harmony couldn't help but join in and make the decision to find a way to enjoy the back of this man's head. As the music continued playing, Harmony stared.

Not long after resolving to accept her situation, Harmony tilted her head, *Huh, this looks like the back of the head of the man at the library last night.* She thought back, recollecting his hair, his shape, his posture. *I think this is him!* Then out of the blue she thought, *I should marry this guy someday, he has impeccable timing.* An internal laugh ensued.

"Please stand and greet your neighbors in Christian fellowship," the pastor instructed while raising his hands to the heavens.

Harmony Hope stood and shook the hand of the girl beside her first. She turned around and shook hands with a lovely young couple seated behind her who looked like they had stepped out of a magazine. Finally, turning forward once again, she found herself facing the most amazing man she had ever seen in her life. He was tall, but not too tall. Perhaps he was just over six feet. He had almost black hair. It was cut short similar to a military style. His eyes were literally the crystal clear blue color of a cloudless sky. And his smile, beamed! "Hi, my name is Cord." He held his hand out for greeting.

"I'm Hope." Slowly her right hand extended itself with no apparent help from her.

Softly clasping and shaking her hand, Cord said, "Hope?"

"Yes. Hope, just Hope."

Thinking her need to add "just" to her introduction was odd, he emphasized his response, "Well *Hope*, it's very nice to meet you."

"Nice to meet you too."

"Hey, I'm not blocking your view am I?" he asked politely.

"Just a little bit, but I'm sure I'll survive," was her honest reply.

Snap out of it! was her pounding thought.

Though neither truly wanted it, their hand release was mutual as he offered his explanation, "Sorry 'bout that. I was sitting farther down the pew, but a large group entered from the side aisle so I scooted down here to the end to give them all room. Since I'm blocking you, I'll just go sit somewhere else."

"No!" *Too much, pull it together*. "Um, no, please don't do that. I'm fine. I'll lean or move over if I feel it's necessary."

Hope finally gathered her wits and was able to relax.

"Well, how 'bout if I sit there beside you then. You can keep your seat on the end. I'll scoot right in and be out of your way."

"Sure, that'll be fine if you want. There's room." She responded in her soft, sweet, southern drawl.

Cord was infinitely thankful that this dream of a human being hadn't gone along with his stupid idea of him moving somewhere else. He was also grateful that she didn't seem to mind him sitting next to her either. In reality, she probably either had a boyfriend, because a girl like this would never be single, or she wouldn't be interested in him anyway. He's just a plain ol' Idaho boy. She looked as if she'd stepped off a runway in New York. Although, she sounded like she'd been carefully plucked out of a country music video, because she was far too pretty to be in it in the first place. *Yes,* he thought, *she's too pretty for even country music videos. I don't stand a chance.*

Cord slid smoothly past Hope. His cologne was hypnotizing. He took his place next to her and looked down. She felt his eyes on her so she turned slowly wanting another glance at them. They exchanged smiles.

I think I just made my first friend, she thought.

I hope I just made a new friend, he thought.

"You may be seated." The pastor guided the congregation by turning his palms face down and lowering his hands.

They sat. They listened.

Cord sat with one ear on the pastor and the other ear on the voice in his head. It was a fifty-fifty battle. He wanted to talk to her. He wanted to hold her hand. At one point, Hope bent down to get a pen from her purse. When she did, her elbow brushed his knee. He jerked it away giving her room to dig in her bag. "Sorry." She had mouthed to him thinking that she had invaded his personal space. He lifted his hand and whispered back, "No worries." He then winked at her while sharing his inviting smile. She swore she heard a *ting* and literally had to bite her lip to keep from laughing at her imagination.

When she rose with her pen, she was still trying not to laugh at herself. Then, *You're ridiculous Hope. This guy is never going like you as anything more than a friend. You've already been in love. You don't get it twice.* Her smile faded and she turned her attention to the journal she had placed in the pew rack in front of her when she stood for hymns and greetings. The sermon began, she reached for her book and opened it to an untouched page. Her pen seemed to move on its own.

At the conclusion of the sermon, just before they were all released, Cord gently touched the back of her hand with his index finger. "Hope," he said softly leaning close to her ear.

She had left this world and entered another. Her heart had joined the message being offered and her mind had to sketch the visions. Startled, she jerked her face in his direction. He was so close. She didn't mind. "Yes," she responded using the same tone she had received from him.

"Your work there is remarkable."

She looked down. On the page, she had drawn a lone rugged cross set on a hill surrounded by barren land. There was a pathway leading away from it into the desert. But the pathway to it was peppered with tiny flowers adorning dew drops. The pastor had spoken of how lonely life is without faith, though with faith, hope and love in your heart, there is eternal peace and beauty.

Hope wasn't fully aware of what she had drawn. She didn't even remember cognitively planning a picture. Her mind simply listened while her hand scribbled. She replied, "Thank you Cord. It's just a pastime. I don't usually let anyone see my work." She remembered how the only person who had ever had full access to her journal drawings was him, Evan.

"You shouldn't hide such beauty. If you share your gift, others may find peace and joy in it." Then he dared to ask, "Can I see the others?" He held out his hand.

She looked at him first with shock, then insecurity turned into contemplation. His question had taken her breath away, and although she had softened and nearly submitted, Hope still answered, "Not yet."

Cord pulled his hand back slowly. He was terrified that he had offended her. How could he have been so forward? He knew having her in his life was hopeless, so he said, "Okay, *after* lunch perhaps." He thought, *why not just put yourself out there Cord? If she is going to run the other way, she might as well go now.* Cord had only sat next to her for forty-five minutes. Life would go on. Although he was very interested in this girl, he'd keep looking for the perfect someone, somewhere else.

Harmony squeezed her journal, but *Hope* mustered the courage to look at him again. By this time, the congregation had been released, yet these two new acquaintances remained unaffected by the exiting commotion that surrounded them.

Wrapping her dainty, soft fingers around his tan wrist, Hope placed his left palm on her journal. She smiled. He was unsure as to whether he was supposed to take it or freeze, so he froze.

"Repeat after me," she began.

He smiled at her and almost chuckled. *I like her.* "Okaaaay…"

"I, Cord what's his name," she said with a serious countenance.

"I, Cord what's his name," he mimicked her tone and expression and clearly suppressed a laugh.

"Do solemnly promise," Hope guided.

"Do solemnly promise,"

"To never, ever, ever laugh at Hope's drawings."

"Wait! What if they're funny?" He tried to negotiate.

"Say it." She was stern and unscathed.

"Fine, I solemnly promise to never, ever, ever, or was it just two evers?" he asked. She raised her eyebrows, he continued, "laugh at Hope's drawings. There I did it, but I don't know why you think I would laugh at your work. If the others are anything like the one you just drew, I can't imagine laughing at them."

Each was now equally mesmerized by the other. Every glance and expression spoke volumes. Hope smiled shyly as she pressed the journal upward with her left hand into his palm. When he curved his fingers around it, she released his wrist. With him sitting on her right, she turned her face and stared blankly over her left shoulder while she waited for him to thumb through the pages. A few wows were whispered. She listened to his breathing. He would take a deep breath every so often. She wondered which ones spoke to him and which ones didn't, but she could not watch.

Cord raised his head and noticed the sanctuary was nearly empty. The only people who still remained were the band members who were tearing down their setup and a few ushers who were picking up programs and coffee cups that had been left behind. Before regaining her attention, Cord took a moment to plan their next interaction. Unsure of how Hope was going to respond, he decided to move forward, but first, he really wanted to see her face. Cord lifted her right wrist and placed her palm on the journal. When she gripped it, he released her.

"It's time for lunch, Hope. Let's go."

His confidence was familiar to her so without hesitation, she turned and said, "Sounds good. I'm ready. Yes, I'm ready."

Chapter 3

"See you two next Sunday," the pastor called to them as they were exiting the antiqued, rustic room. Hope and Cord looked over their shoulders and waved.

Cord walked two steps behind her. The guilt he felt over how enamored he was with her was pecking at him like a tiny bird. He admired her long, softly curled, light brown, barely blonde, hair. It was the perfect compliment to her baby blue eyes that were encircled with a slate blue ring. He realized he was already memorizing her features. Upon this realization, he tried reminding himself that even though he met her in church, it's okay to find her attractive. Affection is affection. There's no rule that says you can't find someone at church attractive. Married couples don't check their hearts at the door, why should he?

Hope could feel his eyes bearing down on her as she stepped through the doorway into the late September, autumn air. There was a light breeze and the leaves had turned yellow, orange and red. A strand of her hair blew across her cheek and stuck to her lips. She looked over her shoulder to Cord just as she pulled the rogue strand away and tucked it behind her ear.

He was silent though still focused on her every move. Relief that she had been raised to make her best presentation in public eased her nerves. You never know who you may meet on any given day. This day, she was glad she had met Cord.

Hope stopped at the top of the steps and placed her hand on the railing. Cord was on her left and he stepped to the opposite side of the iron bar. Her shoulder was bare. *Don't stare. Don't stare. Say something, h*e thought, but alas, he was simply speechless.

Her outfit of choice that morning wasn't selected with the intention of attracting anyone. Hope simply pulled on her winter-white, off-the-shoulder, fuzzy sweater dress. However, Cord was very much appreciating how it only reached down to her mid thighs and it clung perfectly to her young figure. He was even aware of how her high-heeled, over-the-knee, brown, leather boots complimented her style. He wondered if she always looked this perfect. Her presentation from every direction was more than satisfying.

Just try to be normal Hope. Keep it together. "Well, where are we going to eat?" she asked with a perk to her voice.

"That's up to you. Do you have a favorite place?"

"I've only lived here for six months. I hardly ever venture to restaurants and when I do, I stick to downtown mostly because it's walking and biking distance from my apartment. I eat most meals at home… alone." She was immediately sorry she added that last word. *Keep smiling Harmony. Don't feel sorry for yourself.*

"Alone huh? We can change that starting today. Let's go to brunch at the Miner's Ballroom. They have great food. It's ironic ya know? Scruffy miner's eating in a ballroom?"

Hope laughed and asked, "Soooo... am I over dressed or under dressed then?"

"Uh, you're perfectly dressed. Most people go there looking fairly nice. It's a popular place for after church brunches with a lot of the North Villagers. You know, those of us who live here north of downtown?"

"Yeah, I picked up on that title pretty quickly when I moved here. Being a southerner, it was humorous to be called a North Villager the second I took my keys from my landlord."

"You'll have to tell me all about your move here over brunch."

Unsure yet hopeful she asked, "Do you want to tell me where the restaurant is and I can meet you there?"

"No, ride with me." He didn't hesitate to command.

Thrilled by his response, Hope squeezed her shoulders upward toward her ears and grinned. He was equally pleased that she seemed eager to join him.

Cord pulled his keys out of his pocket and Hope tightened her grip on the railing. Descending stairs in those boots was mildly tricky and falling down said stairs in that outfit would be mortifying. Noticing her reliance on the railing Cord thought, *Idiot, why would you put a medal cage between you and this girl. You should have offered her your arm. She's never going to like you, at least not for long.* He smiled at her and nodded his head in the direction of his car, "This way." This time though, he placed his hand on her lower back in an attempt to make up for his previous oversight.

Cord guided Hope to his car and told her they'd return for her's later. As they approached his SUV she complimented his taste in vehicles. "Nice 4Runner! They didn't have one in sunshine yellow? Black was the brightest you could find?"

"You're cute." He opened her door and Hope slipped in like she'd done it a thousand times. He snuck a peek at her thighs as her dress hem slid up a bit. Not noticing his glance, she instinctively tugged her dress downward in modesty. He gently closed her door.

When he climbed into the driver's seat, Hope crossed her right knee over her left and tucked her bag on the floor between her left ankle and the center console. She then fluffed her hair, pulled it over her bare shoulder and let it drape naturally. He actually loved how comfortable she was making herself. They both felt like she belonged right there.

Cord cranked the car, turned on the radio, lowered the volume, and pulled away from the curb.

"So Cord, how old are you and what do you do?" Hope asked with her chin resting on the heel of her hand.

He looked over at her. She melted. Straining to form a clear thought, he stuttered, "Uh, um, I am twenty-five and I work for my dad's accounting firm."

"Hm," she responded.

"That's it? Nothing else to offer? Just 'Hm'?"

"I'm thinking. Give me a minute." She thought about what else she wanted to know about him, then asked, "Where did you go to college and did you grow up here in Riverton?"

Watching the road he answered, "I did grow up here in this valley, but in a town just west of Riverton. I've been here my entire life and I even went to college at Riverton University. I lived in a dorm for two years, then in an apartment for four years. I moved home to save money for a short while. Then, I bought a house in the Village a year ago. I live west of the church. It's walking distance, but as the weather gets colder I usually drive over."

"Same. I live to the east about six blocks, then turn toward the hills and go another three blocks. I've been driving now that it is getting chillier too. Besides, walking in three inch heels is not as fun as it looks." *If he is from here, he probably has a trail of girlfriends around. Who cares? Have a nice afternoon Hope!* She added, "It sounds like you prefer to stick close to home, Cord."

"I do. I like it here. I travel a lot though. I'm single. Most of my friends from college and high school are all still single too, so we take trips a couple of times a year together. My busy season at work is January to May, so I have time to spare during the summer and early fall."

Hope had been so focused on Cord's voice that she hadn't paid any attention to the short drive. When the car stopped, she was still leaning on her elbow on the center console with her attention on him. He looked at her and announced, "We're here."

Snap out of it, Hope!

I think she likes you, Cord.

"Oh, sorry I was staring. I was waiting for you to tell me about your favorite travel destinations." She made up a quick excuse for her ogling.

"We'll get to all of that soon. Let's go eat. I'm starved and there may be a wait."

Cord got out of the car and Hope sat still. She had been taught to allow young men the chance to be gentlemen. He did not disappoint. He opened her door and offered her his hand. She picked up her bag as she slid off of the seat and onto the road. As they approached the entrance to the Miner's Ballroom, Cord scooted ahead and opened the door for her. They entered the restaurant with his hand placed once again on her lower back. She was so glad she was wearing long sleeves because he gave her goosebumps with his gentle touch. She missed that feeling and wanted to turn and give him a hug and a kiss, but she didn't dare.

Once they were seated, had ordered and were enjoying their meal, Cord desperately wanted to know more about her daily life. He was already wondering if she would be willing to see him again and the sooner the better. *I think she might like me, but if not, let's just get this over with.* "What are your plans this week? Do you work or go to school? What do you do for fun?" He took a bite waiting for her reply.

"I work for a doctor. I don't believe he needs me as much as he says he does though. I think he feels sorry for me and wants me to be successful. My personal assessment of the situation is that I'm sort of his employee slash scholarship recipient."

"Well, you can't complain about that. He sounds like a dream. How'd you meet him?"

"He was in line behind me at the market my first weekend here. I had my calculator out and was adding up the cost of the things I wanted and needed. He asked me why I was taking so much time to buy my groceries and I told him I was on a very tight budget because I didn't have a job yet. He said, 'I'll hire you if you'll just move along. I have somewhere to be and my wife will have my head on a platter if I come home without these groceries.' I looked at him like he was crazy and told him to go in front of me because I may have to put some things back anyway and he said, 'Seriously, here's my card. I'll see you at my office Monday morning at seven.' I almost fell over. He's also the person who told me about the church we attend."

"Wow! So you were offered a job just like that?"

"Yes. Dr. Morris was even willing to let me work around my school schedule. I work from seven to three for him and then go straight to school for my four and five o'clock classes. I get home around seven each night, study, read, and then go to bed. Every day has been the same for six months."

"If Monday thru Friday are the same, what are your weekends like?"

"Shopping, biking, hiking, reading, studying on Saturdays, and then all of those with church added in on Sunday's."

"When do you hang out with friends or, um, go on dates?" A casual question followed by, *What were you thinking asking her that?!* Cord scolded himself.

Hair tuck, focused on plate, Hope replied, "I don't have friends or dates." *Don't look up! Act nonchalant and take a bite.*

Wanting her to look up, Cord bent down trying to see her expression but not make it obvious that he was begging for her eyes. "No friends... or dates huh? Sounds lonely or boring."

"I stay busy enough." *Don't look at him yet. You're not ready.*

I've struck a nerve. I'll have to figure that one out. "So back to the calculator, I'm really not trying to be nosey, but couldn't your parents help you out a little bit? I mean if you came all the way out here from the coast of North Carolina, wouldn't they want to make sure you were going to be secure?"

"They were helpful. They said, 'Figure life out Ha, Hope.'" She almost said her other name, which she hates. She continued, "'We'll help you get started and if you ever need anything, call us, but try to do this on your own. Go be alone or find friends or fall in love.'" She regretted saying that last part but continued, "'Just make your own life. We'll all be here with open arms waiting for you to come back whether it's for a visit or forever.'"

She needed to change the focus, "They can certainly afford to support me, but why should they? I'm an adult. I've got this. I get up each day and step through everything that comes at me." *Suck it up! You are NOT helping yourself!* "I've lived like a princess my entire life. I can live in a tiny, studio apartment for a while. It's not going to hurt me to work and support myself. I'm just thankful I only need one job. That's what the calculator is for!" She finally looked up and grinned at him.

Cord gave an agreeable expression. "I guess you're right. What difference does it make if you are in a huge house or a tiny apartment as long as you are happy?"

She leaned on her forearms on the edge of the table and said, "Yeah… happy…" then realizing she was dangerously close to being improper, she slid her hands politely to her lap.

How could she think I care about where the heck she places her arms?

Since they both were finishing their meals, Cord decided to state his position on this brunch. He raised his eyebrows and spoke with definitiveness, "Hope, the check is going to be delivered soon. Please don't get out your calculator. I've got this."

She laughed and thanked him. Then she added, "So you are either my first friend or my first date."

"Wait, you've never been on a date before?" He was shocked.

"No! My first date here, in Idaho, silly!"

"Whew! I was thinking perhaps your parents raised you in a convent or worse, you are some freak!"

Deciding to mess with him, though his second choice wasn't far from her own personal truth she said, "No, I was not raised in a convent!"

"Funny!" He smiled fully aware of her implication. "I highly doubt you are a freak... not that I'd mind anyway. At least you would certainly be a lovely freak."

"Thank you." She closed her eyes and nodded as if accepting a compliment from a royal.

Here goes... "What do you want to do next, Hope?"

She thought, *I'm going to see where this goes today,* then answered, "I'd like to get my car, go home and change clothes, then, I don't know. Did you have something in mind?"

"You said you hike or bike on weekends. Do you want to do something like that?"

"Can we do something less outdoorsy today? Would you be interested in doing something as boring as going to the art museum?"

AW! Why didn't I think of that? Cord's actual response was cool and collected. "I haven't been to the art museum since I was in elementary school. That sounds like a great idea."

"I haven't ever been to Riverton's art museum but I do love them all. I check their website quite often and they have a very whimsical exhibit right now. There'll be a da Vinci exhibit beginning in March. I've been waiting on pins and needles to see that one. I've seen a da Vinci exhibit at the Smithsonian, but it'll be fun to see one way out here in Riverton." Her eyes sparkled and all sorrows and insecurities disappeared when she spoke of art. She knew this about herself.

"March huh? That sounds fun." Cord agreed with excitement though trying not to match hers. He didn't want to seem to desperate. *March, that's a good sign.* "Do you still want to change? You can tour an art museum in that outfit."

"You're right, let's just go straight there."

Cord stood and pulled Hope's chair out for her. She reached for his hand. He took it and for the second time that afternoon she wished she could kiss him. He gently assisted her to her feet. Instead of waiting to see if he was going to release her, she decided to take control and secure her grip into his hand as they made their way out of the restaurant. He squeezed to let her know that he was glad she did that.

The tour of the Picaso like, cubism, novice paintings was entertaining. Cord had a lot of questions and a lot of critiques. They laughed and Hope defended the artists relentlessly.

"My blind dog could do this!"

"Cord! You're missing the point. This is someone's treasured creation. It's colorful and it makes your brain imagine. It forces your eye to look for reason. It simplifies art yet gives snobs something to sound pretentious about during their discussions. Don't you get it?"

"Now that I get! Yes! That all makes a lot more sense. I believe I'm officially ready for every art exhibit in the world. Bring 'em on. I got this."

During their moment of joy and compromise, she took his hand in hers and held his bicep with her other. She pulled him to face her and she smiled looking up into his captivating eyes, "Not all art has to make sense, Cord."

"Well your art makes sense," he said. Then he gently ran the backs of his fingers down her cheek. He whispered, "Your drawings *are* treasured creations."

"Those are just sketches, scribbles from my heart. I have others that I can show you sometime that I'm more proud of."

"I'd love that."

"Wait, did you say you have a blind dog?" She asked unsure of what she'd heard earlier.

"Yup, just one."

"Just one. How many blind dogs to people usually have around here?"

"No, I meant only one of my dogs is blind."

"How many dogs do you have?"

"Three. Lumpy is the blind one. He's old, fat and lazy so blindness works well for him."

Hope huffed a small laugh and pressed her forehead to his shoulder. They gave their position another five seconds and then mutually backed away. The museum options had been exhausted. It was time to take Hope home or time to find another way to cling to the remaining hours of the day together.

"Coffee?" he asked.

"It's four-thirty. Why don't we call it day? I get up early so having coffee past a certain time of day makes for a very restless night. Besides that, my feet have had enough. You can join me for tea at my tiny apartment if you don't mind tight spaces." She offered instead.

"That sounds great. I'd love to join you for tea." Cord gave a slight bow. Hope curtsied in response.

Cord delivered Hope to her car and then followed her home. He parked on the street when he saw her pull into a driveway. The house she lived in was an immaculate, newly updated, Cape Cod styled cottage. It was painted gray with white trim. Judging from what he could see above ground, he assessed that Hope probably was not exaggerating about her fraction of it being tiny.

After getting out of her car, Hope walked to the street to wait for Cord to join her. "My entrance is around back," she said pointing.

As she led him through the back gate, he noted the professionally coiffed shrubs. The hedges were thick and lined both sides of the property. The fence was a freshly oiled, wood, privacy fence. Before they even reached the steps that led down to her apartment Cord stopped her, "Hope, what if you come home late at night? Doesn't walking back here in the dark worry you?"

"If I come home too late or feel uneasy, I have a key to the front door. There's an entrance to my apartment from inside the house too. Garrett doesn't mind me coming through that way. I don't do it very often. Also, he's usually home so if I were to scream he'd probably hear me."

"Is your landlord married or does he have other roommates?"

"No, he's single and he lives alone."

"Hm, how old is he?"

"I don't know?"

"Is he twenty or fifty?" Cord pried.

"Probably in his twenties or early thirties would be my guess."

"You live here alone with a strange man who may be in his twenties?"

Our first date and he certainly is inquisitive. "Can we go inside, Cord? My feet really hurt, and I'm cold."

"Sure. Sorry. I was just curious."

"Mmm hmm... Sounds like it." Hope rolled her eyes at him and shook her head. She led Cord to the back of the house and down the narrow steps that were enclosed by concrete walls. The house wasn't built on a slope, so her basement apartment was completely underground with the standard dugout, concrete, window wells. Her living space was only half of the basement so it was especially small.

"Make yourself at home. I'm going to go change. I'll only be a minute." As she walked away from him she added, "You are welcome to see if there is anything you'd like for a snack or to drink in my kitchen slash dining room slash living room."

He laughed, "I'm good. I'll sit here on your couch slash guest bed slash table and wait for you."

"Ha! Good one. Suit yourself." *He's funny.*

Hope emerged dressed in leggings, a sweatshirt, and thick fuzzy socks pulled up to her knees. She spun around modeling her casual attire and he clapped. After her fashion show, she went to her kitchen to heat water for tea.

"Cord, it's time to eat again, do you want to eat here?"

This is a good sign. She's not trying to get rid of me. "Sure. What did you have in mind?"

"I can make us a big plate of nachos and a salad if you'd like."

"Perfect, can I help?" he replied.

"If you don't get claustrophobic you are welcome to join me." Hope nodded her head toward her location inviting him over.

Cord was excited to get his hands busy. He was nervous and didn't want to sit there and stare at the walls or her. Stepping to her side he said, "Just tell me what you want me to do."

They teamed up and prepared their dinner and tea. Within a few minutes they were seated at her bistro table enjoying another meal together. Hope tucked her feet under her and clasped her warm tea cup in both hands. She did more sipping and Cord did more eating. Conversation flowed naturally between them as they talked about his vacations and her's. They briefly discussed families and siblings, and laughter was shared as they told stories of crazy pets. After an hour of enjoying each other's stories, they cleaned their dishes.

With clean up complete, Hope gathered the courage to say, "Cord, you can stay a bit longer unless you need to get going. You're my first guest other than Garrett and I'm not entirely sure he counts since his visits are sporadic and only to repair something or open a jar. I'm enjoying your company. I've been down here alone for six months. I forgot what it was like to talk to someone other than my boss, co-workers or professors."

"I'd love to stay. It's only six o'clock. I don't have anywhere to be." *Don't say it Cord. I have to...* "I don't like that you're alone here. You have me now, so no more loneliness and no more calling someone else to open jars for you. Oh, I kill spiders too." He felt like covering his eyes and peeking through his fingers to see if she had a 'How dare you!' expression. He held firm and maintained eye contact though.

"You must be pretty darn fast if you think you can get here in time to kill a spider for me. Have a seat Cord."

Cord went directly to her couch and sat in the corner against the wall. Hope followed. Standing over him she asked, "May I sit next to you?"

"You better," he responded with authority.

She smiled and handed him the remote. "Find a game, Cord," she instructed scooting right up next to him. He wrapped his arm around her shoulder, and she leaned against him placing her left hand gently on his chest.

The next thing she heard was, "Hope, Hope," he whispered while delicately stroking her cheek and pressing a kiss to the top of her head.

"Hmm..."

"It's nine-thirty. Time for me to go home and for you to go to bed."

Astonished that she had fallen asleep, Hope pressed her face to his shirt then pulled her body to an upright position. "Sorry I passed out on you. I hope you don't take offense. I guess I was or am really tired."

"No offense taken at all. This was a perfect way to end a perfect day." He then smiled at her and said, "Pressures on, Hope. This day will be a tough one to beat. You up for the challenge?"

She chuckled and replied with the standard, "Challenge accepted."

After they exchanged good night hugs, and Cord took the opportunity to kiss her on the side of her head once more, Hope closed the door behind him. Without proceeding through any of her usual nighttime rituals, Hope collapsed on her bed and fell fast asleep thinking only of one man this night.

Chapter 4

At seven o'clock Monday evening, Hope pulled into her designated parking spot at home. After gathering her assortment of totes for the day, she clambered out of her car. Needing momentum, due to carrying a full load of books, a lunch bag containing empty leftover dishes, a heavy purse, and a backpack complete with her laptop, she shoved her car door closed with her foot.

Stumbling to the gateway of her underground palace, Hope concentrated on the positioning of her possessions. Trying to adjust and shift everything, she fought clumsily to grip the chain that would unlatch the lock. It swung open and she sighed an exhale of relief thinking she had somehow managed to inadvertently open the gate.

"It's been twenty-one and a half hours since I've seen you, Hope."

His voice caused a quick, though shrill, scream to escape her throat. "Geez, Cord! What the heck!? You don't know that Garrett wouldn't shoot you if he saw you sneaking around back here. Why didn't you just call me and tell you were coming over or perhaps you could have waited in your car until I got home? Either of those or a million other choices would have been excellent and far less criminal minded ideas."

"You're funny! I talked to Garrett and asked him if I could wait back here. He said he didn't mind. He has a nice yard. I didn't want to sit in my car. And... I didn't call you because I never got your phone number. You'll be happy to know that Garrett wouldn't give it to me and I didn't want your boss thinking you had a stalker so I didn't call Dr. Morris to try to get it. Waiting here was harmless enough."

"Harmless for you! I could have had a heart attack."

"Well since you didn't, do you want to go get dinner?"

Hope stood with her arms and hands full contemplating all she still had to do before she went to bed to build up strength to conquer yet another twelve hour work day. Her back was beginning to hurt. As if Cord read her mind, he suddenly started pulling her bags from her. Appreciating the relief she said, "Cord, I already ate at school. I pack a lunch and dinner every day. Eating out is not in my budget. Also, I have homework and I'm very tired. Our lives are extremely different. I'm not the girl who is going to be ready to party seven days a week."

"What? I don't want a party girl. I just wanted to have dinner with you."

He was so sincere, there was no way she was going to be able to resist him. No deliberation was needed. A quick nod toward her steps was given. "Come on Cord. Let's put all of this stuff inside. Then, let's get you something to eat." They proceeded to her humble home.

Hope unlocked the door and flipped the light switches. Every light in the main room of her studio illuminated. Cord had collected her lunch bag, her tote and the textbooks that were too large for her full backpack. He placed those items on the table while she walked directly to her bedroom to put her backpack away. Returning to him, she asked, "So what are you in the mood to eat this dark, chilly evening? Oh, and before you answer, I am not in a mood to eat out. I have to study."

Her question significantly narrowed his options solely to whatever she had to provide. So, he replied, "I guess you plan on feeding me then?"

Hope laughed. "I don't plan on feeding you, but I do plan on fixing you something to eat that you are more than welcome to feed yourself."

The mental image he conjured up of her feeding him made him cover his mouth and laugh with such energy even a few gasps for air were necessary. Hope stood straight faced as if she was not amused, although, she truly was. The sound of his joy made her want to rush to him and throw her arms around his neck. Not knowing how he would feel about that, she restrained and finally joined him with a few chuckles of her own.

"Do you want me to just surprise you?" she offered.

"Sure. That sounds perfect."

"Very well. You are welcome to help or you may turn on the TV. I'm guessing there is a football game on that may hold your interest while you await your dinner."

Cord nodded and looked at her television. He suggested, "What if I find the football game *and* help you fix us something to eat?"

Hope nodded and took the two steps that were needed to place herself in the center of her kitchen. He turned on the football game, then joined her.

"Get ready for a culinary delight," she bragged.

"Sarcasm?"

"Mmm... maybe. But, I'm actually glad you came over. I can cook your dinner and my lunch for tomorrow at the same time. You have actually helped me out. If you hadn't shown up like a starved vagrant, I would have gotten right to my studying and reading and just taken a PBJ for lunch tomorrow. Now, I'll have real food to eat." She smiled at him.

"Good. Glad I could help. So what's for dinner?"

"Well, since I am on a budget, we'll be having grilled chicken, homemade mac-n-cheese and baked Brussel sprouts."

"What does all that have to do with a budget? That sounds like a lot of food."

"These are just all very inexpensive basics that can be prepared in less than 30 minutes. That's all."

Cord was intrigued and offered, "Feel free to tell me what you need from me." He watched and waited.

First, Hope set the oven on four-fifty, then she placed a pot of water on the stove top. Next she pulled out one large chicken breast and Cord thought, *Remember to bring food next time.* Slicing it into three fillets, she was sure to leave the center cut thickest for him. Hope planned on eating the top slice tonight and the bottom tomorrow. Before placing the seasoned chicken fillets on the grill pan, she dumped elbow noodles into water and set a timer for fifteen minutes. When the oven beeped, signifying it was preheated, Hope brushed a baking sheet with olive oil, placed halved sprouts face down on the surface, brushed the tops with oil and lightly seasoned them. As soon as the vegetables were in the oven and the noodles were boiling, she put the chicken on the heated grill pan. While all of those items cooked, her final task was to make the homemade sauce for the mac-n-cheese.

Finally, Cord was given his instructions. Hope said, "I'm going to need you to stir the sauce and do not stop."

"Got it!" He gave a salute and a serious nod.

While butter and flour in the warmed frying pan for the brine were being mixed, cream was poured. As the sauce thickened, three different cheeses were added. Cord stirred and watched. No words had been exchanged thus far and he was feeling as if he had really become and inconvenience. He asked, "Hope, do you not believe in socializing while you cook?"

Focused on his attention to his one and only task, though a very important one, she replied, "I hadn't given any thought to what we should say. I'm just trying to get dinner done so we can sit and relax." Hope looked up and winked at him before stirring the noodles and flipping the chicken. "The sauce is done Cord." She turned off the eye of the stove. The timer still had six minutes on it so she suggested, "How 'bout we talk now if you'd like."

In awe of this beautiful, kind, studious, young woman, Cord decided again to be bold and be willing to walk away if his actions offended. He put a plan into motion. Cord placed the whisk on the counter and emptied her hands of the spoon she held from periodically stirring the boiling noodles. "Is everything okay here for six more minutes?" he asked.

Hope looked everything over, cracked open the oven door, closed it back, looked up at Cord, and innocently replied, "Yep. Why do you ask?"

One glance at his eyes and her instincts kicked in. She remembered this look. Her heart warmed but then it panicked. No one had ever touched her or even kissed her except Evan. *He's going to know I'm a complete idiot! What do I do? What do I say? Just wait Hope. See what happens.* She turned her head but kept her eyes on Cord's trying to act mature.

Cord took both of her hands and slowly pulled her toward him. When she was close enough to reach around, he placed his hands on her waist. Naturally, she slid her hands to his arms and held just above his elbows. Cord smiled at her and she easily returned the sentiment. She may have even flirted while welcoming his hold on her.

Making no effort to disengage from this moment, Hope remained in Cord's arms. Completely unaware of what was happening, her eyes were seeing Cord, but her mind was watching Evan lure her. The time she had had with Evan often played like a movie, a favorite movie she would never get to watch again. The two remained transfixed as Cord continued stepping away from the kitchen and toward her couch. Hope was literally following blindly.

"Watch your step," he sweetly cautioned and the spell was broken. She focused her attention back to this moment and was suddenly unable to move. The two had been swaying in sync as if in the midst of a slow dance, so when she stopped, he stopped.

"Are you okay?" he asked.

Needing a moment to decide, she stalled by sliding her hands from his arms to his wrists and she slipped her fingers in between his. Then, lowering their hands together to their sides, she answered, "I am okay, just nervous I guess."

Cord was confident in what he was doing although not so confident moving forward with Hope. He truly didn't want to scare her away by appearing needy or too aggressive. With their fingers interlocked, he tightened his grip and decided to commence their motion toward her couch once more.

You like him Hope. Don't be afraid. Evan moved way faster than this with you. He never gave you an option. Okay stop thinking about Evan. She kept her eyes on Cord's praying he couldn't read her mind.

When they finally stood in front of her couch, Cord turned their bodies so Hope's calves brushed the edge of the center cushion. He released her hands and she placed them on his waist. Then, holding her upper arms, he gently lowered her. Once Hope was seated, he knelt in front of her and placed his hands on her outer thighs near her knees.

With no thought whatsoever, Hope said feeling mildly stressed, "Cord, I have, uh, I haven't ever, um…"

He knew what she was trying to say even though she didn't need to. His thought, *Thank heavens*. His words, "Good. You shouldn't."

Embarrassed, she turned her face and pressed her cheek to her shoulder.

"Hope, please don't worry. I brought you in here so you could rest. I'm going to go finish dinner. I'll bring you a plate in a few minutes."

Hope was shocked. "What? You didn't bring me in here to…"

"Uh, no. I did not. You look tired. You're doing all of the work. And I am more than capable of stirring, flipping, and straining anything. It's not your job to work for twelve hours just to come home and have some guy you just met yesterday begging for a meal. I'll take care of the rest, though I am very grateful. I came over here to take you out to eat. I had no idea you would insist on cooking instead. Please don't think my intention was to cause you stress. Stay here."

Hope stared, then gaped and then smiled. *Perhaps you are growing up Hope. Maybe this is what an adult relationship is like.*

Cord returned to the kitchenette just before the timer went off. He drained the noodles and poured them into the cheese sauce. The chicken was placed on plates and the sprouts were removed from the oven. While he was searching her fridge for condiments, he found a bowl of grapes so placed a bundle on each plate. After scrounging around for all the utensils they would need, he cleared, then set a perfect table. Finally, he called for Hope to join him.

Hope had left this world again. Listening to his plundering and zoning out to the sounds of the football game, sent her thousands of miles away. Monday night football at grandma's meant male relatives shouting at the commentators or players, and female relatives bickering over whether or not grandma's play on the Scrabble board was a real word. How could one woman have such a ridiculous vocabulary? Rarely was she challenged anymore because her opponents had lost every challenge in the history of playing with her.

Will I ever go back? I don't know Harmony. I just don't know. For now, you live here because being there is too difficult for you. Try to enjoy this place. You've made a friend, and he seems like a good one. God's watching.

"Hope!"

Startled, she sat right up. "Yes."

"I've called your name five times. Do you sleep with your eyes open or are you just really good at ignoring people?"

"I'm so sorry. I guess I was daydreaming. You shouldn't have convinced me to sit down. If you want me awake, you may have to let me push through my tasks, but I am grateful to you for finishing dinner."

"Well, come on over. Everything is set for us."

"Okay. Thank you. I guess I am hungrier than I realized."

Hope joined Cord at the table. He waited for her to sit and he lowered to his chair only a fraction of a second behind her. As soon as they were scooted and positioned to eat, they simultaneously reached for one another's hand. Both were secretly pleased that the other gave no thought to saying a blessing before eating. Hope looked to him then bowed her head. Cord proceeded without any discomfort.

"Amen," was said in unison.

Small talk was exchanged about her classes and what a work day looks like for him. Hope explained that she is a bit behind schedule as far as college graduation is concerned because she took a semester off and only takes twelve credits per term due to having to work full time. "I'll graduate eventually. I'm no longer in any rush. I'm content stepping through life one day at a time for now. Plans change so easily that I don't see any point in setting my mind or heart on one particular path anymore." *Hope, stop it. You're going downhill. Change the subject.*

Having an inkling she was referring to a failed relationship, combined with her sudden facial expression that seemed to whisper, *Shut up,* Cord agreed with her. "Life and plans do change quickly sometimes." *Try to get more from her.* "Look at us, we just met yesterday and we've already had three meals together. You even felt compelled to share a very important piece of your private history with me." He cocked his head, offered a silly grin to her and took a bite.

Hope grabbed her napkin and covered her mouth. Even though she was in the middle of chewing she scolded, "Cord! You did not have to bring that up. What is wrong with you?"

Before answering, he swallowed quickly, took a sip of water and picked up a grape. "Nothing is wrong with me. And, I brought it up because it is no secret that I am interested in you as more than just a new buddy to watch football with. I'm curious. You don't need to be explicit… yet… but will you tell me, have you never had any high school or college boyfriends?" He popped the grape into his mouth keeping his eyes on hers ready to read any signs of sadness, anger, or joy.

Hope didn't hesitate in her response. As a matter of fact, it was so quick, it was almost as if she had practiced it. No emotion was shown as she confidently said, "I'd like to keep some mystery between us for now if that's okay with you. You know the most personal thing about me. Why that is still the case can wait." She then offered his mannerism back by cocking her head, sending forth a silly grin and popping a grape into her mouth.

Cord laughed, evaluated her countenance, and simply assumed either she had not dated at all or she suffered from a scarred past. At twenty-one though, how much history could she possibly have with relationships. He wasn't concerned, after all, he had only known her an hour shy of one full day. Why should she be comfortable discussing old flames? *You should be grateful Cord. At least she's not filling your ears with stories of other guys. You can appreciate and respect her wanting some mystery on this topic.*

Seeing he was pondering her request, Hope added, "Listen, I am sorry I revealed very private information so early in this," she pointed back and forth between them, but was at a loss for the correct word. In an attempt to avoid making a big deal out of what could be occurring between them she finished, "so early in this *relationship*."

Cord easily caught onto her avoidance of having to name what they were as a pair. He decided to stay on this track though. "First, don't be sorry. Second, don't feel uncomfortable about using the word 'relationship'. And third, why did you feel compelled to release that particular bit of personal information so soon? What did you *think* I was going to do to you?" To lighten the mood of the question, he offered a silly grin after he asked it.

Hope wasn't uncomfortable answering him. She lifted her brow and dove right in to her thoughts. "Uh Cord! I've seen R rated movies, not many, but I've seen them. And usually when a guy your age starts seductively escorting a woman to the couch, or bed, or countertop," she thought for a quick second, "or beach, or tent, or pool, or—"

46

"Okay, okay, I got it Hope. It sure sounds like you have seen more of those movies than you're willing to admit to though."

"Oh no! That was just one!" she retorted.

"Oh my gawd! You are hilarious. You'll have to tell me the name of that one."

"Not on your life Cord. Anyway, as I was saying, when a guy has that *look* in his eyes," she lowered her voice and turned very sultry, "he doesn't lower a girl to the couch, kneel down in front of her, place his strong hands on her knees, lean in close, then whisper, 'Just relax babe,' sexy wink, 'I'm gonna cook you dinner.'"

Cord laughed harder. Hope shook her head and rolled her eyes. Though he was struggling to catch his breath, he couldn't help but add, "Hope! Seriously, there was only six minutes left on the timer! Did those movies teach you that all those activities could be accomplished in six minutes?" He then raised his brow, cocked his head, looked down at his plate and said, "Because, at the risk of being far too explicit, someone is not doing something right if they are only spending six minutes at it!"

"Agh! Cord! Stop! I don't want to know that information yet and I certainly do not want those mental images while I am trying to eat!"

Bringing his laughter under control, Cord apologized, "Okay, I am sorry. I'll stop. But in my defense, you started it."

Hope pointed her fork at him and said definitively, "I suppose you are right. I did start it, but seeing as how I am an extreme novice on the topic, I'd be more comfortable if we change the subject."

Still working to settle his hysterics, Cord struggled to ask, "Hope! Can we please have dinner together every night?"

"Well, you know what they say, 'I'm here all week folks. Tip your bartenders and waitresses.'"

"So is that a yes?"

Liking that he is entertaining to her as well and she was already getting used to his company, she replied, "That is definitely not a no."

Chapter 5

Meal clean up was shared and afterward Hope invited Cord to relax in front of the game while she retrieved some of her textbooks to study. When she returned to her living room, she sat on the floor in front of him and he immediately protested. "Hope, sit up here with me please."

Continuing the sorting of her supplies she countered, "Just lie down. It's okay. I'm fine on the floor. I'll sit here and get my homework done while listening to you breathe."

"What? Why do you want to listen to me breathe?"

"I don't know. It gives me peace I guess. It's distracting and keeps my focus off of the noise of the television." Hope was already feeling the need to have company, and she wanted Cord's company.

He gave her a strange look then said, "If I lie down, I'll fall asleep."

"Well, suit yourself. Sit up then, but I'm staying here on the floor in front of you. I need to spread my notebooks and textbooks out so I can find everything I need."

Again Cord protested, "Do you *have* to study right now Hope? We don't have much time. I'll leave soon and you can study then. Let's just spend fifteen or twenty minutes together. From what you've told me about your schedule, it doesn't sound like we'll get much time together during the week. Sit with me for thirty minutes, then, I promise I'll leave so you can study in peace and quiet."

Cord's words were too familiar and they almost released a flood of emotions. Before she responded, she was instantly transported back to a previous time in her life when she was sitting with Evan.

Almost exactly one year earlier, Hope had her books and papers sprawled out on her dorm room floor as Evan lay on her bed watching television. She was writing, reading, thinking, and periodically sighing in frustration.

Leaning over her shoulder and stroking her hair, Evan said, "Hope, babe, put all that away. I can't take your misery any longer. Just leave it. Who cares about scores and grades anyway? Your happiness is far more important to me."

Depressed and jealous, Hope replied, "Evan, it's easy for you to say that grades don't matter because everything comes so naturally for you. I have to work really hard just to keep up. I *have* to study."

"No, you don't. All you have to do in this world is be with me. I'll take care of us. Babe, life is too short for all this stress. Please, please just get up here and rest in my arms." He then added dramatically, "Rest with me like there's no tomorrow."

Hope argued, "I can't rest. I'm afraid of failing. I will fail if I don't work."

Evan scooted more of his body over the edge of her bed so he could pull her chin forcing her to face him. Hope's despairing eyes and pinched brow were more than he could bear from her. He studied her expression as he listened to her heart. From the first moment he ever saw the insecure girl of his dreams, he felt compelled to make sure she was always happy, always safe, and always confident.

"I will never let you fail Harmony Hope. Never. Just because a number on a piece of paper may be lower than you anticipated, it doesn't mean you have failed. It means you shouldn't be taking that class. It means you were designed by God for something different. And, just because I am studying business, it doesn't mean you have to. You are an artist and a darn good one. I am marrying a fun, loving, kind, creative genius. I don't want a business woman in boring clothes with slicked back hair styles. I want you."

Remembering his words forced an uncontrollable pressure in her throat and the memory began to fade. "Not yet," she whispered. *Come back,* she thought. It was obvious Hope had drifted away. Cord just observed her demeanor without speaking a word.

Still in her dorm room with Evan, she listened again as he said, "Hope, leave all that stuff there. I'm not asking, I'm telling you, come here now."

Hope put her pencil in the crease of her text book and raised onto her knees. Evan pulled her by one hand with his other on her waist. He then lifted her and flipped her over his body trapping her between the cinder-block wall and himself. She wasn't going anywhere. "There, you're all mine again. We don't have much time. I'm going to go home soon and you can resume your self torture then. For now, let's make every second count together."

"But Evan, how am I going to learn all of that stuff for my management test tomorrow?"

"You don't need to learn all of it. You only need to learn seventy percent of it. I'll bet you are already pretty comfortable with at least half right?"

His assessment and suggestion were making her feel better already. She nodded, "Yes, I definitely know half, if not more."

"I know you do. You're smart. You just worry too much. If you'll relax, the studying and the tests won't seem so daunting and you'll do better on them. Although, I stand by my statement that you should not be getting a business degree anyway."

"Evan, I'm getting a business degree because I hope to maybe, just maybe, open my own art gallery someday."

After a slight gape, he whispered, "Oh, well I feel silly. Why have you never told me that? I can't wait to visit your shop and I really can't wait to watch you create all of your own works that will fill it. You're my pride Hope. I'll forever support your dreams."

"Thank you. I love you."

"I've loved you since I first saw you in that tiny little skirt trying to avoid me."

"Tell me our wedding date one more time," she requested.

Running his fingertips gently from her temple to her chin, his voice almost cracked as he said, "We're almost there Hope. In one year, seven months, and fifteen days, you will be Mrs. Evan Roberts. All of you will belong to all of me on May tenth, two thousand nineteen."

"All of me already belongs to all of you."

"No babe, part of you belongs only to your husband. Let me enjoy being your boyfriend and your fiancé." He reached for her hand and played with the ring he had given her for her high school graduation. "I'll have forever to be your husband."

Hope never argued with him about his beliefs because quite frankly, they shared those beliefs. Evan kissed her the way only he could. She fully returned his affection releasing every school related tension and turning her entire focus to only loving the amazing man God had given her when she was a very young girl.

"It still hurts," she whispered thinking she was the only one in the room.

"What hurts Hope?" Cord asked lovingly though with concern.

Hope squinted when she heard a foreign voice. She turned and a guilt weighted her down when she met Cord's eyes. Her mouth opened to speak, but no words came out. Cord knew she was thinking about someone else, most likely a former boyfriend. This awareness left him speechless as well.

In a stand-off, neither could move. Hope knew since she was the one who had altered the mood between them, it was her place to repair the uncomfortable situation she had created. She closed her eyes and swallowed. Nerves had dried her mouth. Cord had brought his water over with them from the table. He held it out to her without even giving it a second thought. When she opened her eyes, she took it and sipped.

Hope looked to her left at the mess she had strewn on the floor. She then looked back to Cord who sat at the edge of the couch with his elbows resting on his knees and his hands clasped with fingers intertwined. She finally spoke, "Please don't go. Please stay. I don't want to be alone. I've been alone for months. I want you here." And she released a few tears.

No room for doubt was left, Cord knew Hope had a broken heart. He also knew he would have to very slowly peel back the layers to get to the reason for her brokenness. He replied, "I'd love to stay, as long as you're sure you want *me* here."

Hope turned and knelt in front of him. She pulled his wrists unlocking his fingers from one another and slipped into a closeness with him placing his hands on her sides. When he squeezed her ribs and began caressing them gently, she rested her forehead on his shoulder and said, "I want *you* here."

Cord pressed his lips to the side of her head and exhaled a long, slow, deep breath of relief. Hope held onto the back of his neck with both hands while Evan's memory eventually faded.

When Cord was certain he had most of Hope back with him, he urged her to join him on the couch once more. This time he leaned back and she sat on his lap while he cradled her until she fell asleep. Periodically, Cord would kiss her forehead and lightly brush the strands of hair around her face.

I don't care what she's been through. I'll be here for her as long as she wants me.

Chapter 6

A seed of doubt was beginning to take root within Hope. Maybe she wasn't ready to let someone else be a part of her life yet. Maybe she wasn't ready to fall in love again. When she pondered the doubts, she realized there was also a seed of hope wanting to be planted. Maybe she was *already* beginning to revisit the concept of love. At the very least, she had fallen into genuinely caring for Cord. And, she had fallen fast.

Regardless of where she stood on an emotional spectrum, Hope needed the next few days of that week to study. With only two or three hours each night to get her homework done, spending time with Cord was going to make fulfilling her responsibilities very challenging.

Tuesday after work, a polite text was sent. "Hi Cord, I have a couple of tests this week and homework that needs to be caught up. Maybe we can hold off on seeing each other for a few days."

His phone buzzed on his desk. He read the message and thought, *That was quick. I thought she liked me.* Fearing a broken heart was soon to be in store for him, he sent a cool response, "Whatever is best for you." Send.

That's it? That's all he has to say? Cord's message seemed curt and emotionless. *I thought he liked me. What the heck?* Hope sent no reply.

Reading every word from her again and again, Cord decided to send one more message. "Should I call you Friday?" Send.

Okay, so perhaps I didn't scare him away completely. She typed, "That'd be great. Have a good week." Send.

Don't reply. Let it go Cord. You'll look like a desperate loser if you reply. Be strong.

No further correspondence was made by either. Both sat in their respective spots reflecting on what they could have done differently.

* * *

Friday evening, as anticipated, Hope heard from Cord, via text. At seven-fifteen, a message appeared. "I hope you got all of your work and studying done this week. Can I come over?"

"I did get everything finished and I think I did pretty good on my tests. Yes, come on over."

Ten minutes later Cord was tapping on her door. Hope opened it and moved to the side inviting Cord in. Her only experience with a love interest caused her to expect a hug or kiss or some sort of welcoming and personal sentiment, but he simply moved far enough out of the way of her door for her to close it. She sensed a coldness in his countenance so she didn't show any signs of affection toward him either.

"Hey, I, uh, I just stopped by on my way to meet up with some friends to tell you that I have plans with my family tomorrow. I'll, um, call you again soon to see if we can get together."

Is he freaking kidding!? The ultimate sign of anger in body language is a woman crossing her arms. Hope crossed her arms and said, "Fine Cord. Have a good night with your *friends* and enjoy your day with your family tomorrow." She then opened her door without saying another word, a clear signal for him to leave was received without misunderstanding.

UGH! Fine! I'll leave! What is wrong with her? "Have a good weekend Hope. Maybe I'll see you soon." He left and he didn't return.

As for Hope, she went to her room, put on her pajamas and crawled into her bed. The tears she fought this time were over Cord.

She spoke to herself, "I guess it was too soon. I'm not ready. Boy I sure did misread him. Why would he come over just to tell me he's going out with friends? I really like him though."

Pretending that Evan would actually enlighten her, she spoke to him next. "Evan, was I wrong? Did I let myself become too interested too soon? I don't think I know how to be with anyone but you. You made everything work every minute of every day. I don't know how to be with anyone else."

Knowing him like no one else, she recalled things he had said to her in the past during various trials she faced. His voice resounded within her, "Harmony Hope, you learned everything you need to know about relationships from me. You're ready. Don't be afraid to make mistakes. The hills you have to climb make you stronger and when you climb them with someone else, you become stronger together."

"Okay, I'll wait for the next guy to come along and I'll remember that."

"Hope, the door isn't closed with this guy yet. Hang in there. You'll know if it's supposed to end."

"I'll try to hold on. For now, will you tell me a story Evan?"

"Sure. How about the one of us moving me into my dorm?"

"No! That one makes me cry."

"Hope, they all make you cry right now."

"I know. Maybe I should go paint instead."

"That's a good idea. You painting always made us both happy."

Hope got up and went to her easel to work on her moon scape, as she was calling it, since she hadn't decided what the land would be yet.

As she stared at the brightness of the moon and the glow that surrounded it, a memory vaguely appeared in her mind. Wanting to paint and not cry, Hope suppressed the flashback and opened her paint box. While fumbling to find the brush she planned to use, her fingernail caught a piece of paper that had been placed face down underneath her supplies. Completely unaware of what it was and thinking it must have been an old receipt, Hope pulled it out, flipped it over and read it. "Think about me right now Hope because I promise I am thinking about you. Call me. I love you, Evan"

"How long has this been in there? When did you write this? Why am I just finding it?"

Hope pulled out one of her chairs and sat so she could study the note. She could feel the impressions of the letters from both sides of the paper. "He was real. He did exist. He loved me."

Her plan to not cry anymore that night had completely disintegrated. Holding her newest most treasured possession, Hope couldn't help but turn her focus back to the canvas. The memory she had tried to tuck away resurfaced and suddenly she knew why. Her painting was a memory. She hadn't realized it before now, but it was a memory. She was painting a view of the ocean.

A movie began to play in her mind as she floated to a particular time when she and Evan went to the beach to be alone late one night. She had just graduated from high school and he had completed his Freshman year of college. The moon was full, the sky was free of any signs of clouds or even that southern haze that often hides the stars and textures of the moon's face. Evan was not going to miss an opportunity to lie on a blanket on the sand and memorize every crater while listening to the hissing of the waves. He loved the night sky and always thought it was one of the most valued gifts from God. He was fascinated by the heavens.

Watching the couple like an audience member, Hope smiled remembering the time an officer walked up to them and said, "No sleeping on the beach after nine p.m."

They both sat straight up and Evan boldly spoke, "Oh Mister Officer, I promise we are *not* sleeping!"

"Evan!" Hope patted him on the chest to let him know he was embarrassing her. Evan just smiled and squeezed the hand that was resting on him. He was never unsure or regretful of anything he said or did.

"Young man, I need to see your's and the young lady's identifications please." Evan fished his wallet out and respectfully handed his ID to the man.

While the officer shone his light on the license, Evan asked, "Sir, is it illegal to be awake on the beach at night? I promise we are doing nothing here that we couldn't do if the beach were plagued with other humans."

The officer checked Evan's ID and handed it back to him smiling. "Well, I see you are nineteen, but how old is your date Mister Roberts?"

"She's eighteen sir, and we're engaged. You're almost four years too late to get us for making-out underage, if that is against the law."

Hope sat with a worried look throughout the entire exchange, but Evan was confident and endearing. Even the policeman could see that he was dealing with a good person who just really loved and wanted to protect his future wife.

"So you two have been together for four years huh?"

Evan nodded, "Yes sir, just about, three months shy of four years right now."

"You've already out lasted many marriages son."

"I suppose so."

"When's your big day young lady?"

"May 10, 2019, right after he graduates from college." Hope replied grinning with anticipation.

"I can see you'll be one of the most beautiful brides ever ma'am."

"Thank you sir," Hope replied sweetly.

"Oh, she will be sir because she already is the most beautiful girl in the world!"

"Alrighty… carry on you two. Be careful out here. Don't go swimming."

"We wouldn't dream of it. Grew up here. Know the rules and respect 'em sir."

"Good night!" The officer called out while walking away with his hand waving in the air.

Hope gaped at Evan and dropped onto her back. Looking up at the sky she said, "Evan, why does the world trust you and fall at your feet?"

"It doesn't, but if it did, I would have to say… it's the curls!"

Her body jolted with laughter until he placed his on top of her and pressed his lips firmly to her neck. "Hope, how do we hold onto this exact moment forever? I don't think I'll ever be as happy as I am right now. Life just keeps getting better and better with you."

"If it keeps getting better and better, then don't we want the next moments to come?"

"Yeah, we do."

"But, how about if I paint this night for you someday? Would that help you hold onto it forever?"

"Definitely. I want you to give me this night for my wedding present. Will you do that?"

"Of course. I'll have it ready for you by May 10, 2019."

Other than watching them continue making-out on the beach, Hope's memory ended there. She laughed and cried at the same time. After she slipped the note back into the box, because it had been safe there for some time, she replaced the lid and went back to bed.

No painting, no reading and it was only nine.

"I guess I'll shop and run, alone, tomorrow. Good night Evan. Good night Cord." She turned off her light.

When her window went dark and he was sure she wasn't going anywhere, Cord whispered, "Good night Hope," and he went home.

Chapter 7

He's here. What is he doing here? He said he had plans tonight.

Cord sauntered to the Witches, Wizards and Wanderers section of the library hoping that the sad girl he'd seen the previous week would be sitting in the same location. He had given up the possibility of a romantic evening with Hope, where he intended to rekindle feelings that seemed to be fading away, in order to check on this other girl. After the sketchy week the couple had had, and being afraid she would not understand, Cord had decided not to tell Hope about all of his plans for the evening. He knew he'd tell her when there was more trust between them. After all, he had nothing to hide. For now though, he wasn't sure a girl he'd just met a week ago and had only been on two dates with would understand him bypassing time with her to check on the emotional well being of another young woman.

Good, she's here. With his hands in his jeans pockets he stopped about twenty feet away from the stranger and offered a casual, whispered, "Hi."

"Hi," she shortly replied while slinking insecurely back into her comfy corner. Thinking he recognized her, Hope pulled the brim of her hat down and tucked her hands into her long flannel sleeves. She then covered her mouth and nose with the back of one of her hands and drew her knees closer her chest. Embarrassed by her grungy appearance, Hope knew she looked atrocious and certainly did not want the guy she had a crush on to see her looking so boyish and drab. There's a time for such sloppiness in a relationship and it's not until there is actually a relationship established.

Evan hadn't even seen her like this until they'd been together for a couple of months and that was only because he liked to fish and hunt. He made her promise no *prissing* and wearing makeup in a deer stand or in a Johnboat. There was never a question in her mind though that he loved her natural look as much as he loved her glamorous look, but Hope had no confidence in where she and Cord stood at the moment. She did not want him seeing her looking quite this bad yet.

After shifting and hiding as much of her face as she could from him, Hope refocused on Cord.

Judging from her body language, Cord could tell he had frightened her. He introduced himself sheepishly as if he were afraid he would scare her off. "My name is Cord."

"What? Did you really just introduce yourself to me?" She whispered with urgency as she dramatically dropped her hand from her face to express complete shock.

"Yes, is that okay? I'm not trying to bother you or pick up on you or anything like that if you're worried. I just wanted to say hello. I'm the guy who told you to have your conversation in the coffee shop last week. Do you remember?"

"Of course I remember." She gaped and glared at him like he was crazy.

"Soooo... usually when one person introduces himself, it is customary for the other person to return the gesture. Do you have a name?"

"Cord, are you joking?" This time she straightened her back and looked right at him.

"Not really. But, since you know my name, I'd like to know your's." He couldn't quite figure out why she went from seeming terrified to being offended by him.

Hope had to think about this. She truly did look ridiculous and she was also a little miffed at him about the way he reacted to her needing time to catch up with her school work. Maybe she shouldn't tell him who she is. Then she thought, *Can one person truly look so different in various settings that he or she is completely unrecognizable to even those with whom they are acquainted? This is like superheroes wearing masks or just a pair of glasses, huh, or even a ponytail instead of a beautifully coiffed Texas hairstyle. I'm talking, can a real person,* like me, *be unrecognizable just because I change some simple things like my hair, my makeup, and my style of clothing.* After deeply pondering the reality and the personal experiences of late, she answered her own question. *This is real. He does not know that I am Hope.*

She tightened up her accent and in a hushed tone said, "My name is Harmony." *I'm going to see how this plays out.*

"Hi Harmony."

"Hi Cord."

"Can I sit? I'll stay way over here. I meant it when I said I'm not here to bother you or try to pick up on you. I won't stay long. I promise."

Harmony did feel better after hearing him say all of that. "Sure, have a seat. You pay taxes too I suppose. You have as much right to be here as I have."

He laughed at her sense of humor while lowering himself to the floor. Carefully leaning back against a bookcase, Cord raised his knees and stole a quick glance in her direction though he was cautious and intentional not to study her. There was only one reason Cord was there; he was hoping to ease his mind about this girl's emotional state. He knew that would require having a conversation with her. When he had left the library the previous Saturday, he wondered if maybe she was just having a bad day. This week, he needed to see for himself that she was better so he could get on with his life. The obsession of his concern for this complete stranger had been very distracting and he was ready to move on.

Easing into a conversation he asked, "How long have you been coming here Harmony?"

She hated the sound of her name coming from him. Her family members were the only people who called her that. With a mild edge to her tone she responded, "You mean to a library? To check out books? And read them? I guess since I was about two! How 'bout you Cord? Why haven't I seen you here before last week?"

"Last Saturday was the first time I had ever come here to this library. I was bored and tired of television. I wasn't interested in any of the football games that were on so I decided to try getting a book. I didn't want to buy any books because they would just clutter up my house, so I came here to see if I could find one that would interest me?"

"Wait, you consider books clutter?" A hysterical, though muted, laughter commenced as she said, "Oh my gosh! You sit amongst the life works of nameless faceless wonders and you refer to them as clutter! What planet doth thou descend from sir where thou wast taught that such treasures as these are merely clutter?" She waved her arms dramatically toward all of the shelves they beheld.

Able to respect and enjoy her retort, Cord joined in her hysterics. "That came out all wrong! I must sound like an idiotic meathead!"

"Yeah, you do. I wish I could argue with you, but clod, blockhead, dimwit, those are definitely adjectives that also came to my mind."

"That is a lot of adjectives for such a short span of time."

"Well, I think fast. It probably comes from *reading* a lot."

"Very funny. But seriously, I am none of those... well, most of the time. I guess I have my moments though."

"Yeah, like that one, but you can relax Cord. I don't believe any of those words could ever be used to describe you. You obviously are a very well put together gentleman. I'm glad to have met you, apparently twice now." *Uh oh, don't flirt Harmony. He likes you, but not this you.*

Uh oh, she's flirting. Not what I wanted at all. Fix this. "So, why are you here on a Saturday night again as long as we are on the subject of being here?"

"I just like it here. That's all." Her tone did change. He sensed it.

Cut to the chase Cord, tell her why you're back. "This is an odd place to spend all of your Saturday nights Harmony. Maybe you should make some friends."

"Maybe you should mind your own business." Harmony turned her attention back to the pages of her book.

"Harmony, I heard a lot of what you said last week. Then, I watched you cry here all alone in this hidden corner. You weren't just feeling a bit blue, you seemed seriously distraught. I came back because I was worried about you."

"Don't you have a girlfriend you could be worried about?" She snapped at him.

"A girlfriend?" He actually droned out the word. "Can you define the term?"

"I'm not someone who trifles with identities. You know what a girlfriend is. Although, it is none of my business. You don't have to tell me anything you don't want a complete stranger to know about you. Your answer won't offend me nor will it affect my desire or lack there of for you. You should know, I have my own life."

"Boy, you're about to lose me in your commentary. You must read a lot of these period piece novels." She shrugged. He continued, "I'm going to be frank with you. I'm feeling bold and I also believe in honesty. I do not have a girlfriend." Her heart dropped. She held strong and steady. "I did however just meet someone who is already very special to me, so I'm trying not to scare her off."

"So your idea of not scaring a girl off is to spend a Saturday night checking on the well-being of a different girl than the one you are actually interested in? How complex, and risky Cord! You may want to rethink your dating strategy if this is the best you could come up with."

"God you're right." He dropped his head back against the book shelf and a few books slid out of place. He turned and straightened them, then settled facing forward again. Staring straight ahead at the wall that was only three feet in front of him, Cord absorbed her sarcastic truth.

While he sat silently, Harmony noted, *He's not even trying to get a good look at me thank heavens. That means he truly isn't interested in Harmony, or me, or her. Ugh, this is confusing.*

Deciding to further his explanation so Harmony didn't think he was avoiding Hope, he confessed, "I told Hope that I had a family thing this evening."

"Hope huh? Sounds prissy. Did *Hope* accept *that* as an excuse? I thought you believed in honesty. Isn't that what you just said five seconds ago?"

"I was honest. I did have a family thing. My brothers, parents and I all went to visit my grandparents at their retirement home. I didn't want Hope to feel obligated to go. It wasn't a normal occurrence. We have all been very busy lately and we needed to visit them. It happened that we were all free this afternoon and tonight so we made the plans. I have every intention of telling her where I was, but let's be real, I just met her. I think a visit to a retirement community on a Saturday night is a bit *familiar*. What girl wants to spend a Saturday night like that, especially this girl? And besides that reason, I'm also not sure she likes me as much as I like her."

"Okay, those are two very different topics and we will cover them one at a time after I share a small piece of advice. Let your girlfriend decide for herself what she is and is not interested in doing! Do not assume that any girl would not want to spend time with your family and grandparents. Most girls are nothing like guys, at all! Now, I am ready for you to tell me what makes this girl so special?" Harmony sounded jealous. *Harmony stop. He's freaking talking about you, you moron.*

He detected her discomfort, "Thanks for the advice. I hadn't thought about giving Hope the option to decide if she would like to meet my family. And, I get it, everyone is special in their own way."

"No Cord. I'm not being snarky. Tell me, what makes her special. I think if you face it or admit it to yourself, it can help you decide how far you want this new relationship to go." *Whew, I think I saved myself.*

"If you don't mind me being open, I'll tell you."

"Go for it Cord. Let's hear this."

"First of all, I met her at church. Second, she took my breath away. Literally, I couldn't breathe for a few seconds once I saw her. Third, she's funny; she has a great personality. Fourth, she's responsible. She could be a brat, but she isn't. She works very hard and she's smart, like you. Fifth, our first few days together, she made me feel like I mattered to her and was important in her life. And, although there are probably a million unspoken reasons I like her so much, the final reason I can share is that she makes me feel electric."

Harmony listened intently. He was important to her and he had no idea that the reason why was because he was the only person she had ever chosen. Evan chose her, but she chose Cord. She would tell him someday if she decided she could. For now, she had to be Harmony. "I appreciate your reasons, but before we return to figuring out if she likes you as much as you say you like her, you *have* to explain the word electric. That's just weird. Dare I ask?"

"How old are you Harmony?"

"Old enough, but don't be creepy!"

He laughed. "I wasn't planning on it. Have you ever had someone fill your skin with electricity with one very slight almost non-existent touch?"

A pressure eased into her throat but she suppressed it. "Mm hm."

"Hope barely touched my knee at church and I felt a shock shoot through me. When she sat up, our shoulders touched and each time I felt her life. I could actually feel her living. When she touched my wrist, it was like one of the fantasy books you sit among where a wizard sends magic through someone with a wand. There's more, but that should help you understand the word electric."

"I do know what you mean Cord." Her voice was lowered. Somehow she was separating from herself and trying to figure out if she was recoiling back to Evan or if it was Cord's arms she was missing in that moment.

Cord could see she was withdrawing again. Trying to keep her engaged he asked, "Will you tell me why you are here Harmony and why you were crying?"

Back to the present Harmony. Wake up. Keeping her chin down she replied, "Not until we cover the second part of your statement. You're concerned that this girl, Hope, doesn't like you as much as you like her, correct?"

"Yeah, we had a rough week. She said she didn't want me to call her this week, so I didn't. Then, when I did go see her Friday, she didn't seem very interested in me so I acted like I was just stopping by on my way to go meet some friends to tell her I had plans for tonight too."

"Crap Cord! You did that to a girl you supposedly like? What the heck were you thinking? Was she dressed up when you stopped by?"

"Of course she was dressed up, she had just gotten home from work and school. She's always dressed nice during the week."

"How long had she been home?" The pressure in her throat was growing stronger. Now Hope wanted to cry over her exchange with Cord from the night before.

"Maybe thirty minutes."

"Cord! A woman changes her clothes within seconds of getting home if she doesn't have plans. Don't you think that perhaps she stayed dressed because she was expecting you to take her somewhere?"

"Oh gawd! Harmony, don't tell me that."

Seeing his regret and sulking in her own, Harmony spoke up with a rasp while still working to disguise her accent. "Cord don't play games with this girl. Either let her know how much you like her, or walk away. My job as a woman is to look out for other women in these situations. Fix it or leave the poor girl alone."

As soon as those words left her lips, a few tears escaped and he noticed. *She must have been hurt by someone and that is why she is being so protective of Hope.* "Harmony, thank you for your perspective on Hope. Will you tell me now why you come here on Saturdays and sit alone in a corner and cry? I think you've helped me tonight, let me try to help you."

His concern was so genuine that Harmony decided she would be open with him. "I come here because it keeps my mind off of a guy, a guy who left me. Not that it is any of your

74

business, but, I was crying because a guy left me and I want him back. Every minute of every day I want him back." *You said too much Harmony. Too much!* More tears welled and another escaped. She wiped it with her flannel sleeve.

He understood her. He understood how she was feeling. "Harmony, I get it. I had a feeling that you are here because you are hiding from something. You're hiding from your feelings, your loss. You have to get up though. You can hold yourself down in this place physically and emotionally, or you can get up and face each day. You'll find someone else. So this guy left you. So what? It's his loss. You're young, I can tell. I can't tell how young because I can't see your face, but it's obvious you can't be over twenty." She let him think that. His estimate was close enough. She wasn't sure if she was going to let him think that she had been dumped though. "Harmony, call a friend. I've been where you are. I know it's painful, but you'll recover if you let yourself."

Harmony decided to take advantage of her anonymity and see if she could learn something about him. "Cord, what makes you think you've been where I am? All I've said is a guy left me."

"Everybody gets dumped Harmony."

"Huh! Even *you*!?"

"Um, yes! Even me. What's that supposed to mean anyway? I'm no one special."

"Cord, look at you and then take another look at me. There's a distinguishable difference. You're all put together and clean and tidy and... whatever else. While I'm a wreck. I can't even dress myself on a Saturday night. This is supposed to be the one night a week girls get all gussied up and go out on the town. I pull on my ex-boyfriend's overalls and flannel shirt and curl up in the corner of a library. I read, talk to myself a little, cry a lot. I'm big fun!"

"Harmony, I am not special. I've been dumped... big time. But we're talking about you now. I can't handle anymore discussions about me right now. I'm still in recovery from your conjecture on Hope's feelings. As for you, stop wearing some guy's clothes. If I see you here again, you better at least be in something that you bought for yourself. You can start your recovery there."

"I'll try, but if you really want to make me feel better, you'll answer my question about you being dumped Cord. I shared something personal with you, now you tell me something personal. And that sappy story about a beauty queen electrifying you doesn't count."

"Beauty queen Harmony?"

"I'm assuming based on your expression when you talk about her. Focus Cord, an example of you being dumped." *This is so unfair to him but I have to know.*

Wanting to just get this part of their exchange over with, he confessed to this complete stranger. "I dated a girl from the time I was twenty until I was twenty-four. We were engaged. I planned my life around her. Then, she told me one day that she had been seeing someone else for several months and she was moving in with him. Four years of my life were gone. My heart and my identity were grounded in her and in our future. She became all I knew in this world. Then, suddenly, it was all over. I felt like an idiot. I was deceived and I have spent countless days and nights feeling worthless. I've felt like I will never care about anyone else ever again."

He paused before continuing, "I know what it feels like to lose someone. But Harmony, what I learned from that is there's always someone else. When the one you think is 'the one' leaves you, someone else will be there for you. You have to get out of this rabbit hole though. See, I've been alone for almost two years, but I've at least been out there. I may be a complete dope, but I never shut myself down to others, I just waited. Then, this week has been the first time I've had hope in a long time. Huh, and her name is Hope. How fitting."

Harmony didn't respond. She listened to every word looking down at her fingernails. When he finished talking, she pulled her bag onto her lap and closed it up. She wiped her cheeks while asking, "You just met Hope this week?"

"Yes."

"And she already means so much to you that you obviously don't even seem to know how to act around her?"

Cord released a puff of air feeling disappointed in himself. "Yeah. I've probably screwed everything up trying too hard to play it cool."

"My former boyfriend is not coming back to me Cord. You at least still have a chance to repair the damage that you both may have caused equally."

"I'm going to try."

She was done. "I need to go home now." With her bag in one hand and her book in the other, she raised herself to her feet.

"Only one book this week Harmony?"

Looking at the book she had checked out last week that she didn't finish, she answered, "Yeah, just one book. I was distracted by a new friend this past week and didn't have time to read any of last week's books yet. The other four are at home. If things go well in my life, I may not get to them. Or, if things don't go well in your life I may not get to them. I came here to read tonight, but I had to play therapist instead."

He smiled at her twisted perspectives and said, "Well, I'm glad to hear that you have a new friend. It means you're one step closer to letting go of that guy who left you. And, thanks for the honest thoughts on my situation also."

She sniffed, pulled her fists into her sleeves and put her hand up beside her face as she walked past him. He assumed she was embarrassed about crying in front of him.

"Hey, maybe I'll see you next week Harmony."

She stopped and with her back to him said, "I hope not. That wouldn't be a good sign for either of us."

She's not wrong.

Chapter 8

"Wake up, wake up! Wake up, wake up!" *That blasted voice. Do not forget to change that sometime today.*

Hope tapped her phone that was laying on the pillow beside her this morning. After checking it for messages, she stared at it remembering she kept it in bed with her because she had fallen asleep hoping Cord would call.

Next to her phone was the book she was reading about the princess and the young wizard. Still believing the wizard was probably an old man, Hope at least was liking the character and growing attached to him. Deneb, the wizard, was the only being who knew a secret passageway into the heart of the princess. This was important because Princess Vega carried the burden of a deadly spell that had been cast upon her by the evil Queen Lyra, of course. After the queen revealed her curse of death and despair to Vega and Deneb, she used her powerful dark magic to place it in the center of the princess' heart. Although Deneb knows how to release the curse, his deep love for Vega is preventing him from removing it for fear of losing her forever. Keeping his knowledge a secret, he has decided to try to find another way to free the princess from the evils of the queen.

"Huh… I am enjoying this book," Hope muttered before flipping her covers off and rising to face the day.

It was Sunday so straight to the shower she went. The entire time she spent showering she thought only of her conversation with Cord at the library while she was pretending not to know him. The night was nearly a blur to her now and she had almost forgotten about it. As she washed and scrubbed and rinsed, Hope recalled as much of what she had learned from him as possible. *He likes me, a lot. He has an ex-girlfriend who cheated on him. He lived with her! So that certainly means he has an infinite amount of experience compared to my none! He is concerned about Harmony. And, he worries enough about what I think of him that he is willing to hurt my feelings to keep from looking bad. How on earth did you come up with that solution Cord?* Hope's final thought, *Cord better be at church this morning.*

Hair curled and coiffed; makeup ready; mini-dress, tights and ankle boots on; keys in hand; out the door.

Just after Hope curb parked, her door opened, sending a quick jolt of fear through her. She gasped.

"No worries. I'm not here to car-jack you. You just look like someone who is on her way to church, so I figured I'd escort you… if you don't mind." The young man held out his hand to help Hope from her car.

In any other situation, Hope would have probably rolled her eyes at the guy, and she would have truly been concerned for her safety. However, receiving an offer of an escort to church left her having to rethink standard protocol for dealing with a strange man opening your car door without invitation. *Well, this was not how I expected this morning to begin, but I am not going to be rude. This guy seems harmless enough.* Hope placed her fingers in the offered palm of the young stranger before her.

When she stood, he leaned down, pressed the lock button, and closed the door for her. Hope kept a sideways, suspicious glare on him as he placed her hand in the crook of his arm.

"We're off to church. I hope you don't mind if we walk very slowly," he said leaning into her personal bubble.

Hope squinted and pulled slightly away from him adding back into the equation the few inches he had just subtracted. *Boy he's cocky. Definitely my age or younger. Shaggy brown hair, brown eyes, and again, a man with a 'ting' when he smiles. Ugh! Poor guy. He just doesn't stand a chance, at least not today.*

Her retreat from him was not subtle so he tried to ease her lack of trust and stress. Using a tone that was heavily seasoned with sugar and spice and all things nice, he said, "Please don't be worried. I've never seen you here before. I certainly would remember crossing your path. So, when you parked your car right behind mine, I felt like it was fate. I had to be the first person today to greet you and make sure you know how welcome you are here. I don't think anything could ruin my day now and that is all because no matter what happens for the next fourteen hours, I got to walk into church and sit with the most beautiful girl I've ever seen."

Hope halted their saunter and did not hesitate in her rebuttal, "Oh please! You are *awfully* smooth. First, an infinite number of things could happen to ruin your day. Second, just because you offer a fragrant compliment doesn't mean I believe it. Third, I'm not sure there is a scenario where I would be capable of spending my free-time with a guy who stays up until at least one a.m. on a Sunday night." She then softened her voice for her final argument. "And fourth, dearest gentleman, while I am grateful for the escort and conversation as I arrive at church, I wonder if perhaps the reason you haven't seen me here before now is because *you* haven't been here."

Acting oblivious to all she said to him, his reply was, "Why thank you for the compliments. What's your name?"

"What compliments?"

"You said I am awfully smooth, and you referred to me as a dearest gentleman. So, thank you. Now, will you tell me your name?"

He was certainly amusing and she really was not threatened by him at all. "My name is Hope. What's yours?"

"Colton, Colton Cooley. Don't laugh."

"Ha! I'm gonna laugh because it's funny. I love that some other set of parents are as ill humored as mine. My name is Hope Hanover."

They began moving forward again and their exchange became more relaxed since Hope decided this guy was harmless. Colton and Hope chatted casually as they walked down the uneven sidewalk that was laden with a blanket of multi-colored leaves. Although she was listening to her new friend, Hope also had one ear on the soothing sound of the crunching beneath their feet. She also had a piece of her thoughts that kept imagining Cord sitting in the building.

Colton held Hope's hand on his forearm a bit tighter as they ascended the steps into the church. Once they reached the narthex, he pulled her to the side of the sanctuary doors. Hope was beginning to feel mildly discomforted because she was now going to have to tell this guy that she was meeting someone else that morning. Then, she had to hope that Cord showed up so she didn't look like a liar.

As she was preparing her reply, Colton took both of her hands and asked, "Hope, I meant it when I said I'd like to sit with you. I'd also love to have you join me for lunch today after the service. Will you have lunch with me today?"

Before she answered, Hope looked to her left and scanned the half of the sanctuary that she could see through the wall of windows beside them. She didn't see Cord. She turned her focus back to Colton, "I am very flattered by your invitation and I also had one of the most memorable walks to church in my life, but, Colton, I can't have lunch with you today. I'm sorry." Fearing that she would look like a liar if Cord wasn't there, Hope avoided any other explanations.

"Okay Hope, I'll accept that for now. I must warn you though, I plan on walking you back to your car in an hour."

Hope lowered her head and smiled. Not wanting to give him false hopes, she replied, "Fair enough. If after this service you still feel like I need your company as I return to my car, then you are more than welcome to walk with me. After all, I am parked right behind you."

"See you in an hour then." He kissed her on her cheek and she leaned into his embrace before releasing his hands and walking away.

Colton stood perfectly still, fully focused on where she was going to sit.

Hope walked through the double doors into the sanctuary. Her steps were small and very slow. Her heart began to race as she prayed Cord was there somewhere.

Oh, thank you God. There he is. Finding the back of his head on the aisle seat of the pew half way to the altar, Hope proceeded toward him. She had never been the pursuer in a relationship because she had only been in one relationship. Cautiously and quietly Hope positioned herself next to him. Cord jumped to his feet the moment she appeared at his side. He fought every instinct to wrap his arms around her.

"You're here," he commented innocently.

"Of course I'm here. It's part of my routine. I don't know how we never met before last week."

"Me neither, but I meant here next to me."

"Where else would I sit Cord?"

A tinge of guilt over the words he chose stumped him. Cord looked down trying to figure out what to say next. Stammering he mumbled, "I, um, just meant,"

Clearly he was stalling, so Hope decided to get straight to her most pressing question. Gently she asked, "Why did you wait until Friday to call me and then only show up at my door long enough to tell me you were busy for the next two days?"

Cord was not wanting to have this conversation in whispered tones in church. He wanted to pull her back down the aisle and out of the building so he could tell her everything that very instant. Hope on the other hand, knew they still had a few minutes before service began to clear the air. She was holding firm and expecting an answer to her question. Before she was going to sit with him, Hope wanted Cord to either explain why he preferred hanging out with another girl the night before, even though technically she wasn't supposed to know that, or she wanted him to put an end to the very brief connection they had made.

Noticing she had one free hand by her side, he reached and softly caressed the back of it with his index finger. He finally said, "I am sorry I didn't call you much last week."

Electric. He was right last night. I feel it. Hope didn't even want to give him a hint of an idea that she didn't want him touching her. She held very still and let him continue his affection. Her reply though contained an edge, "You didn't call last week or yesterday. You know Saturdays and Sundays are the only days I do have free time." She awaited patiently for another attempt at an adequate explanation from him.

"All I can say is I'm sorry. I don't have any logical reason to offer you as to why I acted the way I did." He hooked her finger with his.

Dang it. He's got me. You have to stay focused though Hope. Do not give in… at least not yet. You need more from him on this.

Not at all satisfied with his inability to verbally ease her fears, Hope let Evan peek through without losing focus on Cord. She took charge just as Evan would have done with her. *Maybe Evan was in control of everything because I let him. Maybe I needed him to teach me how to build and strengthen a relationship.* She could hear Evan's spirit in her words as she spoke them. "Cord, I'm not interested in games, insecurities or lies. I don't have the time nor the energy to allow a guy to play with my emotions. We work this out right now or we end it."

The man she knew existed within Cord arrived. A full grip on her hand was taken, his eyes focused, he leaned closer but not in an assertive way, and he said lovingly, "Hope do not think I am in any way playing games with you. Also, I am not an insecure person nor a liar. I thought your message to me last week was your way of politely saying you weren't interested in *us*. Then on Friday, when I did see you again, you still seemed distant. I was not going to appear *desperate* by trying to convince you to spend time with me, so, I decided I would turn my visit into an opportunity to inform you in person that I had plans Saturday. I left hoping I'd see you here today and we could either start over or pick up where we left off that dreaded Tuesday of last week."

An inner confession was made, *I probably did act distant and uninterested because I was angry that he didn't call me all week. He's got me there.* However, her words had more spice, "Did it ever occur to you Cord that perhaps your attentions toward me would have been perceived as *desire*, not desperation?"

The sound of that point of view was encouraging so without beating around the bush he outright asked, "Are you saying we are going to continue moving this forward Hope?"

"I never said I wanted this to stop Cord. I just need you to understand my situation. I have to work. I have to go to school. And, I have to study. Those things don't leave me much time for anything else. But, if you are willing to work with me to create an agreeable schedule, then my answer is yes, I want us to move forward."

Feeling uplifted Cord finally smiled. The sight and sound of her was filling his heart. The only problem he now faced was that during their conversation, Cord found it difficult to give Hope a hundred percent of his undivided attention. She had gotten about ninety-five percent of it though. In his peripheral vision Cord could see that the guy Hope had been speaking with before she found her way to him never turned his glare away from them. *This is church. He should NOT be looking at us like that. That kid needs to let go of whatever he thinks is going to happen between him and Hope. I'm fixing this now and it won't be broken again.*

Not releasing that grip he had on her hand, Cord moved their hold to her lower back, pulled her to him, and kissed her forehead. He heard and felt her take a slow deep breath at his touch. *Electric,* they both thought. With his lips moved to her ear he whispered, "Round two Hope. You and I are starting round two right now. Get your sketch book out. I can't wait to see what you draw today. Here, take the end seat. I know it's your favorite."

"Round two it is," she replied.

Once her affirmation was received, Cord stepped inward so Hope could take her seat. Next, nonchalantly, he looked for the young guy who had been in the back. After a quick glance around the room, with a scan of as many faces as possible before turning and taking his place next to his girlfriend, Cord sat feeling mildly disappointed that he couldn't find the guy.

"What's up Cord?"

Ugh! There he is! Sneaky devil slithered right up next to me.

Suppressing irritation, Cord droned out, "Good morning Colton. Glad to see you at church. You haven't been here in a while."

"Mind if I sit there?" Colton asked pointing at Cord's location next to Hope.

"Yes I mind! Are you kidding me?"

Colton laughed. "Doesn't hurt to ask?"

Cord rolled his eyes but reached over Colton for a shared hug.

They had Hope's full attention. "Aw, you two know each other?" She asked Cord excitedly before adding, "Colton and I just met." Then looking to Colton, "I'm so glad you're going to sit with us. I was worried you'd be alone back there." Back to Cord, "So how do y'all... Oh my gosh, are y'all brothers? You look a lot alike!"

They both nodded. Colton bore a big grin as if he were up for a challenge, but Cord's expression was simply polite with a hint of cynicism. Cord had one eyebrow raised and he kept most of his attention on Colton as he clearly did not trust him.

"Is Cord the reason you turned me down when I asked you to go out to lunch with me Hope?"

"You asked her out?"

"Of course dude! Why wouldn't I?"

"Because you're at church!"

"Uh Cord, you asked me out at church," Hope interrupted.

"That was totally different," he replied to her.

She shook her head at Cord and then answered his brother's question, "Yes Colton. Cord is the reason I turned you down. I hope I didn't upset you."

"You didn't upset me at all. I was just going to try again when I walked you back to your car." Then turning to Cord, Colton mentioned, "You didn't tell me you were seeing someone."

"Well Colton, you won't need to walk her back to her car. She's leaving with me. And we don't really spend a lot of time talking now do we?"

In a jolly tone, Colton advised, "I'll thank you kindly to allow Hope to decide her own fate post sermon. And you are right, I suppose we don't talk much, but we were all together yesterday visiting the grans. You had plenty of opportunities to share your news with everyone then."

Desperate to avoid any conversations about what he had done on Saturday with Hope nearby, Cord put an end to the discussion by scolding his youngest brother. "Leave her alone. She already told you we have plans. Shh, service has started."

All faced forward reverently.

Post greetings, music and pleasantries, Hope's full attention went to the pastor and her pen began moving. Despite being annoyed by his youngest brother, Cord couldn't wait to see what Hope produced this week.

The week's sermon had been about conquering fear and while traditionally the story of Jesus in the Garden of Gethsemane was reserved for the Easter season, the pastor used it this day to teach about how even Jesus feared so deeply, that blood was shed through his pores like sweat. He said that while fear is a burden of humanity, in the end, we are to trust God to work all things for our good.

Cord nudged Hope with his shoulder to ask her for her book. With no qualms this week about sharing, she handed it to him right away.

Hope's sketch was a night scene of a back view of Jesus kneeling with his arms out-stretched. His robe glowed in the moon light. The finely drawn leaves of the trees that surrounded him also shined as they reflected the rays that beamed down between openings in the wispy clouds. The Savior's hands were facing forward and Hope had drawn blood dripping from them as if He had already been pierced. When Cord pointed at the hands, she explained, "He was born carrying our sins. That pain was always a part of Him." He thought her justification was compelling.

The way Hope was able to sketch the negative lighting with a pen was remarkable to Cord. Before handing the journal back to her, he studied the moon and the way it contrasted against the black sky. Somehow she was able to make it seem as bright and brilliant as the moon in the painting she was working on at her home.

"Wow Hope. Easy on the eyes and talented. Impressive!"

"Colton!" Cord snapped.

"What? I'm serious." Succumbing to his brother's fair claim on this girl, Colton teased, "Hold on tight Cord. She might be a keeper."

Since the combination of the message and Hope's artwork had relaxed him, Cord replied peacefully and with a smile. "I plan on it. We'll see you at Thanksgiving Colton."

"You plan on sticking around that long Hope?"

"Colton!"

Hope laughed knowing very well not to even bother answering such a question at this stage of seeing someone.

Grasping the pew in front of him and sliding to the edge of his seat, Colton began his departure. "I'll see you two lovebirds next week."

"You're coming back to church next week Colton?" Cord asked shocked.

"Yeah! If you found Hope here certainly there's *hope*, for me too. Ha! Get it?"

"Yes, we get it."

Colton added, "Besides, she can't be the only one like her on this planet with how many people on it, seven billion?"

"Yep, seven billion." Hope answered.

"How do you know that Hope?" Cord asked.

She replied, "I thought everybody knew that. People write songs about it."

"I've never heard any songs that say there are seven billion people on earth."

"Maybe we listen to different stations Cord."

"Ha! You're funny too! Oh yeah. I'll be back next week. Do you have any friends like you Hope that you could introduce me to? It would significantly reduce my odds of finding just the right girl. As of right now, according to your information, I have a one in seven billion chance of finding the *one* for me."

"As sorry as I am about your odds Colton, please know, the world is safe. There is only one of me. I don't think I would hang out with anyone who is like me."

The more she spoke, the more Hope's words sounded like Harmony's. Cord thought, *I think I may know where Colton could find someone like Hope, minus the fancy clothes, hair and makeup.*

"Hope Hanover, Cord and I both think you're great to hang out with. I don't know why you feel any different. Hey, catch you two later!"

Colton's farewell caught Cord's attention and he shot her a look containing a very apparent, though unspoken question.

"He asked Cord," she whispered as she stroked his upper arm.

Cord nodded in acceptance.

Colton stood up to make his departure and just before exiting, he said, "Oh, before I go, don't worry Cord, I'll be sure to fill mom in on your new girlfriend. I'm sure she'd pay big for any updates on you."

Trying not to let his peaceful disposition be completely ruined, Cord lowered his voice to a paternal tone. "Colton, seriously. Knock... it... off. And you do not need to say anything to mom. I'll call her this week myself."

Hope enjoyed all of their banter. None of it was found to be insulting in her mind. As far as she could tell, Colton just knew exactly which of Cord's buttons to push. She waved to him with her finger tips as he patted Cord on the back. Then, before he left, when he was sure his big brother wasn't looking, Colton zipped his lips to show Hope he could be trusted. He never had any intentions of telling their mother anything. Cord's relationships were his business, not Colton's. She winked at him to say thank you and he winked back.

Hope put her fingers under Cord's chin and lifted his eyes to hers. "Are you ready to take me to lunch now Cord?"

"Very ready!"

"Good. Maybe you can fill me in on all the fun things you did yesterday with your family."

"Yes. I will gladly tell you all the fun things I did yesterday. Let's go."

Chapter 9

The small talk over their lunch at the Brunchroom was not satisfying for Hope. It was obvious that Cord was avoiding sharing the events of his social calendar from Saturday. Harmony had advised him to be open and honest. She wondered if he was working up the courage to share a confession.

If I bring up his family, maybe I can guide him into discussing yesterday. "Your youngest brother sure is funny. Is your middle brother that entertaining as well?"

"My middle brother is adventurous like Colton but much more reserved and responsible. He works for my dad a few months each season and backpacks around the world the rest of the year. He took off to somewhere late last night. Colton, he seems to be content right now surfing, skiing and flirting. Please don't tell him that you find anything about him remotely entertaining. You'll only encourage him."

"No promises. You should know that he and I already established a pecking order though. I'm in charge."

"That does not surprise me."

"How old is Colton?"

"He's twenty-one. Why? You're not thinking I'm too old for you are you?"

"Oh no. Not a chance. You're not at all too old for me Cord. I like you just the way you are."

Cord decided to take a big risk. "So how old was the last guy you dated?"

She answered, "Twenty-one."

"And how'd that work out for you Hope?"

"I'm living here, not in North Carolina right?"

"Will you tell me which one of you did the leaving in the relationship?"

"He did. He left me. As a matter of fact, the last thing he said to me was that he wanted me to have a completely different life than the one I had with him." *God do not cry Hope! Do not cry!* "Idaho is as different from North Carolina as I could find. I'm here. He's not. Can we change the subject now?"

"Fair enough. I'll drop it now." *At least I got something out of her about her last boyfriend. I can't fault her for being dumped. I was dumped too.*

"You now know two very intimate and private things about me. All I know about you is that you have two brothers, you're an accountant, you don't like it when I have homework, and you have a blind dog. Oh, and you hang out with your friends on Friday nights. None of those things can be classified as personal. Any common passerby could get that information from you. Tell me something that you only want me to know about you."

Cord was ready to have a real discussion with Hope. He was feeling confident that neither would run, or end this, or have a fit. He confessed, "Friday night I sat outside your bedroom until you turned off your lamp, and Saturday night I sat with another girl in the library for over an hour. We talked about her personal life, my personal life, and *our* relationship." He waited for her reaction.

Hope dropped her eyes from his, to her plate, to the crowded restaurant, and then back to his again. "You really have a way with words Cord. Why is it that you can't seem to soften any of your blows? We haven't even kissed yet, and if you plan on one happening in the near future, you should really at least *try* to sugar coat the things you say to me."

Cord couldn't tell if she was joking or serious. He wondered if he had misjudged her new found devotion to their relationship.

"Cord! Aren't you going to say anything?"

The man within arrived. "Hope, I'm not someone who worries about softening anything I have to say just so I won't hurt someone's feelings. I'm not trying to hurt you. I am just letting you know what I did this weekend so you can decide for yourself what you want to do with the information. I care about you, probably too much already. It drove me to the verge of insanity not spending last night with you. I only went to the library because I had a brief encounter with a girl there before I met you and I thought she was suicidal or something. You have nothing to worry about as far as she is concerned. I am not attracted to her. I like her. She's clever and gives good advice, but I am not interested in her as anything more than a new friend. You'd probably really like her. I want you to know about her because I may go check on her again next weekend, but we can discuss that later."

He paused to reorganize his points. "Next, I could not leave you Friday night because I counted down the hours and minutes for four days until I got to see you again. I have not had my soul crushed, like what I experienced with you, in two years. I wanted to be next to you so badly, that I sat out in the cold just so I could be there when you went to sleep."

Hm, is that creepy or sweet? Cord may be as much of a freak as I am, sometimes.

He continued, "And last, I will kiss you soon. Very soon! I will know when we are both ready."

Hope had gotten her confession and then some. She immediately decided she would process how she felt about the library girl later that week. After all, she wasn't jealous about his time with Harmony. She actually felt more guilt over it than anything else. Her focus went to Friday night.

"Cord, until we are further along, I'd appreciate it if you would tell me how you feel. If you wanted to spend Friday with me, like I wanted to spend it with you, I wish you would have shown up with a smile and a plan. Arriving with your hands in your pockets and informing me, before I could even greet you, that you had previous commitments for two nights was piercing. And now, telling me you lied about Friday night hurts even more."

"I didn't lie. My friends were out. I didn't join them because I knew I'd be terrible company since all I really wanted was to be with you."

"Either way, we're done with secrets and worries about what the other will think. Let's just be honest. Our issues last week weren't all your fault. I could have been more affectionate when you came over. I could have been open about how you made me feel right away, and we could have cleared everything up before we both got hurt. I also could have tried to work out seeing you any afternoon or evening last week. I don't want to go into details, but please try to understand that I am very new to the logistics of dating. Even though I had a serious boyfriend for six years, I don't feel like I've ever dated anyone."

Six years! Did she just say six years? Cord tried not to flinch.

Hope decided she shouldn't say anymore about her time with Evan. Anything she could possibly add would only make her sound like she was still in love with him.

A sudden need to excuse herself arose. Hope simply wanted to step away to clear her thoughts. Sitting there with Cord was beginning to make her feel unrecognizable. She wasn't sure who she was becoming and she feared she would anger him again.

No lies and no fears Hope. Just get up so you can go collect your thoughts.

"I'll be right back Cord."

"Where are you going?"

"I need a minute alone. That's all."

"We're talking. Can't your minute wait another minute?"

"I'll be back! I'm not leaving the country!"

He shook his head amused by her retort. "Alright, go."

Hope excused herself but squeezed his shoulder as she parted. *Electric.*

Cord went ahead and took care of their bill since they had long since completed the meal. Most of their serious conversation had occurred after their dishes were removed. He then pondered the 'six years' comment she had casually slipped into their midst like she was just passing him the salt. That would certainly be coming up again. He'd make sure of it. He rubbed both of his hands down his face trying to file the information away for the time being.

Returning to their table, Hope once again had the strangest adoration for him as she watched him from behind. *Why on earth do I know the back of his head so well? God, why am I so weird?*

Before reaching Cord, her wits finally returned and she had clarity about herself. She had become a different person. Everything she wanted to say and do with Cord had felt foreign to her and made her feel edgy, and not in a good way. Somehow, over the past several months of being on her own, Hope had turned into a woman who wanted control in all aspects of her life. She had never had nor really wanted power before, but now, she did. She wanted a perfect balance with the next man she dated. She wanted equal power with Cord.

Hope proceeded to him recalling one of the last things he had said to her. As she stood very silently behind him, she placed both of her hands gently on his shoulders. Her touch first shocked, then calmed him. Cord turned his head only slightly because her lips where already at his ear. Intentionally releasing her warm breath against his neck, she whispered, "I am ready and I don't want to wait for *you* to decide when it's time to kiss me." Hope then inhaled slowly so he would know exactly what she was doing. Then she pressed a delicate kiss to his attentive ear.

Purely by nature, his head tilted her direction. She nuzzled, releasing a barely audible moan. Cord closed his eyes and clenched his fists. *She should not be doing this!* He couldn't touch her but he sure did want to look at her. Unable to open his eyes just yet, he let the sensation of her gently dragging her fingers down his arm and across his back engrave into his memory.

When he heard and felt Hope take her seat, he finally looked directly at her. She had her elbow on the table with her chin resting in the palm of her hand and she was grinning. What could he possibly do but battle every muscle in his face to try to suppress his own grin? Otherwise, he was jumping across to her and he wasn't sure he would be able to control himself.

Finally, his spirit won. He displayed a huge smile and said, "You think you're funny don't you?"

"Mm hm. Because I am, but I also meant what I said."

"Oh! I know you meant what you said, because I felt it. What you just did is the reason I get to be in charge of when we are intimate. You obviously have no idea what you are doing to me."

"Oh no, I know exactly what I am doing."

"Let's go," he commanded.

"What about the bill?"

"I paid it while you were off plotting against me."

Hope laughed out loud. Cord stood. "Let's go Hope."

"Wait. What if I want dessert?"

"You don't."

"Uh! You don't know that!"

"I do now. Up. We're leaving."

She knew she had him. It was surprisingly easy. *Balance. Equality. Symmetry. He's an accountant, these should all be concepts with which he is very familiar and comfortable.* "Where are we going?"

"We are going out that door! Please don't ask any more questions or make any more comments."

She shrugged in agreement. "Very well. You're in charge."

"No, I'm not."

They both smiled and waved as they walked past their waiter. He wished them a pleasant day and they thanked him and returned the sentiment. Cord opened the restaurant door for Hope and she exited imagining they had been together for years. The walk back to Cord's car was silent but Hope stayed a half a step in front of him. She liked his hand on her lower back and she didn't want him to see her silly expression. Cord could tell she must have still been wearing that prideful grin because each person they passed on the sidewalk smiled so widely at her, you'd think she was a clown. He shook his head and counted steps to keep his mind off of the sensation of her breath and lips on his neck and her soft touch on his shoulders.

When they arrived at his car, he had pressed the remote to unlock the doors. He opened Hope's and held her hand to help her lift up into the seat. "Cord, what if I'm not done being downtown? I wanted to shop and walk off our lunch."

"You're done for now. Sit."

She looked at him and raised her eyes but didn't quite roll them. He closed her door and she watched him through the front window as he walked around to his side. Her eyes never left him as he climbed into his seat. He looked so serious.

"Where are your keys?" she asked.

"I thought we agreed you were not to ask anymore questions."

"Hm, I thought we then agreed that you weren't actually the one in charge." She almost couldn't finish her sentence for giggling so uncontrollably through it.

"You done?"

Biting her bottom lip she said, "Yup."

Cord turned his upper body towards hers, slid his left hand behind her ear and pulled Hope to him. At first, his depth was passionate. Then he transformed into seductive with light teases down her neck. When he returned to passionate, Hope thought, *A new life. We have a new life. Together.* She slid her hand to the buttons of his shirt and she pulled as well, though with much less intensity. He was good at this so she wanted him to have all of the control.

Giving them both a pause for recuperation, Cord pressed his cheek to hers and whispered, "I never want to kiss anyone else for as long as I live."

"It's a little early for that type of a decision isn't it Cord?"

"I'm trying out that, honesty when telling you how I feel, thing we talked about."

"Ah, it works! It works very well."

She listened to him regulate his breathing for a few seconds before pulling back just far enough to look into his eyes. Filling the silence she asked, "Did you kiss me so I couldn't kiss you first?"

"As glad as I am to know you were planning to kiss me too, I must say, no, I was not trying to beat you to our first kiss. I kissed you because I couldn't stand another second of not knowing how it feels." He concluded with a quick kiss to her open lips.

"Mmm, great answer. When can I have more?"

"Last Monday, when we were having dinner, you said you hadn't had this in your life yet. Are you sure you want more right now?"

"Just because I don't have much experience at this, past a certain point, doesn't mean I'm not thinking about it right now and wanting a heck of a lot more!"

"So you're thinking about what happens past this point?"

"Definitely." Her whisper about drove him mad.

His left hand was still holding her face very close to his. He brushed his lips against hers and said, "I thought we were going to shop and walk."

"We will, when *I'm* done."

"So I released a dragon."

She nodded. "I think so."

Once again, he fully appeased her and he was not hating it.

* * *

Eventually they managed to remove themselves from his car so they could walk off not only their lunch, but also their pent-up vigor. Incapable of releasing the other's hand, they visited several shops and noted which restaurants they wanted to try together in the near future.

After getting her car, the pair went to Hope's where she changed into her comfy clothes within seconds of walking through the door. Upon her emergence from her room, a surge of envy stewed within, and Cord departed briefly for home to change as well.

"Try to hurry," she requested.

"I'll be gone fifteen minutes."

"The door will be unlocked. Come on in when you get back."

Hope reached up on her tiptoes to kiss him goodbye. *He smells so good!*

I need to leave clothes over here. I wonder if it's too soon to bring it up. "I'll be back."

Only ten minutes later, Cord walked into her apartment and found Hope already asleep on her sofa. He turned on her TV and scooted her forward just enough to lie down behind her. With his arms wrapped tightly around his girlfriend, he kissed her again and again on her neck and shoulder. Hope returned his embrace by pressing against him. Cord closed his eyes for a nap too.

Chapter 10

Monday's schedule allowed very little spare time for either of them. They managed to have a quick, though late, dinner together but no home visits were made.

By noon on Tuesday, Cord couldn't stay away from his new love interest. He left work and rushed to Dr. Morris' office. The waiting area was quiet with a few patients scattered about. As is typical when a person enters a room, all eyes moved to him and most stayed on him for a while. Feeling a bit insecure, Cord slid his hands into his pockets and stepped unnervingly to the receptionist's desk.

"How may I help you?" Her greeting was in a hushed tone.

"I uh, am here to see someone," he replied.

"Is your wife already checked in sir?"

"Um, no. I don't have a wife."

"I apologize, your girlfriend then? Is she checked in?"

Curious about the focus on a significant other, Cord looked around to discover he was standing in an OB/Gyn office. Now that he was aware of his surroundings, he decided to get to the point. "I am here to see Hope. She is an employee at this office."

"Oh! Why didn't you just say so when you came in. We have a lot of men show up here looking for their wives or girlfriends for their appointments. I assumed you were with one of our patients."

"Nope. Nope. Uh… nope."

Seeing that the man before her was quite uncomfortable, the receptionist smiled and said, "Have a seat sir. I'll go get Hope for you."

Cord turned and found a chair by a window a safe distance from all of the women in the room. He sat, crossed his ankle over his knee and sifted through the magazines on the table beside him. Each one had a woman or a baby or a woman with a baby on the cover. *If men come here, why don't they have anything a man would be interested in reading?*

The door that led to the examination rooms opened and the distraction captured Cord's attention. A nurse stood with a clipboard and called a name. It wasn't Hope so he turned and looked out the window deciding counting cars or memorizing license plates would be more entertaining than reading a women's magazine.

A few more minutes passed. Still staring out the window, Cord began to wonder if he shouldn't have come. If it was taking Hope this long to get to him, perhaps it was because she was too busy for company. But, just as he was debating whether or not to leave, the door opened again. Cord looked to the woman in the doorway with so much anticipation, he almost saw Hope's face. However, once again, it was a nurse with a clipboard. His heart sank and he took a soothing breath in an attempt to calm his anxiety.

"Mr. Cooley?"

He heard his dad's name. Stunned, he looked over to the nurse. She smiled and said, "Cord? Are you Cord Cooley?"

"Yes, I am."

"This way please." The nurse had a serious expression that softened to a smile when he stood up to approach her. He must have looked completely perplexed because she waved her clipboard toward the hallway and repeated, "This way sir."

Cord looked around and all eyes were on him. His hands went back into this pockets, he returned a smile to the nurse, and he followed.

"Your wife is waiting for you in exam room three." Before Cord could speak, the nurse opened a door to a room and he saw a bare foot dangling from the examination table behind the door.

He whispered with great urgency, "Oh no! No, no, no. I'm not here for an appointment." But before he could back away, the nurse lightly pushed him on his back and gave him no choice but to enter the room. She then closed the door trapping him inside.

Facing the door, Cord heard a giggle. He refused to look until he heard, "Here to see me?"

He pressed his forehead on the door while gripping the handle for security. "Geez Hope! I almost fainted! What the heck are you doing?"

Hope burst into laughter and had to lie back on the table to catch her breath. When Cord finally turned and looked at her, she pulled her knees to her chest and gasped. "Oh! Cord! Your face when Ellie pushed you and closed the door! Gawd, it was hilarious!"

Cord stood with his back pressed against the door because it was the only thing holding him up. He said, mildly amused, "Okay, okay, you're funny. Congratulations, you can scare the crap out of me and make me laugh at the same time. That was not funny though! That was mean."

Hope settled her laughter a bit and from her reclined position on the table; she made a pouty face and held out her hand to him. Cord took it and moved to her side. Her smile was contagious and her flowing hair sprawled out on the paper covered pillow looked alive. Placing one hand on her head so he could stroke her hair and the other on her abdomen, Cord leaned over her and he did not disappoint. Hope received one of his incredible signature kisses that she had fully expected. Intentionally leaving her wanting more, he pulled away and said, "So this is what this experience feels like huh?"

Hope replied, "Sort of. I'm guessing the real thing is a whole lot scarier and a whole lot more exciting at the same time."

"Yeah. Kind of like what I just experienced then. Complete terror and then excitement when I learned that you were the one in here. I can imagine what it would feel like to be coming in here for real." Her body mildly jolted while she continued to chuckle at him. Still staring down at her, Cord thought, *I sure would like to keep kissing her, but I'll wait. Kissing her in a room with graphics of female body parts plastered to every wall is quite the mood killer. Maybe there'd be less "surprise" pregnancies in the world if there were more of these posters around.*

Cord's distraction was obvious so she asked, "What cha thinkin' about?"

"Don't hate me, but birth control."

She started chortling again and replied, "Yeah, sort of comes with the territory around here."

Although Cord was still leaning over and holding onto her, his eyes were starting to roam. She could tell he wanted to say something else. He leaned to her ear and whispered, "Does your boss offer blueprints on the female anatomy for all of us men who have no idea what on earth we are dealing with?"

"Agh!" She squeaked out a silent scream as to not disturb the business operations of the day while pounding her heels into the vinyl covered table. The paper crackled beneath her.

Cord then added before she could catch her breath, "Or should I just steal one of his lovely pieces of artwork from one of these walls to take home with me?"

Hope wrapped her arms around his neck and pressed his head to her cheek. He adjusted so the top half of his body was laying on hers and his arms were tucked under her back. Cord couldn't help but kiss her neck from that position while she giggled a bit more. When she was able to speak again, she replied, "I'll bring home some pamphlets for you to peruse while I study tonight. Will that work for you babe?"

"Sounds instructive and invigorating. I've always wanted to know how on earth the babies got into their mommy's tummy."

Hope pressed her cheek to his and he continued kissing her neck and ear. With his lips on her he said, "I owe you a sincere apology Hope, so, I am very sorry."

"For what?" she asked quizzically.

"For not being able to hold back. I think I'm going to love you someday."

Hope smiled and didn't feel even the smallest amount of fear when she said, "Then I'm sorry too."

Cord lifted off of her, held out his hands, and pulled her to a seated position. They both looked around the room and were certain they each were imagining what this experience was going to be like for real. Hope loved watching Cord's curiosity and interest in all of the equipment and in the posters. She smiled shaking her head when he left her side to wander from one to the other. "Welcome to my world."

"It's not a boring one is it?" he replied.

Hope thought of everything in her life and said confidently, "Nope. It is not a boring one."

* * *

Hope and Cord both took the remainder of that afternoon off from work. Dr. Morris didn't mind her not being there to file for the three remaining hours of her day. He was happy that she had found a friend and this friend seemed to hold promise for making all things better in her life. No amount of filing was worth missing out on the very first moments of a romance.

Hope and Cord had lunch at one of the restaurants downtown that they had scouted on Sunday. They sat out on the patio in the crisp air and warm sunshine. Outside days were coming to an expeditious end so they were grateful for a slightly warm day. After eating, they walked to a nearby shopping area and Hope tried on clothes. Cord couldn't resist buying her something new to wear and there was no chance that she was going to argue. Posing and ogling in the mirror, Hope flirted, "I'll wear this to church Sunday. Thank you!" He nodded and thought he could hardly wait to see her out in something he had chosen for her.

The afternoon minutes ticked by quickly and soon it was time for Hope to get to class. Cord drove her back to her car and told her he'd keep the bags from the store and pick her up for dinner at seven. The plan was for her to go to his house that night. She agreed and kissed him. Then just before she bounced out of his car and down onto the pavement, he grabbed her for another, much better kiss.

"Let's make every one of them count."

"Good idea," she replied.

Cord's hand naturally placed itself on her chin. She reached and held his wrist. They stared. He could see her anticipation and she could see his desire. They mutually took more time, a lot more time, with this one.

"See you in three hours."

"I can hardly wait," she winked.

Chapter 11

The new man of her dreams had made himself at home on her stairs leaning his back against one concrete wall with his foot braced against the other. When Cord heard the metal latch to the back gate click, the nerves in his stomach rumbled and a smile was impossible to suppress. With his eyes turned upward anticipating her arrival, Cord awaited the vision of the girl who was now living in almost every one of his thoughts.

The first thing he saw was Hope's hand on the railing. It slid delicately to the hairpin curve and suddenly she appeared above him. Although on some level Hope was expectant of his presence, looking down on his shadowed male form still startled her and she froze. Once her mind processed who was before her, she said with humorous irritation, "Why do you sit here in the dark? Again, your car would have been far more comfortable and warm. You also could wait for me to call you and tell you I've changed clothes and am ready to come to your house. You could give me your address so I could meet you there. I have a thousand of these suggestions, stop me when you hear one you find more appealing than sitting like this outside my door."

Cord chuckled while responding, "I am more than aware that there are other options Hope, but none of them afford me the opportunity to see you the second you get home."

Aw… He's so sweet. "I can appreciate that logic, but why aren't you in your car? You could have seen me the second I got home from there."

"I walked here since I don't live that far away."

"I hope you don't expect me to walk back with you. If you are so hellbent on walking, I'll follow you in my car, but *I'm* not walking."

Cord lowered his eyes and huffed a short laugh. "I'm riding with you. I truly had no plans for tonight other than dinner at my house. After I got our food, I had some time to spare so I figured I'd walk over here. I enjoyed the exercise and the fresh air."

"Alright, on your feet so I can get by you and get in my house. I'm starved."

Hope descended the stairwell and just as she reached Cord's side he placed a hand gently on her lower back and kissed her very sweetly. She closed her eyes and leaned into his warmth. A fight was fueled within her to resist being the first to pursue a deeper and more personal connection between them. Being near Cord was quickly releasing a person living within her that she never knew existed.

Afraid she wouldn't be able to control herself, Hope was unable to allow Cord's affection to continue any longer. She touched his cheek and pulled away from him. With her door unlocked, she led the way inside, keeping her back to him so he couldn't see she was suppressing a nervous smile. Cord followed silently and it was quite apparent within moments of entering her apartment that something seemed to be wrong with him. A nagging feeling lingered in the air that suggested Cord was struggling with a decision. He was quiet and his playful attitude from earlier that afternoon had disappeared. Hope decided she'd wait out asking any questions until she was ready to leave. That way she could see if he perked up on his own.

Outfitted in her leggings and a second-skin, long-sleeved t-shirt, Hope returned to her living room where Cord was sitting on the couch with his arms crossed, staring out of the window. A tense demeanor emanated through his body language.

Pretending not to notice, Hope tried using a light-hearted and unaware tone. "Hey, Cord? I'm ready. Are you?"

"Yeah," he replied, but he made no motion towards getting up.

No reason to ignore whatever this is Hope. Let's get it cleared up. She asked out right, "Is something wrong?"

Cord looked at her and she knew he definitely had something to say. Gathering his thoughts, he stood and said, "Hope, I don't want to seem too forward, but would you like to stay with me tonight, all night?"

Hope's eyebrows raised in shock. That was not a question she anticipated this early in their relationship. Her immediate internal debate was evident and Cord felt horrible for asking.

He opened his mouth to withdraw the question but Hope stopped him by speaking first. "How about if I pack a bag and we see how we both feel after dinner? Will that work?"

A smile of relief appeared as his shoulders dropped releasing the anxiety he felt after the words were out and he knew he could not retract them. He replied, "Great idea. I have a lot I want to talk about with you and I wasn't sure how long you were willing to stay. Also, you have fallen asleep on me pretty early the three times I have been with you, so I was thinking I'd like for you to know that it's okay with me if you stay over."

"I do like to sleep and I don't like to get home late. I'll go get something to wear to bed because I don't feel like packing everything I'd need for work tomorrow. We can set an alarm for five-thirty. That should give me plenty of time to get back here and get ready."

The two collected the few things she would need for the night, turned off all of her lights, locked the door, and they headed to her car. Not knowing exactly where they were going, Hope handed Cord her keys and after a minor scuffle over him rearranging all of her mirrors and her seat for a three minute drive, they were finally in motion.

Their relationship was only nine days old and five of those days they didn't see each other, so this was her first visit to his house. Not wanting to be presumptuous, though hopeful, Cord had parked his own car to one side of his garage so Hope's car could be parked inside as well for the night. As soon as her car's engine was dormant, Hope's pulse began to race. Sitting in the car together, both focused blindly out the front window to the dimly lit wall. Then, simultaneously, their heads turned and their eyes met.

He looks worried.

She looks confused.

"Will you tell me what you're thinking and why this dinner is any different than the other meals we've had together?" She asked while offering a comforting smile to let him know that she didn't disapprove of his invitation.

An exhale seemed to release his concerns and a half smile appeared before he answered. "I'm thinking that I just want to spend my time with you. That's all. And, this dinner isn't really any different from the others with the exception of us deciding to spend the entire night together. I'm worried that you're worried."

Hope smiled and never broke their eye contact. "I'm not worried. I'm hungry!"

Cord laughed and felt gratitude that he had chosen someone who can read a situation and respond to it all while maintaining a sense of humor. He replied, "Let's go eat then. We're having chicken and dumplings and steamed vegetables. All was homemade at a local restaurant."

"How is that homemade then?" she asked.

"The owners are an older couple who live in an apartment above the store."

"Ah, that's an acceptable justification."

After a few mutual chuckles, Cord and Hope got out of the car and entered his house. The first room toured was of course the laundry room. It was neat and tidy and looked pretty much like every other laundry room in America. A polite hand was outstretched leading Hope into the kitchen, which was lovely and had been remodeled. Everything in it was new and modern. Without speaking, Hope took it all in. Cord waited for her to process and form opinions. He didn't want to interrupt her thoughts.

"This way," he whispered nodding his head toward the living area. Hope stepped passed him and he gave her a couple of feet of space so she could turn around a few times to absorb everything her eyes were taking in.

Looking up at the walls, down at the floor and side to side at all the room contained, Hope was impressed. His living room actually made her feel happy. It was bright and inviting even in evening. Lamps lit the space and gave it a soft, warm glow.

Cord's house had freshly, resurfaced, original, hardwood floors throughout and Hope was surprised that the furnishings weren't masculine. She had expected black leather furniture with images of cars or color-block styled paintings on the walls. Instead, she was shocked by the retro, mid-century modern decor. It was masculine, but it also had a feminine touch, very gender neutral. The colors were deep aqua, red and gold with a few black and white accents, and the furniture had natural wood trim where each piece wasn't upholstered.

"Very impressive Cord." She looked to him nodding with sincere approval of his style. She asked, "Is this all you or did you have help?"

Testing her intuition, he replied, "You're the artist. You tell me. We may not know each other very well yet, but do you think I conjured up this conglomeration on my own or do you think I had assistance?"

"Geesh! I could have done without the *'not knowing each other very well'* remark since I came here with the intention of spending the night with you! Nice! Thank you for the reminder that I'm contemplating sleeping in the same bed with a man I've only known for a week Cord!"

"Oh my gosh Hope! I didn't mean to make you feel bad. I'm sorry."

"Don't apologize, but do promise me you'll still respect me in the morning," she said sarcastically with her eyes cut toward his and a slight smile on her face.

Cord stepped to her and placed his hands on her waist. "You have nothing to worry about. I told you, I just want time *with* you and nothing else *from* you."

Hope looked into his eyes smiling and said, "I believe you or I wouldn't be here. And you had help."

"Yes, I had help, but only with the kitchen and this room. The rest of the house is all me."

"I can't wait to see it then," she replied very flirtatiously.

Wanting desperately to kiss him again, Hope restrained. Though, she couldn't figure out why he was waiting. *I wonder* if he thinks he is going to offend me or scare me in some way. When Cord loosened his grip on her waist, she decided to take control. A slight tilt to place her bag on the floor beside them, then a gentle grasp onto one of his hands, and Hope boldly demanded, "Come on Cord."

"Where are we going?"

"To your room." She tugged, but he was planted like a tree trunk.

"What? Why?"

"We're going to go set some boundary lines."

"In my bedroom?" he asked feeling unsure.

"Yes. I think this night will be a lot more relaxing if we set some rules and define some boundaries for this relationship. Besides, rules will be easier to follow if we both know them and can hold each other accountable for following them." Hope tugged again, but his feet remained firm.

"Well how is going in there going to help us define our boundary lines?" His search for clarity continued.

"Think of it as a practice what you preach exercise. If we put ourselves to the test, then we can learn as we go. There will be no doubts, no questions, no worries, no insecurities. I think we need to face what is happening between us now and we need to face it together."

Cord's expression screamed excitement. With his eyes widened, he lowered his chin as he said, "Sounds like a fun way to learn to me! I'm in! Let's go!"

Yay! He's back. Hope laughed and shook her head at his enthusiasm. "Which way Cord?"

Without another moment of hesitation, he took the lead and led her to his bedroom. As they entered, Hope paused in the doorway and quickly scanned for any signs of another female in his life. She studied the bedding, the decor, the photos, and the furniture. She prayed that her intentions weren't noticeable. Everything within her vision appeared to belong to a single man. The only photo that even caught her attention was the one she saw sitting on his dresser. It was of five people whom she assumed to be his family since Colton and Cord were both in it with another good looking guy. *Huh? There they all are. Handsome family.*

Noticing that Hope was looking for something, Cord spoke in a comforting tone repeating his previous statement about his home. "I told you the rest of the house is all me."

Feeling as if she had been caught in a jealous or untrusting thought, Hope replied, "I, um, was just taking it all in and trying to get to know you a little better." Her eyes moved from his to the photograph again. "May I?" she asked pointing at it.

"Of course."

With the photo in her hands, the imaginative and creative part of her pictured three little boys fighting over toys in a playroom, wrestling in the dirt on camping trips, and whining about having to dress up to go to church on Sundays. A motion picture of his mom made Hope smile as she imagined this woman threatening, loving, bribing, laughing, and rolling her eyes at the years of mayhem her sons had generated in her life.

Cord enjoyed the smile Hope donned and wondered what she was thinking.

"Your mom looks so sweet and happy," Hope complimented.

"Photoshop. It's amazing. That woman is bossy!"

A burst of laughter was released and Hope defended the lovely stranger. "Well, I'm guessing with three sons who all appear to be very close in age, that woman had to be bossy. Otherwise y'all would have run her straight into an early grave. She probably had to take control to keep from losing control!"

Now Cord was laughing too. "My mom is a saint, a bossy saint, but a saint. She was never going to let any of us get away with anything. We walked the straight and narrow, mostly because we had no choice. Of course, I was an angel anyway, so behaving wasn't difficult for me. My youngest brother was our guinea pig. Carter, my middle brother, and I would convince Colton to do anything we wanted and if he got in trouble, we'd sit back and shake our heads at him like we were on mom's side the whole time. We'd act like we couldn't believe the hair-brained ideas he conjured up."

"And that makes you an angel? You sound more like the devil in that scenario Cord!"

"Ha! I guess that is another way to think about it."

"Yeah! The honest way! Poor Colton. I feel bad for him. It's no wonder Colton is still so mischievous."

"Do not feel bad for him! He would have ended up naughty whether Carter and I messed with him or not. He was an easy target for us because he was already a terror around our house."

"It sounds more like to me, that despite your mother's diligence in raising a God-fearing child, you and Carter tied a rope to him and drug him down a path of menace while wearing camouflage. Here I thought I was in the company of a kind, genteel, honorable, man. I'm just standing here with a scoundrel."

"Hey! I'm not a scoundrel." Cord paused then added, "I used to be a tiny bit of a scoundrel, but I'm all those other adjectives you used now. I promise."

"Hmph. Now that I know a little more about your life, you're going to have to *prove* that you've relinquished your malicious ways."

Ready to change the conversation, Cord slowly took the photo from Hope and set it back on his dresser. With an alluring expression and tone he said, "Gladly. Just give me that time I asked for earlier and I can easily prove to you that I am the kind, gentle and honorable man you want in your life."

Returning acceptance of his pursuits by placing her hands on his chest, she replied flirtatiously, "I never said I wanted only those things in a man. Perhaps I find a hidden scoundrel within to be intriguing as well."

Her response sent a shiver up his spine; instinctively, Cord stroked the soft skin of the backs of her hands. He then bent very slightly so their faces were mere inches apart, and looking into her eyes he said, "It's time to take your shoes off Hope."

His closeness and gaze gave her chill bumps, and she wanted to confess to loving his description of their touch as *electric*. Amusement and excitement were instigating weakness in her knees. Preparing for what was to come next, Hope lowered her head, then returned her eyes to his as she backed away from him.

"Could you please hurry," he insisted.

She smiled finding the display of his demanding side to be very appealing, and the exact moment his request was granted, his voice oozed seduction as he said, "On the bed, I'm ready to find your lines."

She smirked at his sexy expression. "They won't be difficult to find Cord."

He smiled and pointed.

Moving simultaneously, Hope sat and scooted backwards while Cord maintained a safe distance joining her until she was lying across his bed and he was reclined on his side and settled naturally next to her. Cord raised up on his left elbow and slid his right hand over her ribs and to her back. Then, before she could even give their bodies a thought, he pulled her tightly to him. Elated and a little nervous, Hope had watched his every move and processed the feeling of every touch. With an affectionate, though serious, glance of her delicate features, he moved his hand to her face letting her know they were advancing into the next phase of their relationship. Afraid of disclosing how much she wanted this from him, Hope closed her eyes and Cord took control. His kiss sent her into a trance and she held onto his back for dear life while he moved his hold from her head, to her waist, then to her hip, where his strength was unmistakeable.

Hope absorbed what it felt like to have a man other than Evan with her. Cord was heavier, stronger and far more physical. Their age difference became very evident and her heart loved it.

Cord had allowed all of his natural instincts to take over. He wanted all of her but knew very well not to push Hope beyond any comfort zones; although, he had yet to discover any of those lines she said would be easy to find. In a sultry tone he said, "You just let me know when I cross a line." Hope nodded and let him continue exploring. *Perhaps her lines have moved*, he thought.

The heat between them increased. Hope was craving more and more of Cord and he was beginning to worry that he'd have to be the one to declare the rules. With their passions not diminishing, Cord moved his body down, lifted her shirt and began sliding his lips and hands upward. Hope immediately tensed. *Ah, found a line.* Feeling her uneasiness, Cord immediately stopped. He looked at her and asked, "New territory Hope?"

She shrugged.

"I don't know what that means. Words please."

Feeling embarrassed Hope closed her eyes tightly and said, "Hands yes, eyes no."

"Okay. That's something. What do you want from me?"

She offered another shrug but at least she opened her eyes for that reply.

Cord smiled and said, "Well, that's not a no. Again, words please."

Hope shook her head, placed her fingers on his chin and gently lifted him. When his body was placed back in her comfort zone, she pushed her lips to his once more. With one leg draped over his hip, her hands moved to his waist. She pulled and eagerly encouraged him to continue.

He muttered with his lips pressed to her's, "Hands yes, eyes no, it is then."

Hope giggled and added, "For now at least."

"Mmm… for now," he replied.

* * *

Dinner was very late that night and there were no leftovers. Each had developed a serious appetite. And though describing their physical states using the phrase 'nearing starvation' would be an extreme exaggeration, at the time, the young couple would have disagreed.

Once there was no more food to be consumed, with very full stomachs and not one dish cleaned, Hope and Cord returned to his bedroom to continue their search for boundary lines.

Night time routines were shared and surprisingly neither felt uncomfortable about their casualty during preparations. As Hope completed her final tasks alone she felt confident and eager to return to Cord's arms. Teeth brushed, makeup off, hands moisturized, hair brushed, and one more glance in the mirror. She thought as she viewed her reflection, *Good night Harmony. Good night family. Good night… Don't say it. Just go to bed.*

Closing her eyes and erasing her thoughts, Hope put on a smile remembering where she was and who she was with. This was their first night together and she was grateful to have Cord in her life now.

"The light switch is outside the door Hope."

"Oh, that helps. Thanks."

Hope stepped from the bathroom, turned off the light and walked around to what was to be her side of the bed. Before climbing in to join him, Cord said, "You're beautiful Hope, just the way you are. You're beautiful."

Offering a side glance, Hope tucked her hair behind her ear and thanked him. Something about the situation forced her to suddenly fight an internal urge to think about Evan. Every night for so many months, when she lifted the covers, she pictured Evan there waiting for her. She would even stretch her arm out and reach as far across his side of the bed as she could. This night, as she drew back the sheet and blanket, a man with dark hair and clear blue eyes lay there, and he was not afraid to let her know he was completely unable to look away from her.

Her heart beat slowed then raced as she realized her world was changing yet again. *This is the man I want now. This is the man I need now.* She wondered if he truly wanted and needed her too.

Chapter 12

Every night that week was spent together regardless of assignments due, after work stress, or simple exhaustion from life's routines. They had moved into one another's lives and homes.

Late Friday night after they had been out with friends, Cord reached up to turn the lamp off but Hope stopped him. "Cord, I want to see your face for a little while longer. Leave that on."

Thinking her request was headed toward a playful interlude, Cord replied, "Mmm... works for me." Hope welcomed his advances and his smooth placement down her center.

Not long after he began enjoying his girlfriend's seemingly receptive body, Cord began to sense Hope pulling away. He immediately stopped. His intuition told him exactly what was going on but he asked anyway, "What's wrong?"

"I can't stop imagining you with someone else Cord."

"How can you imagine me with another girl when you've never seen me with another girl?"

"Imagining? I said imagining. I don't have to see something to be able to picture a scenario in my mind."

Cord pondered his reply. This was not a topic he wanted to have to continually evade.

Throughout that week during a meal or just before the lights were turned off at bedtime, Hope would inquire, with what she thought was subtlety, about Cord's past. Because she had spoken with him as Harmony, she knew he had lived with someone for four years, but she didn't know her name, if he ever still thought about her, or God forbid, talked to her.

"Hope, babe, there's nothing you need to know. I have nothing to tell you about any other women, nothing at all."

"I am sure there are things you could tell me. And, I'm not asking about *other women*, I'm only curious about one. All you've told me about her is that you two dated for a long time. You haven't told me anything else: not her name, her age, where she lives now, if you have seen her since you broke up, how long you were together, nothing."

Even though he really wanted to ease whatever fears Hope seemed to be developing, frustration was creeping into Cord's tone. "Have you seen your ex since you two broke up Hope? What's his name? You haven't shared any of the information that you want from me, *with* me, either."

"You know things about my ex. I told you he was twenty-one and we dated for six years and I have not spoken to him." She kept her eyes on Cord's as she continued, "I have not spoken to him since the last time I saw him seven months ago."

She thought, *Why are you doing this Hope? You have to stop.*

Her reply to herself, *I don't want to lose him and I don't want to lose him to another woman. I need to know he is never going back to her.*

Cord studied her face. Hope's fear must have been resonating because Cord relaxed. *Maybe she was cheated on too.*

"Hope, six years was a very long time to be with one person." He paused and took a breath before continuing. "I know that because you dated only one guy from the time you were fifteen until a few months ago, you don't have much to compare me to. Please trust that I am here with you because this is the only place I want to be."

She interrupted, "Just tell me something!"

"Fine, we were together for four years. We are the same age. She does still live here in town. Our paths have crossed, but not since last summer. The last time I did see her, she was with her boyfriend. And, I didn't care! Please Hope, please let this go. We broke up almost two years ago and she's forgotten. At least she was until each time you decided to ask about her this week. Look at us. Right now. Look."

Hope lifted her head from their pillows and tried her best to see anything but she couldn't because Cord was on her from her ribs, literally to her toes. "I can't see anything but your face, shoulders and chest Cord. You're squishing me."

"Good! Then I've made my point. Do you see anyone else here with us?"

"Lord no. Don't be silly. That's gross."

"Now you know how I feel when you ask me about someone who doesn't belong here with you *or* me. This is about us. This room, this bed, this position, this relationship," he smiled. She exhaled a pleasant sigh. Not wanting anymore questions, to prove his feelings for her, Cord pushed his hips and left her no choice but to accept his kiss.

Not another word was spoken. Many lines had been erased that week and even more were erased that night.

* * *

The gift of waking up in Cord's arms and not having to rush off to work was sensational. Hope couldn't believe she had been so ridiculous about his past the night before. Lying there with him she wondered if the reason she pried each night was because she was weakened by fatigue. In that moment, his warm exhale just behind her ear combined with his smooth, muscular body curved to fit her's in every way, gave her an awareness that no one else did exist who could come between them.

Cord's arm was under her's and his hand was tucked under her chin. She held it with her fingers interlocked between his and her lips pressed to his knuckles. When she opened her eyes and saw that the sun was shining, the joy of a brand new day filled her. Pressing her back into him, she whispered, "More. We have all day babe."

Slowly his arms tightened around her while his body pushed against her's.

"Cord, I can't breathe." Hope choked a little and giggled.

"You asked for more."

"Yeah, but I'd like to live through it." They both laughed and he loosened his grip, but only so he could roll on top of her.

"I like the sound of all day together Hope, but we already erased every line except the finish line."

"So! Now that all the other lines are gone, we have the entire track and field to play on and there are no rules. Let's start from the beginning and play again... and again... and again." She shifted so he was as close to every part of her as possible. There was no mistaking where she wanted his touch.

"Oh, you're fun. I do enjoy playing with you."

* * *

After their early morning escapades, Cord joined Hope in her Saturday routine. They had coffee and a crepe at the downtown market and then hiked for a few hours before returning to her apartment for a late lunch.

Even though the day had been perfect, while putting away their dishes, once again Cord's disposition shifted to one of tension and uneasiness. The last time he quieted, he wanted Hope to spend the night with him. She wondered what he had to say or ask this time.

"Good grief Cord. Stop moping and spill it. What do you want?"

He got right to his question with no hesitation. "Hope, do you mind if we don't go out tonight?"

"I might not mind if you're willing to tell me the truth about why."

Cord took a deep breath then admitted openly, "The girl I told you about after church on Sunday, I'd like to visit her again. I think, uh, well, I think she's a friend who may need me."

"A friend huh? I thought you just met her right before you met me."

"Yes, I did just meet her, but still, she's just a friend. I promise. I told you, you have nothing to worry about with her."

"Hm? What's *her* name?"

"Please don't be jealous Hope."

"Who says I'm jealous? All I did was ask you her name. Last night I asked you your ex-girlfriend's name and you refused to release such confidential information. If this girl is just a friend, then I think I should be allowed to know her name."

"I didn't refuse to answer you last night. I refused to discuss my ex while we were both mostly undressed in bed together. There's a difference."

"Ah. So, what's this other girl's name? We're dressed now, so you can talk about another woman for a few minutes."

Cord shook his head at her sarcasm and smiled. "It's Harmony. Her name is Harmony. I told you a week ago that I met her at the library, and that I would probably go see her again? Remember?"

"Oh yes, it's coming back to me, the suicidal girl."

Cord confessed, "I don't know that she's suicidal. She seems to be having a rough time right now though, and I want to stop by the library again to see how her week went."

"This is the same girl you said you shared our personal lives with right? You said you talk to her about us?"

Cord felt very guilty hearing that repeated from Hope's mouth. He tried to explain so it didn't sound intrusive and revealing. "Hope, Harmony is going through a breakup right now. I just told her a few things that were relevant to show her I understand how she feels and hopefully to help her see that her life will get better."

"I'm guessing Harmony can't afford a real therapist then?"

"She doesn't need a therapist. She needs a friend. Harmony sits alone in a corner crying and looking homeless."

"Harmony goes to the library to cry?"

"No. She goes to read. Listen, do you have a problem with me going or not?"

"Are you going to go regardless of how I feel about it?" Hope raised her eyebrows as if daring him to answer the question incorrectly.

Cord smiled at her because he was figuring out that she was messing with him. "Hope, I'm going either way, but I promise I won't stay long."

Without stating her opinion on his decision, Hope said, "Enjoy your night. I'll read or paint or both. I'll see you at church in the morning."

"Hope, I'm not leaving right now! And, I'll come back here as soon as I am done there."

"Aw... thank you for letting me be your second stop on your Saturday night outings. I'll be anxiously awaiting my knight in shining armor's return."

"Very funny. I'm staying with you tonight. *You* are my girlfriend."

Hope smiled and kissed him to let him know that she truly didn't have a problem with him visiting a friend for a little while that evening. *I better beat him back here after their visit. I can't wait to hear what he has to say.*

Thankful for her acceptance, he picked her up so her legs wrapped around nicely, walked her to the couch never losing contact with her lips, and sat down making sure she stayed right where he wanted her.

Chapter 13

"You're ba-ack," Harmony droned in a creepy, cliched tone all while diligently disguising her voice with a raspy whisper.

"And you're in those exact same clo-othes," Cord retorted and laughed from his spot on the floor a distance away. Not only did Cord have no desire to sit close to Harmony, but he also did not want to intrude on her space. His other thought on his proximity to Harmony was that he did not want Hope to casually walk in and see him anywhere near another girl.

"Same book?" he asked.

She tilted her novel, read the title and replied, "Yep. I stayed busy all week so tonight's the first chance I've had to read since last weekend."

"So how was your week Harmony?"

"Decent. No complaints. We can focus on you tonight if you'd like. Get right to it. I can see that you have something to say."

Cord didn't look at her when he quietly puffed out a yielding acceptance of her observation. He was picking at the palm of one of his hands as he began their discussion. "I had a near perfect week and I'm going back to her apartment when I leave here."

"Hm. Why did you say *near* perfect and why do you look like you don't believe it?"

"Hope asked me a few times this week if I ever think about my ex when I am with her. She has asked me if I compare her to Kendal or if I ever wish she was like my ex. Why can't she understand that if I wanted Kendal, I'd be with Kendal?"

"Kendal huh? Is she as pretty as her name?"

"Focus Harmony."

"I will, but help me step into the situation."

"For heaven's sake, yes! Kendal is attractive but so is Hope. Hope's even prettier though because she is so different from Kendal. Hope is natural and happy, most of the time."

"Got it. Pretty ex, pretty current. Current is feeling insecure because she is ignorant about ex."

"That's about it. So, what do you think?"

"Speaking strictly from a girl's perspective, because that is the only one I have at the moment," Cord smirked. "it is my belief that Hope is worried you are thinking about girlfriend number one when you two are together. This is just my guess because I know exactly how that feels. Does Hope have much *experience*?"

"I don't know the depth of her *experience* with anyone other than me, but I do know that she says she is waiting for marriage and I am so glad for that."

"Well then she is definitely worried that you are comparing her to that woman you were with for all those years. I mean, Cord, seriously, you lived with someone for four years. You are certainly not inexperienced in all of the happenings of a marriage. If Hope is holding back and she knows, or is fairly certain that Kendal did not hold back, then she's afraid you are either comparing, or will soon be regretting, your time with her."

"Harmony! That's ridiculous. I love Hope. Kendal never crosses my mind when I am with Hope. Heck, she never crosses my mind at all anymore. My past relationship is long gone and it was strictly physical. I know that now. I want Hope to know that too."

Harmony groaned, "Ugh, thanks for the image Cord. Listen, why don't you share your past with Hope and ease her mind about being compared to other women?"

"Woman! Not women. And, I don't share details about my past because Hope doesn't exactly share much about her past. She acts like she is very forthcoming, but in reality, she is very vague. I avoid conversations about Kendal because she avoids conversations about her ex. I'm not trying to upset her when I refuse to answer her questions. I do it because I think deep down, she really doesn't want to know as much as she says she does."

"Boy your life is complicated. How long has this been going on between you two?

"Two weeks tomorrow."

That was an eye opening statement for Hope. It caused an implosion of dread. *Why am I destroying this relationship? Evan? Help me.*

Harmony responded, "Cord, this sure is a young relationship for you to have so many doubts."

"I have no doubts Harmony. I mean it when I say I love her already."

Oh my! He loves me? He's in love with me?

Her hands got a little shaky but she controlled her voice and remained on topic. "Why do you think she seems to be so insecure about you then?"

"I feel like she is probably putting her past baggage on my back. What I mean is, I have so many friends who all complain about how much they hate it when a girl they are dating brings up former boyfriends. I have experienced that too and I always thought it was aggravating. But now that I am in a relationship with someone who is completely shut down to discussing her past, it worries me. I can't tell if she is hiding something, or still hung up on this other guy, or if she is emotionally scarred because of something he did to her. How can we move forward if she has insecurities due to her past that she won't let me help her with? And, I can't, for the life of me, figure out what all of this has to do with Kendal."

"Let me try to see if I can offer a possible connection. Remember all of this is worth what you've paid for it so don't hold me accountable for any mistakes. I don't need any malpractice suits Cord."

"I promise. I won't sue," he snorted.

"Perhaps Hope is worried about your relationship because her other one ended badly and she doesn't want that to happen again. Hope is threatened by your past relationship because until she recovers from the scars of her own loss, she's afraid you'll go back to that other woman seeking the comfort you had together. Could that be it?"

"Wow! That could all be what's happening with her. Nice job. So how do I help her get over that other guy who seems to have really done a number on her heart. Six years they were together, what the heck did he do to her? I'd give anything to meet him. I want to tell the jerk thank you for leaving her. I'm glad he's gone from her life."

Hope almost came unglued. Hearing Evan referred to as a jerk reminded her of how truly perfect he was. She wanted to defend him as she was suddenly flooded with emotions. There was no end to her love for him. *Cord wants to thank Evan for leaving me!*

Realizing she was playing a dangerous game, Hope had to respond and then she was letting it go. "Cord, as a girl who was just left, please do not take pleasure in Hope's misfortunes. If they were together for six years, you can bet she planned her life around him. She sounds a bit lost now from what you've told me. You may be the first stable thing in her world since their relationship ended. You invited her in, deal with what you are getting or get yourself out."

He heard Harmony sniffle. She tugged the brim of her cap and wiped her nose on the back of her hand that was tucked into her sleeve. She was still hurting. He knew their conversation was triggering her own lingering pain. "You okay Harmony?"

"Yes." Not wanting to talk about her, Harmony changed their focus. "Cord, my next question may seem off topic but it's not. Tell me, why are you so confident telling me about your private life?"

"I guess because I don't know you at all. I don't think I could even pick you out of a crowd or recognize you if you walked past me on the sidewalk. You've never walked past me on the sidewalk have you?" He asked with a raised eyebrow trying to lighten the mood.

"I have not yet, but I probably wouldn't speak to you even if I did. If you like the anonymity, I'd let you keep that."

"No! I'd want you to say 'Hi' because I'd want to introduce you to Hope. She would love you. You two are exactly alike, and at the same time, complete opposites. I'd bet you'd get along great. I'm sure she would love to meet you. She doesn't have any friends besides me right now, but I know she had a lot of friends back home. I think she's just been trying to get used to work and school and being alone."

"I get it. I like being alone most of the time too."

"Yeah, that's why you're always here Saturday nights."

"I'm seeing someone but he's busy on Saturdays. I don't mind. I get my reading done."

"I'm glad your seeing someone. That was quick. Do you like him?"

"Why the heck would I go out with someone I don't like?"

"Good point. Stupid question."

A span of silence ensued.

Cord spoke again, "I wonder if Hope reads since I'm not with her on Saturdays."

That's a good sign. He at least wonders what I am doing when he isn't with me.

"Probably so Cord. That's probably why she doesn't get upset with you for ditching her to sit here with me."

"This is truly a strange relationship you and I have isn't it?"

"More than you know Cord, more than you know."

He huffed a small laugh and they sat in silence again. Harmony pretended to be reading her book for a moment.

"Harmony?"

She looked up, "Hm."

"How much longer are we going to do this?"

"That's up to you Cord. I don't ever plan on stopping my visits to the library. You are the one who shows up here to talk to me."

"Are you going to be sad if I just don't show up anymore?"

Harmony didn't want to hurt his feelings but she was going to be honest. "Cord, I've always known this time with you was temporary. I'm not attached to you coming here. We both belong with someone else, so, no, I actually won't be sad when you stop coming here. I may even be glad because I'll finally be able to get back to reading instead of playing therapist."

"Huh, got it."

Harmony Hope, you better make your exit before he does.

"I'm leaving now Cord. I think covering the intimacy of your past and the lack of intimacy of Hope's has been more than enough information for one night. I'm afraid if I stay any longer, we might decide to discuss something even more private than that."

"What's more private than that?"

"MY love life! That's why I'm leaving! We've had an equal exchange of information this evening. Let's call it a night. Go see your girlfriend. I'm sure she misses you."

"I miss her too," Cord said smiling with his head lowered as Harmony walked past him.

Once she was a distance away, he watched her until she disappeared from his sight. Cord liked that he felt no emotional attachment other than friendship to this horribly dressed young woman. He knew there was a guy out there who loved her just the way she was and he was glad for her. She was getting over a bad breakup and he was at peace knowing she had a growing love interest to support her through it.

Hope walked quickly around the corner to her car. She threw her hat off and pulled her hair down from the shaggy knot it was tied up in. The only part of that evening that replayed in her mind was the part where Cord said he was glad

Hope's boyfriend had left her. Hope could finally cry. She drove home wiping her tears and gasping.

Harmony's voice scolded her, *Hope, this charade is backfiring on you. You show up to get information from Cord, but Cord is replanting Evan in your heart.*

Chapter 14

Cord stopped by his house before going over to Hope's apartment. This left Hope time to get home, clamber out of Evan's overalls, wash her swollen face, and settle into bed with her book. The amount of time that had passed left her wondering if Cord was going to show up or if he was afraid she would pester him again about Kendal. After reminding herself that she was not supposed to know that name, she hoped he would take Harmony's strategically placed advice and come back to stay with her.

Nestled in her bed between her flannel sheets and beneath her electric blanket and down comforter, Hope delved into her book.

Princess Vega was falling more and more in love with the wizard and it terrified her. Historically, everyone knew that wizards were always temporary in the lives of people. The princess had been warned by the evil Queen Lyra to not trust the young wizard, but Vega couldn't help herself. She kept defending their attachment by believing she was different and he would never leave her. Hope still feared the wizard was going to end up being revealed as an old man, though she was beginning to think he'd be endearing and more of an old soul than a creepy, wrinkled up, bearded, grandpa type character.

Deneb, the wizard, continued searching frantically for a solution to save the Princess Vega. He definitely could not use his knowledge to open her heart now because Prince Alastair had been introduced to the story. Although the prince was vying for Vega's heart, she remained faithful to Deneb. "For now at least. Everyone knows the prince always gets the princess." Hope complained. "So predictable."

Only two chapters were completed this weekend because there was a tap on her door. Suppressing a grin, Hope flipped her covers off of her warmed up body and she shuffled quickly to the door. Seeing Cord's face again through her window made every negative emotion evaporate. The thought of making a joke about his time away from her crossed her mind, but she decided against it because she just wanted him by her side.

"Hey!" she said opening the door while vivaciously stepping out of his way.

"Hey to you."

Thank God, he looks happy.

His grin looked genuine, so with her eyes, Hope invited him nearer. Cord clasped the front of her tiny shirt in his fist and boldly pulled her to him for a salacious kiss.

When he ended it, she murmured, "You know that's not enough for me Cord."

Enlivened, he lifted her up to him so she could wrap her legs around his waist. "Even more?" he asked once she was secure in his arms. Hope nodded, never opening her eyes. Knowing he came with the purpose of staying the entire night, Cord reached back and locked the door before walking them to her room.

Without releasing her, Cord crawled on his knees to the center of her bed and placed Hope on her back. Sitting on his heels, wearing a wanting expression, Cord took in the vision of the woman he now openly admitted to loving. Hope simply absorbed watching him enjoy her. She had aged enough and grown comfortable enough with their relationship to wear nearly nothing to bed with him. The only outer garment she wore was a little tank top.

The first thing he asked was, "Are you all mine tonight Hope?"

Confused by his question she scrunched her brow and answered, "Of course."

He gave her an alluring nod. Then he asked, "Cygnus Enduring?"

"What?" She couldn't figure out what he was saying.

"I said, 'Cygnus Enduring?' Your book? Right there, beside you."

"Oh! That was weird for a second. Yes, Cygnus Enduring. Cygnus is the swan constellation. It's brightest start is Deneb which is part of the Summer Triangle."

"Stars and constellations? Fantasy novels?" he asked.

"Yes. I like a little bit of everything." She tried hiding her obsession with the genre.

"What is Cygnus *enduring*?" he inquired with a tinge of humor in his tone as he picked up the book from her pillow.

Hope used the opportunity to take the book from Cord realizing that her check out receipt was being used as her book mark and her library card is under the name Harmony. She answered, "Cygnus is enduring existence Cord. He's just enduring his existence."

"So why does he just have to endure existence?"

"He's sort of like God in this book. He is the king of all wizards, and the wizards are the guards of the human-type beings. Cygnus has to trust every being under him to work out their problems without interfering: evil curses, saving potions, magical spells, love, jealousy. The characters all have issues. I haven't read far enough in though to learn their specific issues. I just know at this point, Cygnus is enduring existence, his and everyone else's."

Cord looked at Hope unsure if there was any significance to her summation. "Huh, sometimes I guess all we can do is endure. However, those times don't usually last too long before relief is given, trust wins and joy takes over. I, uh, hope that Cygnus survives his trials." He smiled at her and she smiled back both knowing that although there was a parallel for them in that story, discussing a novel was not a priority for either.

Not sure if Cord was going to take his time moving forward this evening, Hope leaned and dropped the book onto her hardwood floor. The loud thump of it landing flat startled Cord. "So jumpy," she said soothingly. They laughed while she sat up and rolled them over placing herself atop him. With her hands tucked behind his neck and his rubbing up and down her back, they enjoyed the comfort of one another's warmth.

* * *

When Hope woke up Sunday morning, Cord was already awake and watching her. She raised her hand and slid her finger tips softly from his temple to his chin. He closed his eyes and kissed her palm as it passed by his mouth on its way to rest on his chest.

"Did you enjoy last night Cord?" Hope whispered to him from her pillow.

His eyes squinted open and in his raspy morning voice he replied, "Of course."

"Good. What did y'all talk about?"

Cord's eyes shot open and his voice cleared and raised. "What are *you* talking about?"

"Harmony. You went to the library to see Harmony right? That's what I'm talking about. What did you think I meant?"

"Hope, you and I speak very different languages. Remember two weeks ago when I walked you to your couch and you thought I was taking you there to have my way with you?"

She laughed. "Yes! That was hilarious!"

"Well when you ask a man in your bed, who spent hours last night allowing you to have your way with him, if he enjoyed his night, I promise you that man is not thinking about some weird girl in a library who probably doesn't shower nor do laundry more than once a month.

Hope turned away from him roaring with laughter. It took several minutes for her to stop. Cord never moved from his position on his side facing her. His smile grew wider and wider as he watched her joy.

Catching her breath Hope said while still chuckling, "I haven't laughed that hard since Ellie shoved you into the examination room at work last week. And before that, I don't even know the last time I laughed that much."

"Good babe. I'm glad I can make you laugh."

In her elation, she looked at him and sighed, "Ah... I love —" and she froze.

As soon as she paused, Cord scooted immediately to her and pulled her face to his neck. Even though he was ready to face those feelings, he knew she wasn't. Hope cried for the first time in front of him. And once the tears were flowing, she couldn't hold them back. Every emotion she had pinned up that had to do with Evan and Cord both was released. Cord held her as tightly as he could and there was nothing in him that felt the least bit jealous or worried about her feelings for him. He knew Hope needed to release all of her fears and pain.

"I'm sorry Cord. I'm so sorry," she cried. "I don't want to hurt you."

"Hope it's okay. You're not hurting me. I'm okay. You do not have to say or do anything with me that you are not ready for. Shh..."

After a few deep inhales, Hope kissed Cord on his cheek and then settled back into the crook of his neck and shoulder. "Thank you for putting up with me," she whispered.

"I kinda like putting up with you. I'm learning you have some interesting kinks in your chain, but we'll get them worked out."

Hope snickered and said, "It's because I'm a freak, sometimes."

"Aren't we all babe?"

She remained silent resting in his strength and maturity.

Cord stared at the ceiling waiting for her to either speak or get up. Then, when she did speak, he was surprised by what she had to say, or ask, as it was.

"When will we cross the last line Cord?"

Shocked and amused by her question, Cord remained very still but tightened his grip on her for his reply, "Hope, you can't even *tell* me you love me without breaking down and crying. How are you supposed to *make* love to me?"

He felt her tiny jolts. "You're making me laugh again, Cord."

"I can tell."

"I'm sorry I cried when I was telling you I love you. I do love you. I mean it."

"I love you too, but you're still not ready to cross the last line. We're waiting. We'll get there together. You have to accept though, we will make love when I feel like you're ready. When *I* feel like you're ready."

"Why do you get to decide?"

Cord laughed and said, "Because I'm the oldest, so I know best. I was right about our first kiss wasn't I?"

"Definitely."

Hope giggled, sniffled and wiped her wet cheeks on his shoulder. "Sorry Cord, I don't have any sleeves to wipe my face right now so your skin will have to do."

Her comment touched something in him, but he wasn't sure exactly what it was. He responded sweetly, "It's fine babe. Your tears,"

"And drool," she added.

"yes, and drool and whatever else don't bother me. Besides, I plan on showering before church anyway." He kept his lips pressed to her forehead until he was certain that she was ready to begin their day.

Chapter 15

Refreshed. Showered. Fed. Coffee to go in their hands. Ready for church.

"Hope, you've been working on your painting."

"Oh yeah. Haven't you noticed?"

"No. I didn't. Do I see mountains?"

"Yes. You do." She nodded standing beside him as an observer.

"The moon looks bigger and brighter too," Cord noted.

"Thanks. It's the focal point. It's supposed to make you believe you are there."

"I do believe it. It's hard to look away. I love full moons over mountains when I'm camping. I can't wait to take you with me next summer. Mmm... you're going to love it."

Thrilled that he was thinking that far ahead, Hope squeezed his arm and pressed her cheek to it. She was glad Cord seemed to love her work.

"Hope?"

"Yes?"

"Can I have this when it's finished?"

Be strong Hope.

"Of course you can. It's for you. It was going to be a surprise."

He kissed her and she melted in his arms.

"Are we driving or walking to church Hope?"

"Driving. It's gotten cold. Does is always get this cold so early?"

"Mid October is usually pretty chilly here. We may start getting snow in the next few weeks. Where's your coat?"

"I don't have one. It sounds like I may have to adjust my wardrobe. Maybe my parents will send me some money for shopping. Certainly they won't want their only daughter freezing to death. I'm not sure my budget can handle my taste in clothing."

"You moved to Idaho and didn't bring a coat?"

"I can't remember the last time I owned a coat."

"You're going to have to have a coat. Heck, you should already have one."

"I'm figuring that out pretty quickly."

"Hope, don't suffer or freeze to death. If you need anything. You've got me now. I can help you out. Come on. Let's go."

She smiled and he wrapped his arm around her.

The three minute drive to church was just enough time for one song. Pushing buttons, Hope happened to land on a station that was playing the one about the seven billion people on the planet. "Hey it's your song Hope. It's my new favorite!"

"I'm glad you like it. You do know I didn't write it though don't you Cord?" She sang along and danced like a crazy person until Cord parked the car.

They were still laughing as they approached the front steps. Cord had Hope tucked under his arm trying to keep her warm and she was holding onto him shivering.

"Hey you two? Where've you wild love birds been?"

"Colton, what are you doing sitting out here?"

"I am waiting for you guys to arrive. I missed you, *both*!"

Hope laughed but Cord just shook his head at him.

"Hope, do you need an escort to service this morning?"

"I, uh, think I'm good Colton."

"Cord, mind if I sit with y'all again?"

"Of course not. Don't be ridiculous. You are always welcome to sit with us."

"Thanks. Shall we." Colton waived his arm as if he were part of the welcoming committee.

When they stepped inside, Cord turned to Hope, "Hey babe, why don't you go in with Colton. I need to check on something in the church office real quick. I won't be but a minute or two. I'll come find you two when I'm done."

Hope looked to Colton and he already had his hand held out for her to take it. She looked back to Cord and he said, "Colton, don't scare her with your overbearing personality. She's still new to you."

156

They all laughed, and as Cord walked away, Hope and Colton turned to enter the church. "Before we go in Hope, tell me two things that are interesting about you."

"Like what?"

"Oh don't waste time. Just say two things. The first two that come to mind."

"Okay, I'm left handed and my dad is a retired major league pitcher."

"What? I can't take you in there now. I have to hear all about your dad! I love baseball!"

Hope laughed. She was used to that reaction from people when they found out who her dad was. The reason her dad was one of the first things to come to her mind was because she was freezing, she needed money, and of course, she was a daddy's girl through and through. "We can talk about my dad after church. I'll tell you anything you want to know."

"Will you have lunch with me after church today?" Colton asked sweetly.

"How about if we all have lunch together today Colton?"

"Great idea. My parents are going to be expecting it."

"Your parents?"

"Yep. They are right there waving at us. No turning back now." A very nice looking couple was standing in front of their pew on the far left side near the wall. They were looking back expectant of their sons' arrival. They were clearly not expectant of Hope's.

"Colton!" She whispered her scold. "You didn't tell either of us that they are here."

"I wanted to surprise Cord. I promise this had nothing to do with you. How was I supposed to know Cord was going to disappear as soon as we all got in here? I'm not worried about you Hope, so you don't worry about them. Look." Colton pointed and waved. "They love you already."

Mrs. Cooley was waving frantically for them to come and sit. Not even realizing what she was doing, Hope held on tightly to Colton's hand with both of hers. Suddenly she wasn't so cold anymore, she was terrified instead. At that moment Colton was the only person holding her up and not only did he know it, but he felt alive because of it. "I'll never forget this day Hope."

"Colton! Stop it!" She offered another whispered scold.

How did you get into this Harmony Hope Hanover? Your first impression with these lovely people is going to be that you are cheating on one son with the other. I'm not sure you can think this in church, but, I'm going to kill Colton Cooley!

The instant they reached the pew where the Cooley's were sitting, Cord arrived and casually slipped his hand in between Hope's and Colton's. He whispered, "I know you're just messing with me Colton, but it's about to go seriously wrong. Grow up." The three all kept smiling while Cord kissed his little brother with excessive pressure on top of his head and said to him, "You are so lucky that I love you so much buddy."

Mr. and Mrs. Cooley didn't seem to notice any unusual exchanges. They both had kept their attention on Hope the entire time. Colton and Cord stepped aside to let Hope enter the row first, then Colton pretended that he was going next, but Cord shoved him and rolled his eyes. Colton snickered and Cord couldn't help but smile at him. They all sat and Mrs. Cooley instantly held Hope's hand.

Their arrival was a bit later than usual and they had missed the greeting segment of the program. The sermon was beginning. As the pastor asked the congregation to open their Bibles, Cord bent down and pulled Hope's journal and pen from her bag. Colton watched every move like a hawk. He was happy for a distraction, any distraction. When Cord held the book out for Hope, she shook her head at him.

"Dude your girlfriend is left handed and mom has a death grip on her," Colton whispered in Cord's ear.

"How do you know she's left handed?"

"Uh, because she sat in here drawing for an hour last week with her pen in her *left hand* doofus and she told me a few minutes ago, even though I already knew it."

"Why would she tell you she's left handed?"

"Shh!" Colton hissed in reply. Their mother looked at both of them with an evil eye and Colton gave her a wink and a thumbs up as if he were taking care of business for her.

Mrs. Cooley looked at Hope and said, "Those boys..." while shaking her head.

For the first time in a long time, Hope listened to the sermon instead of drawing it. When it was over, she was so glad that her hand was preoccupied the entire time. The pastor had preached about the union of marriage in Heaven. It doesn't exist in Heaven. Hope was glad for the message because she felt like her first husband was there. She knew she would marry someday and she was glad that she wouldn't have to choose between the two husbands when she did get to Heaven. There was no way she wanted to draw that sermon.

Maybe I'll draw it some other time.

Cord picked up Hope's bag for her because his mom was still holding her hand. They each exited the row and when Hope was freed from the close quarters, Colton grabbed her arm and smiled at his mom. "Mom, Hope will be out in a minute." Mr. and Mrs. Cooley continued down the aisle thinking their children were all following close behind.

"Colton? What are you doing?" Hope asked.

Cord was right there. "Colton, let her go. This is not the time."

"Cord, Hope will be right out. I just have to ask her a quick question."

"You can ask it in front of me," he insisted.

"No, I can't. Just give us a minute. It's one question."

"Hope? You okay?"

"Sure, Cord. I'm fine. We'll be right out."

"Do not mess with her Colton. One question." Cord left after he gave Colton a threatening glare and Hope a gentle kiss.

When they were mostly alone, with only strangers passing by them, Colton turned Hope to face him. "Who died Hope?"

Her brow pinched. She looked at him unable to speak.

"Hope, who died? I watched you throughout the entire service and you lived every word." He waited. She opened her mouth but no words would come out. He asked again, "It's okay. I won't tell anyone. I promise. You can trust me. Who did you lose recently?"

She confessed. "My fiancé died. We had been together since I was fifteen. We were supposed to be married this coming May. Everything was scheduled, planned and ready. We had everything but my dress, because I wanted to wait until this winter to buy one. Please don't tell Cord. I'll tell him soon."

"What was his name?"

"Evan Roberts," she said lowering her eyes momentarily.

"Did you get to see him before he passed?"

"Yes. Please stop," she begged.

"Okay. I'll stop. I'm sorry." Colton hugged her and she let him. Hope stood perfectly still while he wrapped his arms around her. He was smaller than Cord. He felt more like Evan. She raised just her hands and touched his back very gently as if she was in shock. When the comfort of someone else knowing her secret set in, she returned his embrace and buried her eyes in his shoulder.

Cord hadn't seen the entire exchange between them because of the exiting congregation down the aisle. He did see their hug though, as did his parents.

"How do they know each other Cord? They seem very familiar."

"They met here last week. You know Colton, he wins everyone over at first smile. That's why we all love him so much. I'm sure he's asking her about the sermon or her artwork. He's very curious about it."

"She's an artist?"

"Yes. A very good one."

Before Colton and Hope walked up the aisle to the family, Colton said, "By the way Hope, my question is, where was Cord this morning? My parents and I stopped by very early to get him for breakfast, and he wasn't home. They're going to ask him the same question. It's up to you, but if Cord wants to know what we were talking about, you can tell him that. Be ready."

Hope tried not to look shocked because she had just hugged him, and she didn't need to have to come up with two excuses. She said, "Thank you," then smiled and walked away.

Proceeding directly to Cord, Hope felt as if she couldn't get to him quickly enough. When she had almost reached him, she nudged her head so he knew to get her alone fast. Cord's arm went directly to Hope's waist and his lips went straight to her forehead. He said, "Mom, Dad, Colton, we'll meet you at the Miner's Ballroom. We can do formal introductions there."

Hope looked to Cord's parents and they each greeted her with a slight hug and kiss on the cheek. Colton stood with a huge smile and both of his arms open ready to receive his hug too. One was given only because she didn't want to look rude to the people she already thought were going to be her future in-laws. Cord gently took Hope's hand pulling her back to him and they all left.

Never relenting in his manners towards Hope, Cord opened her door, helped her into her seat, closed her door gently, and then joined her. As soon as they were both seated, he looked to her before turning the key and asked, "So what did Colton have to ask you that was so urgent?"

"He asked me where you were this morning?"

"He asked you that?"

"Yes. Don't be angry."

"Why didn't Colton come to me instead of you? Why did he have to pull you aside privately to ask you about that?"

"He only created the situation so I wouldn't be anywhere near you and your parents when they brought it up. He was basically telling me what they were going to be saying to you. He was afraid I'd freak out or feel uncomfortable."

"I suppose that is logical enough. My mom did want to know where I was this morning before we were even out of the sanctuary."

"What'd you say!?"

"I told her the truth. You and I decided to have an early breakfast together before church. It's no one's business how early we decided to eat."

Cord was so smooth and collected. He thought through everything. Nothing seemed to shake him. Even the times that

Hope teased or taunted him, he always took control of the situation, regulated it, and added humor purposefully or not.

"What did you say to Colton, Hope?"

"Nothing. He didn't want a response. He just wanted me away from y'all. I stood stunned. I didn't know how to react. Cord, the way you and I live is new to me. I have never had to deal with what someone's parents think of me. I met my last boyfriend when I was fifteen. A child! His parents adored me from the start. Our brothers are still best friends. Our families still spend holidays together."

"Still?"

Whoops! Too much Hope, too much. "Um, yes. Well, we all spent Easter and Fourth of July together. We haven't had any other major holidays since then. I guess we'll have to wait and see on that though, won't we?"

"Are you saying that if I go home with you for Christmas in two months, his whole family may be at your parents' house for the day?" There was undeniable irritation in Cord's tone.

Hope dropped her eyes to her hands and stammered, "I, I, I'm sorry, Cord. I really don't know. I haven't spent a vacation apart from them in so long. I, I'm sorry." She looked back to him afraid of how she was making him feel.

Her expression crushed him. "It's okay babe. This isn't something we have to worry about right now. Everything you said just caught me off-guard, that's all." He pulled her chin toward him. "Look at me."

When she did, he made her forget her worries again.

Chapter 16

Cord and Hope arrived a few minutes behind the others for their group lunch date. Mrs. Cooley was so anxious to meet Hope and have time with her that she stood outside the restaurant pacing until she saw her oldest son and his new girlfriend come around a corner toward her. She waved excitedly. Hope scrunched her shoulders upward and sent the same energy back to Cord's mom in her return greeting. Colton was standing behind and to the side of his mom mocking her every move. Hope and Cord laughed when Mr. Cooley jabbed him in his ribs with his elbow.

When Hope was within reach, Mrs. Cooley grabbed her and hugged her like she was the long lost daughter who had been missing in her life for years. "Hope! I'm so glad to meet you!" She stepped back, took both of Hope's hands in hers and looked Hope up and down. "Look guys! A girl! She's a girl!" Mrs. Cooley cheered.

Colton jumped at the opportunity to chime in, "I think that discovery and announcement was made at her birth mom. You're twenty-one years too late."

"Oh zip it Colton," she commanded.

"Hope, my life is full of boys, sons, men! I hope you don't mind that I am overjoyed to have a woman to sit with and talk to."

"I get it, Mrs. Cooley. Thank you for the welcome."

"Oh! Cord, did you hear her voice? She's southern!"

Cord kissed his mom's cheek and said, "Yes mom. I have heard her speak. We prefer talking as our means of communication."

"Uh, so sarcastic. You boys and your wit. You all think you're so funny."

Mr. Cooley gave Cord a hug and then shook Hope's hand for their introductions. He then instructed his family, "Our table is ready everyone. Let's continue this inside."

In a maternal tone, Hope heard, "Hope, where's your coat?"

"I don't have one Mrs. Cooley. I'll get to work on that this week."

"Babe, we'll get to work on it this week," Cord added as he kissed the back of her hand. His mom beamed with pride and joy at her son's admirable manners and affections.

Hope smiled at him and spoke so only Cord could hear, "If you keep feeding me, I'll be able to save up for one in no time."

"Hope, you have people who can help you."

"I told you, I'm trying to survive on my own. It's a coat not a car. I'll figure it out."

"We'll discuss it later." Cord couldn't bear thinking that Hope would skip meals and walk around cold until she had a few dollars to purchase a basic necessity. Hope thought of it as a challenge.

During their meal, Cord and Hope were grilled repeatedly about how and when they met, what they do for fun, where she works, how school is going, and other informative topics were brought up as well. Neither had a problem with the attention.

Colton was finally ready to join the conversation and hunt for background information too. He decided to go about learning more from Hope by sharing instead of asking. "Hey Hope?"

"Yes Colton."

"I like that dress you're wearing. I think I've seen you in it before."

Cord cut a glare to him trying to figure out where he was going with his statement. Colton glared back and then turned his smile to Hope.

Very confused, Hope replied, "I don't know where you would have seen it. I don't think I've ever even worn it here in Idaho. I've worn it back home, but not here."

With his arms crossed in front of him and his elbows on the table, Colton offered a dramatic nod while saying, "Oh... I know where I've seen you in that. It was at a dinner party in Cooperstown."

Not caring that she was sitting with people she did not know very well, Hope stood up with obvious intention and she pointed to the door. "Outside Colton!" Turning to everyone else at the table, she politely said, "We'll be right back."

Colton smiled at Cord and his parents behind Hope's back as she had already stepped away from the table.

Cord stood up and grabbed his brother's bicep, "Colton, what did you just do?"

"Nothing. I swear. I'm as curious as you are about what she has to say to me. Wait here. We'll be right back."

The three at the table shook their heads and decided to let Hope and Colton work out privately whatever issue he had generated. "You know your brother is harmless Cord. You know that."

He replied, "I thought I knew that, but he has been pushing her buttons since he met her last week."

"Cord, he's just jealous. He'll get over it. Why don't you tell us more about you two? That'll keep your mind off of them." Cord sat answering more of his mom's questions.

Out on the sidewalk, Hope was building up her mental strength so she could set Colton straight. "Colton take a very good look at me right now!"

"Not a problem for me."

"This is what 110 pounds of your butt being kicked looks like if you dare hint that Cord and I stay together, hint that I have shared very private information with you, if you embarrass Cord, or if you poke your nose in my business. You know nothing about a southern girl's temper."

"It's like you don't know me at all Hope."

"Exactly Colton! I don't!"

His amused demeanor turned sweet, "Hope, I would never do any of those things to you. You can trust me. Trust me."

"What were you implying in there then? Why on earth would you bring that town up?"

"Go back in and I'll tell you."

"Tell me now."

"No and you can't stand out here all day. You have to go back in or they will be out here within the next ninety seconds."

Hope knew what happened most recently in Cooperstown. She just didn't know why Colton cared or felt he should share that she had been there with everyone else present. "Fine. I'll go, but you better tread lightly. Cord and I both will pommel you if you make me look bad."

"You're squeaky clean Hope and pretty as a picture. A dead rat on your head couldn't make you look bad."

She laughed but didn't want to. "Please Colton, please don't embarrass me."

"I wasn't planning on it."

Colton opened the door for Hope and they returned to the table. Cord did not want Colton to say again whatever he had said that upset her in the first place. He had actually zoned out of the conversation the moment that Colton spoke so he didn't hear what triggered Hope into a fury. Mr. and Mrs. Cooley had heard but only Mr. Cooley knew the significance of the town Colton mentioned. He wasn't going to bring it back up though because clearly it upset Hope. Although, he would have openly admitted his curiosity was piqued.

"So, may I continue Hope?" Colton asked for her permission this time.

"Colton," Hope paused. *Obviously he jumped on the internet. Should I trust that he will keep his conversation light? Will Cord go online as well and start a search?* "Colton, please don't."

"Enough Colton," Cord demanded. "Enough."

"Fine! Fine! Hope nice dress. It's very photogenic."

"Colton! Out...side!" Hope fussed once more as she scooted her chair away from the table.

Cord went out with them this time. "What are you doing to her Colton?"

"Nothing I was just going to surprise dad with who Hope's dad is?"

Hope felt bad about yelling at him. She thought he was going to talk about the many pictures that were out there of her and Evan from a dinner celebration they all attended in Cooperstown. The pictures were not bad, but they were taken of very intimate and loving moments between her and Evan and they had a lot of captions about their engagement and how happy the young couple was. Hope had been to many dinners in Cooperstown so the real reason they were usually there, hadn't crossed her mind.

"What did you say in the first place?" Cord asked.

"I said I had seen her in that dress in Cooperstown. That's all."

"Cooperstown? Where the Baseball Hall of Fame is located?"

"Yes!" Colton answered.

Cord turned to Hope, "Why were you there? Were you visiting? What's the big deal Hope?"

"I visit there all the time. My dad is Harmon Hanover."

"The pitcher!?" Cord was shocked.

"Yes."

"Why do you care if my parents know that about you?"

"I don't! I thought Colton was trying to embarrass you by showing you that he knew something about me that you didn't."

That was a quick lie. Hope and Colton both thought at the same time.

"I really was just going to surprise dad Cord."

"Hope, I know you just met Colton and he does have a way of making people edgy and suspicious, but try to trust him."

"That's what I said to her!"

"And you, stop being so goofy with her around."

"That I can't promise."

"Can Colton share your news Hope?"

"Yes. I'm used to it. I was trying to protect you Cord."

"I don't need protection from Colton. *I'm used to it*! Let's go. All of our plates are going to have to be reheated."

Cord opened the door and held it for Colton and Hope. "Harmon Hanover. Wow!" Colton repeated, sounding very impressed.

"Yes Colton. Harmon Hanover or Daddy as I prefer to call him. I was named after him."

"Huh, another bit of information I didn't know about you until now," Colton added quickly.

Although Cord heard it all, he had mostly ignored their exchange. He was allowing Colton to be star struck and at the same time letting Hope learn how to deal with his brother.

Returning to the table *again*, Colton said, "Cooperstown dad!"

"Yes, Baseball Hall of Fame, what about it?"

"Hope's been there like a dozen times!"

"Ah, are your parents baseball fans Hope?"

"Yessir."

"Dad, Hope goes to *formal* dinners there."

"Ah, so are you trying to tell me she has an inside track to some Hall of Famers?"

"Yes! Her dad is Harmon Hanover!" Colton blurted.

Mr. Cooley perked up and a new line of questions began. Colton searched a few pictures on the internet to show everyone and managed to type in a combination of words that only pulled up family photos of Hope as she grew up attending games, dinners or appearances with her dad. Cord and the others were all intrigued by her past and present.

"Hope babe, I only have one question," Cord whispered privately in her ear. "Why on earth are you saving up for a winter coat if your dad is actually loaded?"

She pressed her cheek into the warmth of his breath and smiled. Focused on the color of his eyes, with their noses almost touching, Hope whispered back to him, "I told you, I want to do this on my own."

"I told you. You have me. You aren't on your own anymore. Those seven months are over for you." He kissed her very lightly. She bit her bottom lip and then kissed him back. As most young couples will do, they forgot anyone else was in the room.

"Please keep her Cord!" Mrs. Cooley begged.

"I'm giving it everything I've got mom."

Cord's dad paid the bill for everyone and they all bid adieu. Plans were made for when Cord would be bringing Hope to visit his mom. Hugs were exchanged and while Hope was being entertained by Mrs. Cooley, the last words spoken were from Colton only to Cord's ear. "Cord, don't you dare sleep with her!"

"I already *sleep* with her and it's none of your business."

"Fine, then don't you dare have sex with her."

"Colton, you need to rein in your obsession and stay out of our relationship."

Chapter 17

Theories and research prove you can get used to almost any situation or circumstance. However, the oddity that Hope and Cord had grown accustomed to was the reverse of what most people experience. In general, humans need space. It is actually one of the absolute necessities of a livable habitat. For Hope and Cord though, that space requirement had vanished. Neither could concentrate or even sleep without the other now. Not only were they restless when not together, but their proximity to one another had to be one that allowed constant physical connection. For example, sharing a pillow might seem impossible, but for Hope and Cord, it was the only way they could sleep... every night. And even though their contact was imperative, Cord was still holding firm in his decision that Hope was not ready for the ultimate and final commitment to their relationship.

Hope on the other hand, was growing more attached to her role of equality. She was bold and playful and convincing. Cord remained strong and let her know he was loving her persistence, but that they were waiting. There was no rejection felt by Hope. After all, Evan had held her at bay for the last couple of years they were together. Being in love with, and having Cord to herself, was satisfying enough.

After a week of meshing their routines, another Saturday rolled around. Hope actually needed to go to the library. She was meeting a study group on campus for a few hours, so Cord went to his parents' house for the day.

Late that afternoon when the group dispersed, Hope packed her bag, threw it over her shoulder and stood for her exit. Before even taking a step, a pleasant surprise appeared a short distance before her.

"Colton!" she whispered. "Coltuuuuun!" she whispered again while trotting to him. *Oh he has his ear buds in.* Hope tapped his shoulder and waved happily.

Colton pulled the tiny pieces from his ears and slid them into his pocket. He then hugged Hope and kissed her on the cheek. "What's up Hope? Did you have a good week?"

"Yeah! Wanna get a study room so we can talk or are you busy?"

"I'm not busy at all. I'm just looking for ideas for a project I have coming up soon. My final for my graphic design class is due in four weeks so I need to get moving on it."

"Ooo. What level?"

"It's a 500 level. I'm working on some grad classes to keep my full time status until I graduate in May."

"What's your major?"

"Art."

"Are you serious Colton?"

"Yeah. Hey let's go get a room?"

"That's not funny!"

"No, I mean a study room. You're the one who suggested it!"

"Oh yeah!"

They walked toward a back wall laughing and joking about her air-headed moment. The first room they came to was unoccupied and they both were shocked. Usually the rooms were full on Saturday afternoons because that was when most people in study groups could all get together. They both plopped their heavy backpacks onto the table top as the door slowly and quietly closed behind them.

"What are you doing here today?" Colton asked.

"Meeting with some people for a marketing project."

"Business major?"

"Yes."

"Why not art?"

"I've always had a natural attraction to art and instead of playing sports or taking dance or horseback lessons, my parents hired me an art tutor of sorts. I'm getting a business degree so I can open my own gallery or shop someday."

"Wow. Great idea. So what year are you?"

"This is my third year of college but I'm not really a Junior. I don't take many classes each semester. I took some time off and now I have to work. If my load was too heavy, my grades would fall and I really want a good grade point average so I'm taking my time. Life has taught me, the hard way, that time goes by fast and we don't get much of it, so why sweat the small stuff?" *Hope! Shut up!*

Hope, please don't ever stop talking. Maybe she'll tell me more about her fiancé.

"I know it's a sensitive subject, but I've been curious since church last Sunday; how did Evan die Hope?"

She knew the question would come up. She was ready, at least she tried to be ready. "He had a heart condition that no one knew about. He died of heart failure at twenty-one."

"Can you tell me more?"

Hope took a deep breath and released it very slowly with a sigh. "Sure. I haven't talked about it to anyone. Back home, all of our friends know the story because it's common knowledge. No one out here knows who I am or anything about me. It's been weird to be so alone, until Cord found me hiding in plain sight." Colton smiled and waited silently for her to share.

"So," a tear was already being suppressed. He watched ready to listen to every word.

"So, early last March, Evan and I had spent an evening in his dorm planning our upcoming Spring Break trip. We were so excited because he and I both had saved up enough money to pay for a condo on the Gulf Coast of Florida for a week. We had planned the trip the summer before and both got jobs and worked like crazy to earn enough to take care of all of the expenses ourselves. We were absolutely not going to be asking for anything from our parents. The trip was two weeks away and we were counting the days.

"As usual, our conversations would veer off track and we would end up talking about our wedding and our future and how many children we were going to have. Evan always had a way of making everything seem like a dream. He loved using his imagination. He loved describing the perfect world he lived in. He loved painting a mental picture for me of our future. But this night, after the dreams were shared, he did something he'd never done before. He decided to keep me grounded instead of letting me continue soaring in the clouds." Tears began to fall. She tucked her hand in her sleeve and wiped them. Colton remained very still, eager to envision her experiences.

"Around eight, when it was time for Evan to walk me back to my dorm room, he said, 'I think I'm going to hold you all night tonight Hope. We spend a lot of time dreaming about what it's going to be like someday for us. But tonight, I think we should face that sometimes, someday doesn't come.'" More tears fell and more were wiped. Hope stayed focused though. She wanted to be in that moment again no matter how difficult it was for her.

"I didn't argue at all with him and we both knew his roommate wouldn't mind. The most difficult part would be keeping me hidden until seven in the morning when girls were allowed in his building again." She fidgeted with her sleeve before continuing.

"Anyway, Evan held me all night. I slept but I have a feeling he didn't. The few times Evan and I had stayed together for an entire night, we were usually awake for most it just talking or listening to waves or watching stars."

Colton could tell she was enjoying some of her memories with Evan. He was glad he asked.

"The next morning, Evan kissed me goodbye and said to me, 'If you have to Hope, someday, if you have to, will you go find something, somewhere that is completely different from everything we've had together?' I asked him why he would say such a thing and he just repeated himself, 'Find something completely different with someone else. Please Hope. Promise me.'"

The intensity of her crying was becoming almost too strenuous for her to continue. Colton moved to her side and she cried on his shoulder for a few moments. He stroked her hair and held her. When she was ready, she lifted her head, wiped her face again and went on.

"I promised him but told him he was being ridiculous. I didn't want to even think about a life without him, so I sort of laughed at him, kissed him and told him I'd be back in a few hours after my classes."

"When I returned, his hallway was full and his roommate ran to me saying, 'Hope where have you been? Evan's been taken to the hospital. He collapsed an hour ago and we couldn't revive him. An ambulance came and got him. He's at Baptist.' I grabbed my phone while running out the building heading to my car. I called Evan's mom and she said, 'Get here. Now.'"

Hope pressed her eyes into both of her palms with her elbows braced on top of the table and she bawled.

Through bursts and coughs, Hope finished her story. "I got to the hospital and Evan was gone. He was alive, but gone. His family held off on removing him from life support just so I could get there and say goodbye. His heart had stopped, he had been without oxygen, he had brain damage, and he would not survive on his own. Our families were all together when he slipped away from us. His mom and I both laid our bodies across his stroking his blonde curly hair while his last bit of air released from his body. He's gone Colton. He's gone." Hope crawled to the floor, pulled her knees to her chest and she cried so hard she couldn't breath. Colton lowered to the floor with her and kept his arm around her. He cried too.

Neither had any idea how much time had passed. As Hope settled, Colton released his hold and after a few minutes he asked, "So how'd you get here Hope?"

"I took the money we had saved together and fulfilled my promise to him. Spring Break, instead of going to the beach for a visit, I came to the mountains, to live."

"Can I see him?"

"Sure. I still have thousands of our photos on my phone." She sniffled pulling her phone from her pocket.

Colton flipped through photo after photo. He studied every one. He smiled and laughed at a few. He finally said, "He is one good looking guy. Please don't think I'm weird for saying it."

"I don't think you're weird. He was very good looking. He was brilliant, athletic, kind, loving, funny, and handsome. He had it all."

"He did have it all," Colton paused then added, "because he had you too."

Hope smiled, "We had each other Colton, but I was the lucky one. He was stuck with an artsy freak. Somehow, I ended up with the cool guy. The world is a strange place."

Colton looked at the time on her phone as he handed it back to her. "It's six o'clock Hope. What time is Cord expecting you? I'm sure you two have plans tonight."

"No, we don't. Cord goes to the library on Saturday nights." *Oh shoot. I need to get to the library.*

"I'm sorry, what did you just say?" Colton laughed hysterically. "Did you really just tell me Cord goes to the library on Saturday nights?" *Oh crap! What if Cord is cheating on her and just says he goes to the library!?*

Hope laughed too and said very convincingly, "He does. He goes to the downtown public library on Saturday nights."

"Alright, if you say so."

"Hey Colton, do you have your car by any chance? I stayed here way later than I thought I would and I don't want to ride my bike back home. The sun's down and it's cold. I still don't have a coat ya know? Would you give me a ride?"

"Of course I'll give you a ride. We should get going."

Colton and Hope left the library and when they were walking to his car she asked, "How many times do you think we've passed each other here on campus Colton?"

His reply was quick, "Zero. There is absolutely no way I would have let you get past me."

"You're funny."

"I'm honest!"

"Hm. Hey thanks for talking to me. Sorry I was such an emotional basket case. My life has been kind of tough these past few months."

"Man, don't apologize. I'm sorry for everything you've gone through. Why don't you tell Cord all of this?"

"Cord hates the thought of him, my 'ex' that is."

"That's only because Cord doesn't know the truth. You should tell him."

"I know, but the problem is, I'm afraid that Cord will be hurt by how much I still and will always love Evan. He might not understand."

"Hope you are talking about a man who kisses his little brother when he is furious instead of punching me. Cord will understand."

"I don't know Colton. He's pretty sensitive about me."

"That is true! I haven't ever seen him so protective of someone. He doesn't let you out of his sight. I saw that in him the first Sunday I met you. He saw us walk in and he kept an eye on you the whole time. I thought he was staring at me, but now I know it was you he was guarding."

"Yeah. We have both grown very attached to one another. I'll tell him. I will."

Chapter 18

The drive to Hope's was mostly silent. They enjoyed the radio and Hope enjoyed not having to ride her bike in the cold. When they got to her house, she expected to see Cord's car nearby, but he wasn't there. *Hm, maybe he went to the library early. Shoot! I keep forgetting, I have to get to the library.*

Hope thanked Colton for the ride and they gave each other a hug goodbye. "See you at church tomorrow?" she asked.

"I'll be there."

Hope bolted from the car to her apartment. Once inside, she rushed to her bathroom first and when she was done in there, she repacked her backpack. While switching out her books, her phone buzzed. Cord had sent a message. "I'll be by soon babe. On my way."

She replied, "Can't wait."

Standing by her bed, Hope pulled open the drawer of her dresser and took out the engagement photo she had hidden in there. She hugged it, touched the glass atop Evan's face, and she touched the image where the ring was on her finger.

Tap, tap, tap.

Hope gasped and shoved the framed photo under her pillow. She ran to splash her face with water and rinse her mouth before running to open the door for Cord.

"That was fast!" she said panting as she opened the door.

"I was just down the street. My message said I was on my way."

"I know. What I should have known was that you meant it. I was in the bathroom."

"Sorry 'bout that." His eyes widened and he shrugged smiling at her.

"I was going to brush my teeth!" Hope clarified.

They laughed. Cord grabbed her face in both hands to kiss her and he immediately noticed she was puffy. "Why have you been crying Hope?" She jerked away from him and ran to her mirror. He knew she was stalling. He put his hands on his hips as he called out to her, "Hope, no lies. We cleared up that lying thing two weeks ago."

Ugh! What the heck! What do I say? Oh no. I'm going to lie. I can't stop myself. NO Hope! You're not!

"I was at the library in a study room crying because I was really homesick. I'm better now though."

"What do you mean homesick?" Cord asked suspiciously.

Hope emerged from her room and stood in the doorway out of his reach. "I miss home. I miss my family. I miss everything."

"I'm going to drop this Hope, but I don't want to."

"I'm okay. I promise." She changed the subject. "Are you still going to see Harmony tonight?"

"I won't if you want me to stay with you."

"I'll read Cord. You know I love to read. I spent all day doing homework, so it'll be really nice to have a quiet night. You will come back here though, right?"

"Absolutely. I can't be away from you all night." Cord curled his fingers motioning for Hope to come to him. She moved slowly to him, thrilled to have him in her life.

When their snuggling was concluded, Hope offered to make her and Cord something to eat. He gladly accepted and asked if he could help. Hope felt she could work faster without having to tell him what she needed so she declined his offer. She moved to the kitchen to get to work and Cord got comfortable on the couch.

"What time are you leaving Cord?"

"Eight-ish."

"Will you tell me all about it tomorrow?"

"I won't be gone long. I can tell you all about it tonight if you'd like. I really just want to check on her. She's interesting."

"So you've said." Hope then asked, "How much longer do you plan on making these visits to this homeless, depressed girl?"

"This might be the last. Thanks for not minding that I go see her."

"Huh! Who says I don't mind?" Hope mumbled.

Hearing her phone buzzing, Hope asked, "Hey Cord, will you go get my phone? I hear it. Someone is calling."

"Yep. Where'd you leave it babe?"

"In my room on my bedside table."

After a bit of confusion between them, Cord returned with her phone but she had missed the call. "Who was it?" she asked.

"Nathan?"

"Yeah, he's a study group guy. I'll text him back and tell him what I found after group ended."

Cord returned to the couch until their food was ready. He and Hope then cuddled on her couch until it was time for him to go see Harmony.

"I won't be gone long Hope."

"'Kay."

Hope rushed to her room, threw on her grungy clothes and a baseball hat, she snatched her backpack from the corner, and out she ran to her car.

* * *

How did I beat him here? Straining not to pant, Hope dropped to her corner and pulled out her book. A genuine attempt was made to concentrate on it. The words were sinking in until she had a horrifying thought, *What if Cord went somewhere else or worse, went back to my house? Wait, which would be worse?* Keeping her eyes down, her heart raced. She panicked. "This is it! I am done with this Harmony act. Well, it's not an act. I am Harmony, but I am done being Harmony. Ugh!"

"I like Harmony. You don't need to be anyone else?"

Hope gasped and Cord scared her so badly she choked too.

"You okay Harmony? Did I scare you?"

Coughing she replied, "Yea, yes!"

"Sorry. So you're back to talking to yourself and you're in the dude's clothes. Bad week?"

"Not too bad. My day was a bit rough, but it's ending okay. My book is good, my boyfriend is happy, and I think I'll sleep very well tonight."

"Why the rough day then?"

"I spent the afternoon with a new friend and he seemed to think I should spend more time facing my past. Here I am trying to forget my ex and he thinks I should face the situation because there will be more healing that way. Instead of being bitter and hiding everything, I should be open and forthcoming."

"Are you lying to me so you can try to convince me to be more open with Hope about Kendal?"

"What? No. I thought you asked about me!"

"I did. I wanted to make sure you weren't feeding me a line because I did want to hear about you. So all that really happened to you today?"

"Yes."

"Then you and I are not only in the same boat, we are sitting on the same rowing bench."

"Oh, what's your story this week?"

"Mine is a today story as well, but first, Harmony, what does your boyfriend think of me?"

"Ha! If he knew you existed he wouldn't like this at all. He's more of the 'I'm your only one' type. He's not jealous, but he would certainly not want me spending every Saturday with another guy, even someone who truly is just a friend."

"So I am pretty lucky to have Hope then huh?"

"Only you can answer that. You sound like you have doubts. If she is anything like your description, I would argue that she must be some sort of freak Cord to let a guy like you hang out with another girl every week. I'd worry if I were you."

"She calls herself a freak all the time."

"I think most girls do. Fill me in on what's bothering you. You questioned that you're lucky to have Hope. Why the worried look?"

"Harmony, I learned something about Hope this week."

"Do tell. That is why we are here." Harmony's tone was sinister yet inviting like she was ready for a scandal.

Cord laughed and said, "This is serious Harmony."

"Okay, I'm sorry. Tell me what you learned."

Cord took a deep breath and began nervously wringing his hands. Hope was starting to feel a bit nervous. She coaxed, "Spill it Cord. We don't have all night. Let's talk."

"Hope's in love with someone else, her ex-boyfriend to be exact. I'm sure of it. I found proof, I found it *accidentally*, but proof nonetheless."

"That was an excessively loaded accusation Cord. Are you sure you want to stand by that epiphany because you know the questions and judgements are coming?"

Cord looked down at his now gripped hands that were being held near his heart and said, "I stand by it. I'm sure. Ask away." He finally looked toward Harmony and even without eye contact, she could see that his dreary eyes contained not even a hint of joy.

"I heard three things in that statement Cord. First, you said Hope is in love. Second, you said she's in love with someone else. And third, the one I am actually most disturbed about is, you said you *found* proof. I repeat *found* proof."

Cord replied quickly, "Boy you sure did read a lot into what I said. You're supposed to focus on the 'she loves someone else' part. Nothing else."

Harmony's voice lowered as if she was mildly scolding him. "Cord, I am a single girl who also lives alone. When I hear that a guy 'found' proof of something in a girl's apartment, it can only mean that he was snooping and poking his nose where it probably did not belong. If not being able to figure her out was so hard on you emotionally, maybe you should be asking her questions. Maybe you should be spending time with her instead of me. I don't know how many times I'll have to say that to you. For now though, you better tell me about this proof and how it was acquired before I refuse to ever see you again."

Cord wasted no time defending his statement. "Harmony, it was an accident. I told you that. Basically, I was at her house this evening and she had just come home. She was in the kitchen starting dinner. We were talking and she heard her phone buzz. She asked me to go get it from her room for her. I went into her bedroom and didn't see it. Hope told me to check the bedside table. It wasn't there. She argued that it was there

189

because that's where she left it. I rolled my eyes and told her the table is not so big and I am not so blind that a phone could be hidden or camouflaged. I thought perhaps it was under her pillow because I know a lot of girls sleep with their phones under their pillows. I lifted her pillow to check and there was a picture of her with another guy right there. I thought my heart would burst. I couldn't even breathe. The phone buzzed again and I found it on her bathroom counter. I looked at the photo once more and saw that she was wearing an engagement ring. I have no doubts that Hope is still in love with her ex. I am also upset that she never told me they were engaged." Cord's voice softened, "Harmony, there was no mistaking how they feel about each other. There was no doubt that she was holding on to someone she dearly loves."

Silence. Hope had to process what he was saying. A decision had to be made about how she was going to respond to this as Harmony and how she should handle this as Hope.

"Uh... um... Cord,"

"Yeah?"

"Did it occur to you that if Hope wanted to be with that guy, she would be?"

He looked at her but she feared holding eye contact with him. She continued, "Cord, if Hope was meant to be with him, then perhaps she would be."

"Harmony, it all makes sense now. She keeps me at a distance. She won't discuss her past. She is very secretive about him. I think she plans on trying to get him back. At the very least, I think she misses him and wishes that she was still with him." His tone grew angry, "Why else would she keep a picture of another guy under her pillow?"

Cord's assessment that he thought Hope would go back to Evan and that she misses him and wishes she still had him was too much for her to bear. Fighting tears so her voice wouldn't crack, Harmony became insistent, "Cord, work this out with your girlfriend." She proceeded to pack her bag.

"Harmony! Wait. Don't leave. I don't know what you are so upset about."

She replied with an angry whisper, "Ugh! Cord! Why do you think she keeps you at a distance? Have you done anything to draw her closer to you outside of your beds? Instead of fighting a nameless guy in a photograph, pull her closer to you and find out why she has the picture under her pillow."

"Harmony, please don't imply there is anything of ill repute happening between us. We love each other."

"Then why are you here with me and why are you worried about her feelings for another guy!?"

"I just want to know why a girl would keep a picture of another guy under her pillow if she didn't still love him? I am not being paranoid."

"Do you stay with her often?"

"Yes."

"Then I doubt she *keeps* the photo under her pillow. Maybe she was looking at the picture because she longs for what it represents to her, being close to someone again. It is possible

Cord that she isn't after that particular guy anymore. Girls don't search for the exact same guy over and over. They search for the *connections* they had when they were in love or were loved."

Cord's expression lightened. He almost smiled. Harmony was still fighting tears and she was not making herself feel any better.

"So, it's possible that she looks at the picture of her former fiancé because she wants another relationship? It's not because she misses him?"

Now she couldn't hold back. "Ugh! Cord! Good night."

Harmony stormed away exiting down a different row so she didn't have to step over him. He thought nothing of it.

Cord sat for a while pondering all of the ideas Harmony had placed in his mind. Although he was glad he had been open with her about his thoughts and feelings, he was realizing that they had reached the beginning of their end. To strengthen his bond with Hope, he needed to be having these conversations with Hope.

One more Saturday here. Maybe one more Saturday here. I'll see how this week goes.

Chapter 19

Hope raced from the library home. She had to prepare herself for Cord's questioning. She knew he was coming and he was ready to find out more about her past, the past she had been refusing to share with him.

Hope had time to change from Evan's overalls and flannel shirt into her pajamas. By the time she had her hair up and her teeth brushed, Cord had arrived.

Even though she was so nervous she could vomit, her greeting was casual as she opened the door, "Hey Cord, come on in. Harmony not at the library tonight?"

"No, she was; she left already."

His discomfort was blatant so she tried to keep the conversation light. "Huh? That was a quick date."

"It wasn't a date Hope. Believe it or not, I don't even know what the girl looks like. We sit pretty far apart and just talk."

"If y'all are so far apart, how can you hear each other in a library?"

Cord was afraid Hope would get suspicious if he said they were sitting in a secluded corner where no one else ever seems to appear. Therefore, he chose to embellish the truth a bit.

"Harmony likes weird books, so there's never anyone looking in the section where she sits on Saturdays."

"Is that right Cord?" She paused then added, "I don't care where y'all sit. I assumed you two had a private study room or something. That's where I sit when I meet people at the library. It certainly makes talking a lot easier. I pictured your conversations more like counseling sessions." She rolled her eyes, turned and walked away from him toward her living area.

"Are you mad Hope? You sound irritated."

She felt bad for sounding jealous of herself, she stopped, looked over her shoulder and said, "I'm not mad at all Cord. Just because I don't have friends here doesn't mean you shouldn't. Keep visiting your friend. I really don't mind. I promise."

Relieved, Cord walked over to Hope and took her hand. "Are you on your way to bed?"

"Yep. Are you ready for bed now?" she asked.

"Almost. It's kind of early still. We should talk." He smiled and pulled her face to his for an enticing kiss.

Uh oh. Here it comes.

When he pulled away from her, he said, "Hope, I know you're talking to your ex again."

Calmly she responded, "No Cord, I am not. I promise."

He said it again but with more conviction, "Hope, please don't lie to me. I can handle anything but lies. Admit it, you're involved with your ex again."

"No Cord. I won't admit to that because it's not true. Why are you saying this?"

Hope immediately regretted asking that question. She had rushed home from the library and gotten changed so Cord wouldn't see her in Evan's clothes. In her panic to hide her pretense of being Harmony, she completely forgot about her engagement photo with Evan being under her pillow. Her distress was visible through her eyes. Cord could read every thought.

She's terrified. It's still there.

"Hope, tell me why I think you're talking to him again."

Hope pulled away from him and lowered her eyes. Cord knew she was giving him permission to go retrieve the evidence he was going to use to prove his point in this discussion.

Moving to her bedside, Cord paused. "Should I proceed?"

She nodded. There was no reason to lie or hide. She had not done what he was accusing her of.

Not wanting any deception from the woman he hoped he had a future with, Cord lifted her pillow and picked up the framed photograph. Guilt and hurt appeared on her face.

Cord decided to study the picture more closely since the proverbial cat had been let out of the bag. Hope watched Cord's eyes and prayed he wouldn't show any signs of anger towards Evan. She was afraid she'd lose her temper and throw him out if he did. Her heart would forever protect Evan's memory and his image in anyone's mind.

A decision to talk his way through his thoughts was made so Hope would know exactly what he was thinking. "He certainly is handsome. Clearly, in this photo, he loves you. His eyes don't lie. He definitely loved you when this picture was taken." Hope held back tears by taking a deep breath. Cord continued, "He must be young, because you're young and he must have had access to money because that ring is, well, it's a nice ring. It had to have been expensive. You two are on the beach," he looked to Hope when he said, "and that makes me wonder if he is the reason you can't decide between the beach or the mountains for your painting."

"Cord, please!"

"No Hope, I'm not done yet. I get to finish my thoughts." He stared. Then he crushed her, "Obviously the guy in this picture is full of life. This guy lives each day to the fullest. That's another reason his smile is so big and probably the reason you seem to struggle alone. Perhaps his zest consumed you." He looked to Hope and sadly asked, "How'd I do babe?"

She buried her face in her hands and for the second time that day, released a river of tears. She wrapped her arms around her waist and gave in to the pressure to gasp for air.

Cord watched feeling angry but also sorry for hurting the girl he had decided to love. Wanting information, he asked, "How old were you here Hope?"

"Nineteen." Her reply barely audible.

"Do you still want him? Is that why his picture is under your pillow?"

She shook her head, "No. I promise, I will never be with him again."

"That wasn't my question. My question is, why is his picture in your bed, the same bed you now share with me?"

"Colton asked me about him today. I showed him pictures on my phone. When I got home, I pulled that one out of my drawer. While I was *just looking* at it, you came home and it scared me, so I shoved it there."

"Now I have even more questions. How long were you with Colton and why didn't you tell me? That certainly should have been mentioned. That upsets me. I deserve to know why you withheld seeing Colton today from me."

Her tone was laden with guilt and sorrow. "Cord, I am so sorry." She turned and screamed, "Gawd!" Then looked back to Cord, "Can I get near you?"

"Yes. Come on. Let's sit on the couch. This could take a while. There is so much I want to know. We very well could still be sitting here this time tomorrow."

Hope laughed a little. "Thank you."

Cord sat and when Hope joined him, he pulled her legs over his lap so she was sitting sideways and able to face him. He then draped her blanket over their legs.

Colton was right, even when he's angry, he is loving. Don't screw this up Hope.

"Back to Colton Hope. Oh unless you want to go for a run, read a book, shop online, get a drink of water, or bake a cake."

She laughed again and said, "No. Let's do this."

He nodded in agreement.

She began, "Running into Colton today was one-hundred percent random. He was at the library. We decided to sit in a study room to talk for a few minutes so we wouldn't disturb anyone. You can't argue with me about that Cord; those rooms are for meeting and talking."

"I'm just listening. Keep going."

Hope inhaled and continued, "Colton and I talked about our majors and graduation, and I mentioned that I'm off schedule for an on time graduation because I took last semester off. He wanted to know why. Then, hormones or something kicked in. I spilled my life story while crying like a freaking baby. He drove me home. I took out that picture just before you came over. Now you are all caught up. Except, I need you to take me to get my bike tomorrow." Hope felt much better about herself.

"That certainly was a jumbled mess of what I am sure is an abbreviated version of the whole truth. So, you get more questions. First, what did Colton say about your life history with that guy?"

"He looked at the pictures on my phone and told me I should talk to you more."

"Geesh, pictures on your phone?"

"Mm hm."

"That aside, I will admit Harmony told me the same thing; I should talk to you more." He paused, then added, "I won't let you seeing Colton at the library upset me anymore. That would make me a hypocrite since I did go see Harmony tonight."

Yeah! Colton and I met by chance, not on purpose. Don't you dare say it Hope!

Cord asked, "Can I see your phone?"

"Are you checking it to see if I have calls from my former boyfriend?"

"Actually I was not. I want to see a few pictures for myself. Only a few. Wait, is his number still in your phone?"

Her defensive side kicked in, "Yes, but you are not touching that. It's my phone. I can have any number in there that I want. I bet you that your ex-girlfriend's number is still in your phone."

"Fine. We'll both let that one go too. Back to the photos, can I see them?"

Hope thought for quite some time on this one. Cord watched her face carefully. Her response finally came to her, "I don't want to see pictures of you and your old girlfriend Cord. I truly don't. You are supposed to be mine now. If I see you with her, in my mind, it will completely remove me from your life. Pictures of the two of you will take me to a time when I didn't exist in your world. We are supposed to be moving forward each day, not backward. As for her calling you, if she did, I will trust you to tell me. You have to trust me too. So, you have seen one photo of me with him and it hurt you. I don't think seeing others will make you feel any better."

Cord let her words sink in. She had very valid points. "I still need to ask, why do you have photos of you two on your phone?"

"Welcome to the twenty-first century. That's where they are and where they will remain until I put them on another device for storage. You better not dare ask me to delete six years of my life. If you are even thinking it, you can leave right now. I won't ask you to delete four years of photos from your phone or life."

"Ha! I don't have four *days* of photos on my phone."

Shaking her head and feeling glad they both could laugh again, Hope tried to finalize their discussion. "I never want to hurt you Cord. I am sorry about putting that photo under your pillow, if we are being technical. I, um, I guess I was remembering my past. I was remembering a time when I felt truly secure and felt like my future was headed in one direction. The end of our relationship threw my world into a blender and the grinding and noise and sadness wouldn't stop. I am getting better now though and that is all because of you. You are the only person I have allowed into my life in almost a year. Then you opened a flood gate and brought your whole family with you. Can you try to imagine what it was like to be with one person for as long as you can remember back, and then wake up one day and that person has left you? I took our picture out because I wanted a memory of my life that is now gone forever. I chose to leave all of that to start from the very beginning again. I've been alone for a long time. I will confess that I will probably look at old pictures from time to time, but trust me when I promise you, he is in my past."

Cord decided to assume that Harmony's assessment was correct and that was, that Hope missed the connection of being with someone she loved. He caressed her soft legs beneath the blanket and he turned his face upward. Hope hugged her body waiting for Cord's response.

He lowered his head and looked at her, "Are you tired yet Hope?"

"Very. It's been a hard day."

"Go get in the bed. I'll walk with you and join you in a few minutes."

Cord tossed the blanket to the side and helped Hope to her feet. They walked to her bed together and he picked up the photo before pulling the covers back for her. When she climbed in, she moved to the far side and rested her head on a pillow facing Cord. Once she was settled, Cord studied the picture one more time. *There's more. There's so much more. This guy doesn't look like he ever planned on leaving her. This guy was in love with her.* Cord finally opened her beside drawer, placed the photo gently upside down, and he quietly closed the drawer. Hope watched, wondering what he was thinking.

After closing the drawer, Cord looked at the young woman before him. In her eyes he saw uncertainty. While they held each other's focus, Cord decided he would not let this obstacle alter his feelings until he knew the full story. If Hope wasn't asking him to leave, she must still want him around, at least for the time being.

Unwilling to waste another moment idle, Cord turned and went into the bathroom to change into his shorts that he kept at her apartment. Hope had closed her eyes in relief the instant he turned away from her. Not drifting into sleep, just waiting restfully, she listened. Cord opened the door, turned off the light, then walked into the kitchen to turn off all of the other lights. When he returned to her room, Hope was lying on her back wiping her face one last time with her hand tucked up her sleeve. With no words exchanged, Hope looked up at Cord and the two stared once more.

Harmony does that, he thought.

Unable to take his silence any longer, Hope pulled the covers back inviting Cord to join her. Finally a smile from him was gifted, and she returned the peace offering. Cord slowly stretched his body the length of hers and slipped his right arm under her neck. As she positioned her head on his shoulder, he held her with both arms and kissed her relentlessly. Feeling comforted by him, Hope wasted no time shifting them both until Cord was resting entirely down the center of her body.

He whispered, "It's getting much harder not to cross the last line Hope. This position doesn't help us."

"I know, but this is where I need you right now."

"Okay babe. I'll stay right here then."

Chapter 20

Another Sunday was upon them and since learning of the existence of a new love in their son's life, all of the Cooley's were attending the same service time as Hope and Cord. Positioned to her right was Mrs. Cooley, with Cord on her left, Hope was able to sketch. Her new family members found her talent to be impressive and they too made conversation pieces of her work during lunch. This week's gathering was much less dramatic as Colton sat quietly simply taking it all in. Hope and Cord were feeling secure and had no reluctance openly sharing their connection.

The newness of their love was still overpowering and they continued to spend each night together. Cord was beginning to contemplate inviting Hope to move in with him. He watched closely, without bringing up the subject, to see how attached she was to her own space. The longing to have her at his house everyday made it difficult to remain objective, but he thought she would be better off with him. *Maybe if she doesn't have to pay rent, she can work fewer hours and she can finally buy a freaking coat! Man she is stubborn.*

Mid-week, Colton stopped by his dad's office to help with an advertising design project, and while he was there he decided to chat with Cord for a while. After hugs and small talk that included jokes and insults, Cord couldn't help but disclose his most recent idea to his brother. Colton always had a way of putting other people's ideas under a microscope and revealing the near invisible details, also known as flaws, to them.

"I'm thinking of asking Hope to move in with me."

"Oh my gawd! You cannot be serious Cord! You don't even know her!"

"Yes I do and what I don't know I'll learn. I want to marry her."

"Live with her? Marry her? How long have you known Hope?"

"We've been together a month."

"Ah! Brilliant. One whole month." One of Colton's relationship awareness ideas surfaced because he already knew what Cord's response would be. "Cord, why don't we all go out together Saturday night. You can see how she is in a crowded place besides church. You can watch her interact with others and actually talk to someone besides you! You two seem to keep to yourselves and I don't know if that is her choice or your's. So, let's all get out and have fun, Saturday night."

"Saturday won't work for us. Hope likes to stay home and read or paint."

"And what about you Cord?"

"I have plans this Saturday, but I'll talk to Hope and maybe we can all go out the next Saturday."

He is such a jerk. He is meeting some other girl. I'll revisit the idea of them moving in together.

"Plans huh? Well, the next Saturday will work for me too. Tell Hope to clear her busy reading and painting schedule. As for the topic of you asking her to move in with you, I can't get on board with that one Cord. You lived with Kendal for four years and look how that turned out."

"Colton, certainly you can see that Kendal and Hope are two very different people."

"They are right now, but if you ask Hope to move in with you, I'll bet you the world, you'll turn her into a Kendal: a self-centered, miserable, head-case. Please don't lead Hope down that kind of a path."

"I'm not leading her anywhere."

"Fine, then don't *drag* her down that path!"

Huh! That's the same thing Hope said about me and Colton. Wait. Is he right?

"Colton, I don't want to talk about this after all. I shouldn't have brought it up. Forget I mentioned it."

"Forgetting it is not going to happen. I don't have some sort of brain damage Cord. You need to think about getting some space from Hope. She's trying to survive on her own. Let her figure things out for herself. Stop trying to mold her into what you want for yourself." Colton stormed out of Cord's office.

He did it. He put my good news under his Colton shaped microscope and turned my future with Hope into my past with Kendal. Then he had the nerve to tell me I'd change what I love about her. He's so frustrating. I should have never said anything to him. I'll give this another week before I bring it up to Hope though.

That night, with his conversation with Colton fresh in his mind, Cord showed up to Hope's with groceries. He had been buying everything they needed for meals in hopes that she could save up for anything else she may want or need in her life. While he was unpacking the bags, Hope sat on her floor reviewing notes and highlighting her texts.

I have to know how she feels. I was going to wait, but I need to know. "Hope, why are we always here at your place? We have so much more space at my house?"

Without looking up she answered, "We stay here because this is where all of my stuff is babe. I get up earlier than you and I also don't want to lug my books back and forth every night."

Hm, that's all logistics. Maybe she would want to move in with me if her stuff was at my, I mean our house. "Hope, we can take all of your things to my house."

He got her attention. She knew what he was hinting at but she couldn't react. She kept her head down acting like they were just having any normal conversation. Tapping her lip with her pen she said, "Um, nah, I feel comfy here. This is all mine. It's me. Your house is you. I like my things right where they are. Thanks for trying to make life a bit easier for me though."

Geesh! How on earth could he possibly think we are ready to live together? We haven't made it through a week without arguing over our pasts yet.

"Hope, look at me." His tone was serious now.

She emptied her hands and gave him her attention. "Yes Cord."

"I do want to make things easier for you. I really love you and I need you to feel safe and happy and like you have everything you need."

She didn't need anytime to respond, "I told you the day I met you that I have every *thing* I need in North Carolina. I don't care about things right now. I care about finding out who I am and what I want out of this life. I can't do that in your house. This space is mine. I am safe here and thanks to you, I am becoming happier here. I'm sorry. I hope it doesn't upset you, but I don't want to live with you, not right now at least. We are too new."

Cord walked to her and knelt beside her. "I'm not upset. I don't know how else to show you how much I'm falling more and more in love with you every day."

"You can just say it and show it by the amazing way you treat me. Those will be fine."

He whispered, "Okay, I'd like to start with, I love you and I'm cooking you dinner."

"Nice work. I love you too and I am starving! I'll keep an ear open for the dinner bell." They chortled, kissed, and went back to their respective tasks.

Her eyes were on her books, but her thoughts were on their relationship. He spends one night a week with another girl. *How on earth could he expect me to move in with him? We have so much to learn about each other. I'm still waiting for him to choose me. I would also like for him to talk to me the way he talks to Harmony.*

* * *

Saturday arrived. Cord ran errands while Hope painted. The Saturday market downtown had closed for the winter season and the gray, cold air was too icy for Hope to feel like going for a hike. She fixed a cup of tea and took her canvas and paint box out. Before getting comfortable, she removed the lid and took out Evan's note.

Hope had thought about this treasure many times since its discovery and she had decided right where to put it so it would be safe. With Evan's handwriting pressed very delicately to her lips, she went to her beside table and took out their engagement photo. Hope slid the back off so she could place the note safely behind the photograph.

Shock consumed her as she read, "I'm always carrying you my Love. No matter what decisions you face, good or bad, I've got you. I trust you. I believe in you. I love you." *Another note? Evan when did you write these?*

"He touched this. He wrote this. He's still with me," she whispered to herself.

After some time was spent with Evan, Hope was careful to place the frame back in the exact same position as she had found it in case Cord checked on it sometime. As she slid the drawer closed, she thought, *Why am I so afraid of what Cord thinks? This is my house. Something feels off. I don't know if I am doing this right Evan.*

Slowly, Hope stood and went back to her canvas. Her paint brush began to move and the ocean appeared.

Hours after she became consumed by her work, Hope cleaned up her mess and made herself presentable. Cord had said he would be back around five. Feeling lethargic, she returned to her couch to wait.

Cord knew that the door would be unlocked for him so he entered as if it were his own home. Hope had fallen asleep.

"Hope. Hope, sweetie. Wake up." He stroked her hair lightly.

"My head hurts and I'm tired," she mumbled.

"Are you sick? Can I get you anything?"

"Maybe some water and something light to eat?"

"When was the last time you ate? It's five o'clock."

She shrugged and closed her eyes. Truthfully, she had lost her appetite when she found another note from Evan. Then, she got so busy painting that she lost track of time. Before she realized what was happening, she was dizzy and dehydrated.

"Why haven't you eaten?"

"I was busy painting."

"Oh." That excuse left him less concerned. "I'll get you something right now."

After bringing Hope a cut up apple, some crackers and water, he helped her sit up so she could eat. When she was upright and color was returning to her complexion, he walked over to the canvas. He commented, "I thought you were painting the mountains. There's an ocean here now."

"Yes, but look closely."

"Ah, why is it half beach scene and half mountain scene?"

"I don't know yet. It's still evolving, growing, changing."

Cord listened to her melancholy tone. *One afternoon without me here and she's depressed again. This is why she needs to be living with me. And after the week I've had, I need to be with her.*

Chapter 21

"Off to see Harmony tonight?" Hope dreaded his response. She was in no mood to leave home to go pretend to be *herself* again.

"Last time Hope. The girl is doing good and truthfully, she doesn't seem to have any problems at all anymore. I'm only running over there to tell her goodbye and that it's been nice chatting with her these past five weeks. I'll be home soon."

"I like the sound of that. It means I get to have my first Saturday night date with the very same man who thinks I should move in with him."

He heard her derision and guiltily contemplated her point of view. Before turning the door knob he looked back to her. "Do you want me to stay?"

"No," was her only reply. Her thought, *I want you to want to stay!*

"Hope, honesty please."

"Ugh! Go!" She calmed her tone before adding, "Cord, I don't feel well. Just go. I am going to be horrible company tonight. I'm going to bed. I'll meet you at church in the morning." *As long as he agrees, I won't have to rush home to change clothes and then have to act perky.*

Cord returned to Hope and knelt in front her. "Look at me Hope. I need to see your eyes." He pulled her chin upward so he could feel her breathing on his lips. He watched silently.

Hope's eyes were tired and she was straining not to blink. Very softly she spoke, "I'm tired today. Go. I will meet you at church in the morning. This will all be better by then. It always is. We seem to disagree on Saturdays, then make up on Sundays. You're the accountant, you know those aren't horrible percentages for the amounts of time we are truly happy."

"I'm happy all the time because you're mine," he sweetly replied.

There was no energy for another argument. "I love you Cord, so much. I promise I love you." *But this isn't working.*

"I love you too. Get a good night's sleep. I'll see you in the morning. Since I won't be here tonight for the first time in weeks, I'll give you your bedtime kiss now." His kiss was so consoling and honest, she almost forgot what they were even talking about.

When he finally got up and left, Hope released and internal scream of frustration over having to go out into the freezing night and give relationship advice to her own boyfriend. Deciding to forgo the overalls and flannel, she put an old sweatshirt over what she was already wearing, wound her hair up in a bun, and pulled on her dad's old baseball cap.

Hope arrived panting and opened her book. Once again, she was shocked that she had gotten there first. *He has got to be stopping somewhere before he comes here.* Taking her seat under the direct beam of the canister light in the corner, Hope shifted her hat so her face would be shadowed.

Confident that she was hidden in plain sight, Hope wasted no time in becoming engrossed in her novel. "Let's see, Deneb is fading back and Prince Alatair is beginning to shine. There is still no resolution to the dying heart of the princess. Deneb is going to have to use his secret or watch her die. Alatair's solution, kill the evil queen and you kill the evil spell. Not so fast hero, if you kill the queen you could very well kill Princess Vega too. Deneb seems to know Queen Lyra better than you. After all, he does come from the wizardry house of Cygnus. Be careful prince. Slaying the proverbial dragon isn't always the solution."

"I know that book!"

"Oh geesh Cord! Don't sneak up on people."

"I'm not. I walked right up here and you didn't hear me. I'm not sure you would have heard a tornado."

"Funny. I was reading smart guy."

"Yeah, I heard. Hope is reading that book too."

Cover it up Harmony. "I'm sure she is. Everyone reads this book. That's why they are making a theme park out of it."

"They are?!"

A whispered sarcastic scold ejected, "No! *They* are not. However, it is a classic to Fantasy freaks. Sort of like Super Spiderman comics."

"That's Superman and Spiderman and they are from two totally different superhero conglomerations. One is DC and the other is Marvel."

"So you are a nerd like me?"

"No. Everyone knows the difference between those two groups Hope."

"What did you call me?"

"I mean Harmony. Sorry. I guess I'm thinking about Hope even though I'm talking to you."

"It's okay. We can get right to the therapy session. You said last week that this will be our final meeting. You still feel that way?"

"I'm thinking yes."

"Okay then. Let's hear it. Hope is consuming your thoughts. Cygnus has mine. The sooner we get to talking, the quicker we can get to solving. Is everything okay?"

"Yeah. It's all good with us."

"You don't sound or *look* very convincing. You're fidgeting and moping. Did something happen between you two? Did you decide maybe she's not *all that* for you?"

"No. Definitely not."

Harmony raised her chin more to show him he had her attention. "Soooo…" she coaxed.

"So, I told her I was coming here to check on you again."

"And she was okay with that? You know if she was truly okay with you coming here to see me again, then you've got the one in a million."

"I do have my one. Hope says that the world is lucky that she is one in seven billion. Which is funny because isn't that what you said the first night I saw you here? There are seven billion people on the planet?"

"Clearly you are avoiding something. Why am I not convinced that you believe Hope is your one in seven billion? You seem awfully nervous or insecure about something." *He's not being very open even with Harmony right now. He must be really upset about something.*

"I'm mostly nervous, but it's not Hope I'm worried about, nor my relationship with her."

"Oh, that's right. It's *me* you're worried about. Well don't be Cord. I'm fine. I promise." Harmony sat in her corner now with the side of her head resting against the wall to her left. Cord sat in his same place about twenty feet away from her leaning against the bookshelf. Though this time, he was turned at a slight angle away from Harmony's direction.

When he made no immediate reply she persisted, "Cord, spill it. Tell me what's bothering you."

He whispered, "Kendal called."

Her head lifted. "What?" She shot back at him though maintaining a raspy whisper. *Don't be crazy. Let him talk. You're not Hope. Now try it again with more reason and intellect.* "I mean, what? When did she call you?"

"She didn't actually call, she texted several times this week."

"She must really want or need to get in touch with you. What does she want? Did she say?"

"She wants to see me. She says she misses me."

"Oh, of course she does. She's a woman who has nothing better to do than mess with men. What did you say to her?"

"Nothing. I didn't reply. I don't have anything to say to her."

Whew! That's a relief but get more information. "If you have nothing to say to her, why are you bringing this up to me? Obviously you are at least curious or you feel like there's something left unsaid between you two. Otherwise, this would not be a topic of our conversation."

He sat for quite a while in a silent struggle. Harmony understood, Hope would not. He finally said, "I live in the same town as her. She was very important to me. She hurt me. Our paths cross. I want her behind me, and I thought she was until I got a message from her. Harmony, I know I don't love her, at all, but there's a part of me that wants to see her, make sure she's okay, and I want to tell her about Hope."

"Why are you so concerned about making sure the women in your life are all okay?"

"I don't know."

"Yes you do, so say it."

"I was genuinely concerned the first time I saw you and now I like coming here because our conversations help me with my relationship with Hope. As for Kendal, I am curious about why she's calling and I want to know that she's okay."

Jerk!

"If you are concerned about Kendal's well-being, then why do you want to tell her about Hope? What difference will knowing about Hope make in that girl's life?"

He hesitated, then admitted, "I want her to know how happy I am."

"You mean you want to try to hurt her."

"No, not intentionally, not deliberately. I just want her to know how truly happy I am."

"I'm not buying it Cord. If you were so secure with Hope and completely over Kendal, you wouldn't have a care in the world as to what Kendal knows about you. The only reason you would want to tell her about your new girlfriend is because you still care enough about her to want to know what she thinks."

"Harmony, I want Hope and only Hope in my life. I don't —"

"Stop talking Cord. You don't need to make any excuses to me about your *girlfriends*. You can lie to yourself but you can't lie to me. It's pointless because I have nothing invested here. That's also why I'm not afraid to tell you the truth as I see it. There's something, I know it's something very small, but there is something about Kendal that is still tugging at you."

When she stopped talking Cord looked at her waiting for more words, any words at all, so he didn't have to speak. She obliged, "Go see her. Go meet Kendal. Tell her 'Hi' for me. Tell her whatever it is you feel you have to say."

"What do I tell Hope?"

217

Hope was immediately disappointed and angry that he didn't argue with her at all, but Harmony had a role to play. "Don't lie to Hope."

"I wouldn't. I wouldn't do that." He braced his head in both of his hands as if he was trying to make a life altering decision. He added, "If I were to meet her, I don't even know where we'd go. I don't want to be alone with her."

"Cord, don't over think this. Make a decision. The geographic location of your conversation is irrelevant. Meet her at a freaking coffee shop like every other human does these days. Go to the Bean Counter. It's big. There are lots of windows, lots of people, lots of noise. No privacy there. Your location really does not matter. It's the meeting her that matters."

He still had his head down. Hope couldn't tell what his struggle was, but Harmony knew he'd been hurt and even though he thought he had healed, he hadn't yet. She could not influence him in either direction. Cord had to decide this on his own. She advised, "Cord, do what you want, but either way, you better tell me all about it. Maybe you're not here to help me. Maybe you actually needed me to help you."

Just then he realized that he honestly did want to help her. He was being selfish. "I'm sorry Harmony. Are you okay tonight? Has this been a good week for you?"

"Yep. I think we balance each other quite well. I had a great week. I told you I'm fine." *Until now!*

"Why are you here on Saturday night again?" he asked.

218

"Because my new boyfriend is busy on Saturday nights."
That's how you don't tell a lie.

Cord assumed that must mean her new guy works. Since Harmony seemed okay, he decided to ask, "What would you do Harmony? What would you do if Evan called you and wanted to see you again?"

Her heart stopped. Every molecule in her body tensed. Hope nor Harmony had been prepared for that question. She had to keep it together. "How do you know my ex-boyfriend's name is Evan?"

"I heard you mumble it the first time I saw you here. I heard you mumble that your name is Harmony too."

Holy cow! I sure am glad I've been withholding Evan's name from him these past few weeks. "You have good ears or a nosey disposition."

"Good ears. I don't usually care about other people's problems."

"Yeah right! That's why you're here every week."

"Well, other than your's," he added to defend himself.

"And apparently Kendal's!"

Cord dropped his head back so the books on the shelf held it up. The mention of Kendal replaced him into their conversation and his dilemma. He thought. He pleaded. "Tell me what you would do Harmony."

"I'll tell you that next week," Harmony said with mild derision.

"What? No. You could change your mind by then. What would you do? I want to know?"

"I won't change my mind. I won't change my answer. I only have one answer, but I'm not going to tell you until next week. This decision is all you. What I would do has nothing to do with what you should do. We are in two different situations."

"I won't be here next Saturday. I told Hope that this would be the last time I meet with you. I want to spend an actual Saturday with my girlfriend."

"Ha!" Harmony laughed. "That's probably the best idea you've had in a while Cord. It's about time. You planning a visit with your ex on top of spending Saturday nights with me may be more than any woman deserves to handle."

"So you still think I should meet Kendal?"

"No. You are not putting that on me. *You* make that decision, but don't lie to Hope. Don't do that to her, please."

Her anger caused Cord to assume Harmony had been lied to in the past. He had no idea the strain this was putting on Hope. She was almost done.

"I'm going to see her Harmony and I'll tell Hope about it afterward."

"What if Kendal wants to see you during a time that you are with Hope?"

"I'll just tell Hope that I have an errand to run and I'll be right back to her. I need to get this over with. I need this door not only closed but bolted and then walled over. I just feel like there's something left unsaid."

"Good luck Cord. I'm leaving. You've worn me out." They exchanged hidden smiles.

"Don't forget you promised to tell me what you'd do Harmony. You promised. Can we meet here Thursday?"

What is wrong with him!? She rolled her eyes even though he couldn't see her frustration. "Yes Cord. Thursday. But don't you dare lie to your girlfriend."

Chapter 22

Cord returned a text message to Kendal first thing Sunday morning, "We can meet, but not for long. I have plans. When and where did you have in mind?"

"How about church, then lunch?" she suggested.

"Two o'clock at the Bean Counter," he replied.

"Alright. Can't wait."

Dear God what have I just done? Cord squeezed his forehead staring at the screen of his phone. He deleted the message already terrified that somehow Hope would accidentally see it. Cord placed his phone on his beside table and turned over onto his stomach. *What have you done? Why are you doing this?*

The very next thought, *Hope.* "I had a horrible night without you. I couldn't sleep." Send.

"Same. Maybe being apart wasn't such a good idea last night. Although, I did enjoy having my own pillow to *not* sleep on, and I did feel like a queen in my big bed. I had no idea it was so large." Send.

Cord laughed. "Glad you had a royally rough night. You want me to pick you up or meet you there?" Send.

"I'll meet you there." Send.

Cord drug his tired, sore body out of the bed and got ready for church.

Although she had to pretend like she knew nothing in her texts, Hope had already been up getting ready and panicking over this bomb that she knew was going to drop. She knew what he was going to do and after only five weeks with Cord, she was terrified of losing him. "Evan, did I get too wrapped up too soon?" Hope swallowed down silent screams every minute until she was ready to leave for church.

Turning the key in her bolt to lock her door, Cord arrived to pick Hope up for church. "Hey!" His deep voice startled her from the top of her stairs and she screamed.

"Cord! God, you scared me to death! Don't do that. Call me. Text me. Wait by my car, by it, not in it! Do anything other than freaking me out with your surprise arrivals."

He began laughing as he jogged down the concrete steps to her.

"Hope? You okay?" A voice called from above their heads.

"Yes Garrett. Thank you."

"He's fast. He does look out for you doesn't he?"

"Yes and he believes in the second amendment like all good Idaho boys do." She reached up and gave him a quick kiss even though her heart was pounding in not a good way because of him. Hope still found the color of his eyes, his dark hair, his voice, his tall muscular physique, and his impeccable style irresistible. When she opened her eyes, she asked with pure jealousy, "Why the heck are you still so tan and you haven't seen the sun in two months? It's infuriating."

Laughing he said, "I tan in the winter too. I don't know, I guess my skin just absorbs rays even through the clouds."

"I would ask you to be quiet, but I had that coming since I asked you the question!" Hope rolled her eyes and demanded, "Since you're here, you're taking me to get a coffee. I was leaving early so I could run by the Perky Brewer on my way to church. My craving for whipped cream is driving me crazy. No sleep means an extra thousand calories for some reason. Our bodies are so primeval. Feeeeeed meeeee!" She droned hanging on Cord's sweater after her long ramble about coffee.

Cord could not stop smiling at her. Even cranky and random, she looked like an angel. Hope still refused to wear jeans to church so she was in an ivory mini skirt and another off-the-shoulder sweater, a pink one this time. Tan booties this week tied her ensemble together. Every clothing item had been selected very intentionally this day. Hope wanted to make sure that Cord would be thinking about her every second... well, except during the sermon. She smirked at her own possessiveness.

"I can't look away from you Hope."

"Then don't." She tilted her chin upward and smiled softly in anticipation of one of his unique, signature kisses. She got one, a good one. She loved how each time he had kissed her, he treated it like their first. *Maybe he changed his mind about seeing*

Kendal which would mean he's done with Harmony too. Maybe I am enough.

Cord took her hand and led her to his car. He opened her door as always and she slid onto the warm leather seat that he had already turned on for her knowing that she'd be in a skirt or dress regardless of the cold weather.

Her coffee was purchased, handed to her, and her moaning and enjoyment of it made him want to take her back home. "Hope stop making out with your coffee please."

"Agh! You can't say that when we are on our way to church!"

"I'm saying it *because* we are on our way to church. It's driving me nuts and making it impossible to clear my thoughts of anything but you and your tight little outfit. Now stop!"

"My sweater isn't too tight. It's just right."

"Yes. I can see that." He cut his eyes to her legs, her short skirt and her soft top.

She noticed. "Mmm..." She moaned once more and then burst into laughter almost spraying her coffee out her nose.

"Please don't spew sticky cream all over my dash babe." He laughed with her shaking his head. She giggled and reached for his right hand to hold for the remainder of the drive. He pressed his warm, soft lips to the back of her frigid skin.

Once the car was parked, before they got out, Cord collected one more kiss from her. Hope wondered if it was because of the enticing way she enjoyed her coffee, or if it was because he was carrying a weight within. She enjoyed it either way.

They walked into church hand in hand in plenty of time to greet and be greeted. His parents had saved them seats and they arrived still clenched to one another.

While the music was still playing and hymns were being sung, Hope's coffee kicked in and she had to excuse herself. When she stood and began to scoot past Cord, he squeezed her hand for assurance that she was okay. "Coffee babe. I'll be right back." She got a snicker and an eye roll from him. Her reply was a shrug.

Cord watched her expeditious walk down the aisle and out of the sanctuary. He rolled his eyes again when she stopped just past the open double doors and started looking frantically to the left then to the right. She must have jerked her head back and forth six times before she found the sign pointing to the restrooms. Cord thought about helping her, but watching her was much more entertaining. He returned his focus forward.

Tugging her skirt down and shifting her sweater back into a seamless fit, Hope stepped from the ladies' room and closed the door behind her. Three steps later, "Hey," a soft masculine voice pierced through her.

An outright scream was withdrawn, but not the scolding that usually follows it. "What is wrong with you people scaring the wits out of me? Colton! Why are you slinking around the door to the women's restroom? You look like a pervert."

"Stop with the compliments and the flirting Hope. We're in church."

"I was doing neither funny guy!" They both chuckled silently together until she asked, "What *are* you doing out here?"

"I saw a chance to talk to you alone so I took it. I was sitting in the back when you left the service. I waited for Cord to turn back around then I followed you." Hope knew Cord would have been watching her. If she is within range, his eyes are on her.

Now that she knew Colton a lot better, she was beginning to consider him her only friend. She didn't mind him seeking out a minute to chat. "What did you want to talk about?"

"I wanted to know how your week went. Last time I saw you, you weren't in the best of spirits and Cord was meeting some other girl that night. You doing okay? Are you and Cord doing okay? You're here together again so I assume you two are good."

Hope didn't want to lie to Colton. She had no reason to withhold how she was feeling about the Harmony, Kendal, Hope triangle that Cord stood in the middle of. After all, like her other situation, Colton had no investment in this. He could be objective. She did want to make sure he was ready for her version of the truth though. "Do you want to know how I really feel Colton or do you want to hear, 'Everything is great! Thanks for asking!'?"

"Truth, please!"

"Fine, I'll tell you the truth. The Harmony situation is very weird. Please don't ask. I'll explain it to you some other time.

He does go see her and he has been seeing her for five weeks. He told me he is done, but I know he's going to see her again Thursday of this week." Colton nodded and listened. She hesitantly continued, "My big problem is that, that,"

"Say it Hope."

Colton's eyes gave her strength. She knew she could trust him; Cord was right. "My big problem is that Cord is going to have coffee with Kendal today. I'm not being paranoid. He is going to meet her somewhere. And again, please don't ask me how I know, but trust that I do."

"I won't ask. I believe you."

"Colton, you don't sound surprised that he is going to see Kendal. Why aren't you experiencing a state of shock? Why is this casual, almost common, knowledge?"

Colton thought about her questions before responding. "Hope, do you trust Cord? I mean really trust him?"

"First, don't think I didn't just notice you avoiding my questions by asking one of your own. That doesn't look good for Cord. Second, I think I do trust him, but," she lowered her eyes to the floor.

"But what?"

Returning to Colton's eyes she said, "But, there is no mistaking that he is unsure about us on some level or he is still unsure of his feelings for Kendal. I can't tell which. Now, why aren't you surprised?"

"I won't meddle too much in Cord's personal life Hope, but I will say, my brother is not going to change. You are getting a version of him that has always existed. He loves deeply and he is not someone who will be unfaithful. He is someone who is trying to build his world around his expectations and his desires. Cord wants you now, but that doesn't mean that he isn't still trying to manipulate where he wants Kendal placed in the scheme of things. She hurt him. He remembers."

"I'm not asking him to change. I'm asking him to feel that I am enough and feel it with all of his heart. All of it. I need to get back. He's going to come looking for me and I don't want to have to make up excuses about why we are talking or what we are talking about."

"I agree. Give me your number. I want to check on you later. If you are sure that Cord is going to see Kendal, you may need a friend in a few hours."

Hope gave Colton her number and afterward they mutually reached for a hug. Their embrace lingered longer that a normal, friendly hug, but that was only because Hope was absorbing how relieved she was to be next to someone who knows her and listens to her.

He's Evan's size. That's why I can't let go.

She's been through too much. I need her to know that I'm here for her. That's why I can't let go.

Finally, Colton placed a friendly kiss to the hair that covered Hope's neck and he released her. "Go. You have some drawing to catch up on."

Hope returned to Cord and sat. He looked at her with question marks in his eyes. She whispered, "Don't ask."

"I wasn't going to. I'm just glad you're not lost or trapped in the basement." She smiled and tried to focus forward, but Cord leaned to her and asked, "Hope, is something wrong?"

"No, why?"

"You're shaking, trembling. Are you cold?"

"Um, I don't know. I didn't realize I was shaking." She hadn't realized it. She was so nervous her heart was pounding, but she wasn't aware that her body was matching her heart beat. "I'm sorry." Hope tried to scoot away to give him space thinking she was distracting him, but he just wrapped his arm around her shoulder instead.

"Maybe you should wear actual sweaters during the winter." He smiled at her and rubbed her bare skin. She turned her head to the left, leaned a bit and kissed the back of his hand that was working to comfort her. Then, she placed the fingers of her left hand over his while placing her right hand gently on his knee. He covered her chilled hand with his own.

Is this what Heaven feels like? he thought.

How can this be the same man who plans on lying to me today? He's so perfect.

They remained in contact for the rest of the sermon.

Chapter 23

After church, without discussing it, Cord took Hope straight to a little hidden pizza place downtown. They enjoyed their lunch alone and she was grateful for the surprise. They ordered, sat and indulged.

Midway through their meal, Cord wiped his hands and began rubbing them together. Hope noticed but waited. What she expected to hear from him was completely different from what she did hear. He asked, "Can I trust you Hope?"

Her thought, *That's a weird question since I'm not the one contemplating visiting another woman and possibly lying about it.* Her response, "You can try."

He looked at her quizzically feeling very unsure of what that meant. Cord then asked, "Do you trust me?"

"I try. You haven't given me any reason to not trust you yet. You even tell me about that girl you spend Saturday nights with. I'm not going to follow you around and spy on what you do with that other girl, so all I can do is trust you. It's sometimes a bit difficult, but I try my best."

"I'm not visiting her this Saturday. I want to go on a date with you."

"Alright. I'm free." She took a bite and with her mouth partially filled, she mumbled, "So why the weird questions? Did you do something that I should know about?"

"No, I didn't. I just want to know if I can trust you to trust me."

"Ah… hence the 'Can I trust *you*?' question. Well, I don't know Cord. I'm pretty independent these days and even though I worry constantly about hurting you, I also don't want to get hurt. I'm honestly trying to let you see this other girl without acting like some crazed girlfriend because I want to see where this goes between us. Although we are very new, we should be honest with ourselves and each other. Either of us could walk away at this point in our relationship and we would recover. You and I both came out of very serious, very long term situations. I love you and I know you love me, but we'd survive. With all of that said, I think instead of wondering if you can trust me, you should be pondering what you are planning that seems to make you afraid that you could lose me."

"You talk like Harmony." *Oh crap! What did I just do? Oh crap! She's going to hate me for comparing her to another girl.* "I mean… I mean…" he stuttered.

"Stop talking Cord. Don't dig your hole any deeper. Just be quiet. Let me recover."

They sat in silence for a few minutes until Hope said, "Eat your pizza, it's getting cold and I'm ready to go home."

"Hope, I, I…"

"Will you please eat? I think we need to…" Hope widened her eyes and placed her index finger over her lips in the universal "Shh" sign. She then let him off the hook by winking at him and taking another bite of her own slice.

After a few more moments of silence Cord said, "For the record, I don't plan on changing that you are my girlfriend. I plan on seeing where this goes too."

Hope raised her eyebrows at him and retorted, "Ever? Because if you don't plan on ever changing the fact that I'm your girlfriend, then you and I have very different ideas about relationships and that is what we should be discussing over these meals."

Cord shot his chair backward, stood from his seat, took one large step to Hope, pulled her to her feet, and kissed her. When he released her, he whispered in her ear, "You're my girlfriend for now, but I want to do that to you every day for the rest of my life. Do you believe me? Does that statement help you understand where I plan on this going?"

From her trance, she summoned only the ability to nod.

"Good."

* * *

Entering Hope's tiny apartment after lunch, Cord walked directly to her painting to study it.

"I'm anxious to see this finished. Is it still for me?"

"Yes it's for you. Why would I change my mind?"

"I was just making sure." He looked closely at different brush strokes and stood back to take it all in. "Why is it nighttime?"

"Because that's when you see the moon?"

"No, I mean, why isn't it a daytime piece? This is awfully dark for a full moon to be shining, especially this moon. It's enormous."

Hope hadn't given the darkness any thought. This painting began with a pitch black sky. Next, the full moon was added and for months the only changes she made were enlargements to the moon. Knowing the history and the original intent of the piece made finishing it very difficult. It was supposed to be a moonlit beach, then mountains, but now this was a gift for Cord instead of Evan, so the evolution of the landscape would remain a mystery until she could decide where she feels most at peace.

Cord stood before the painting. Hope watched his expression, and she could tell he was trying to figure something out about her through her work. Her sketch journals shown clarity in her feelings, but this painting had him stumped. She stood beside him and stared at it as if it weren't her work. She wondered what she would think of it as an outsider.

"Cord, you don't have to stay here with me if you're bored." She brushed her fingers down his arm to the back of his hand.

Although he loved her touch and wanted more, he felt relieved because he had an appointment. "I'm never bored with you, but I am going to leave for a little while. I'll miss you though. I'll only be gone for an hour or two."

"I'll be here."

He kissed her goodbye. Before she closed the door behind him, she asked, "Where will you go for now?"

Dang! I wish she wouldn't have asked that! Don't lie! "I have an appointment at two. I'll tell you about it when I get back. I promise."

"Have fun. I'll see you in a little while." She forced an ignorant, loving smile knowing where he was actually going. They offered each other a subtle wave and she closed and locked the door behind him.

Hope leaned her back against the door. She checked the clock, one thirty-five. "Turns out I do have time to follow you around and spy on you. Gawd I'm going to hate myself for this."

Leggings, sweatshirt, running shoes, gloves, ponytail, hat... "God, I know this is wrong, but please don't make me regret it."

The one thing Hope knew was the absolute truth in this situation was that she needed to run! Not only had she eaten pizza, but her nerves were about to explode under her skin one by one. Her heart felt as if a jackhammer was in there trying to get out. She was jealous.

Once she was dressed, she stretched then jumped up an down a few times inside her apartment. Door locked, key and wallet secure, and she was off to see if they were at the Bean Counter.

Every step she took she begged herself to stop and turn around. All the begging, pleading and reasoning got jumbled in her ears. Harmony would never do this. The girl her parents raised would never spy on a guy. That girl loved herself enough to know that if a guy was being unfaithful or lying, then she was better off without him. That girl would let God handle it all.

Evan fell in love with Hope. That is the girl he knew first. Then slowly, she let him get to know Harmony. He decided he wanted to marry her because he loved them both. Evan loved her, every part of her, every mood, every tear, every talent, every habit. She never doubted his complete love. A true relationship is knowing all about someone and not only loving them anyway but loving them because all of their experiences make them complete.

Why couldn't she trust that Cord would love her completely too? He doesn't think Harmony is a freak even though she wears her ex-boyfriend's clothes. He accepts Hope and her sarcastic wit. He kisses her and tells her he wants to do this forever. *Why don't I trust him!? Why do I feel like he is going to leave me!?* She screamed inside her head. She continued running.

Suddenly, just before talking herself out of this insane escapade, Hope found herself at the coffee shop. Shaking her head like a cartoon character, she tried to snap out of her nightmare. Her hands were placed on her sides as she bent over in frustration. Gasping and panting, Hope stood by the window and peered inside. *The back of his head... He's there. He's right there. She's there. She's right there.* Hope's legs felt wobbly, but her body felt rigid. The jackhammer stopped pounding. Air stopped flowing. All she could do was stare.

Harmless. This is all harmless. He is here to tell her he loves you Hope. He is here to build a wall, a brick wall. Why is she smiling at him? Hope covered her eyes. When she uncovered them, Kendal had both of Cord's hands in hers and she was kissing his fingers. *He's not even pulling away from her!* She shoved past the glass door. To calm herself, she turned her face to the back of the room. After removing her hat and tucking it in the back of her leggings, she fluffed her hair. There was no way this girl was going to see her looking like a sweaty, crazed, tomboy, freak. Hope turned and approached them.

"Hey," she said casually.

"Uh! Um! Hi," Cord choked out, his hand still in Kendal's grip.

Hope politely held her hand to Kendal and said, "Hi, I'm Hope."

Apprehensively, Kendal released Cord and gently shook Hope's hand. "Hi, I'm Kendal." She immediately reinstated her hold on him.

"It's nice to meet you Kendal. I've heard so much about you."

Kendal replied clearly confused, "Uh, that's nice, and you are..."

"Oh, I'm nobody special. I go to the same church as Cord. Service was great today wasn't it Cord?" She smiled brightly at him. He nodded. Hope couldn't quite figure out what he was thinking. "Well, nice to meet you Kendal. Maybe our paths will cross again someday." Turning to Cord, "Maybe I'll see you next Sunday Cord. Maybe. I might try a new church. I haven't decided yet. Anyway, you two have a nice time."

Hope pulled her hat from her waistband and tugged it down over her ears. Then, as she turned to leave, Kendal called her name, "Hope wait!"

"Yes?" She asked with the pep of a true southern girl as she looked back over her shoulder and down to where they sat.

"If you go to Cord's church then you must know Colton too right?"

Now suspicion resounded and a head tilt was added, "Yes, I do know Colton. Why?"

Kendal got excited, "Cord, you should set Hope and Colton up on a date. We could double baby. It'd be fun."

Run Hope. Just leave! She thought to herself. Her eyes went back and forth between them like a ping pong match. Each time they went to Cord, the ire and betrayal was evident in them.

Kendal continued, though no one had responded to her when she made the comment the first time. "Hope would you go out with Colton? This Friday? You two would make the perfect couple. I can see it. Are you 21 yet? Colton will want to go out downtown. Cord and I will be with you guys the whole time, unless you'd rather be alone." She winked.

"Oh gawd. I have to go. Nice meeting you Kendal. Bye Cord." Hope twisted on her heels and left the Bean Counter in a fury.

Cord finally realized that he had allowed Kendal to hold his hands that entire time. He jerked them away, pushed his chair back and said, "Wait here. I'll be back." Cord chased Hope out the door.

"Hope! Hope stop!"

Although she had managed to travel the distance of two store fronts away, and she could easily have kept running away, she stopped for him. Pulling her hat off once again, she looked over her shoulder and felt as if she may faint. Her weakened legs carried her body to the wall of the building on her right. She rested her forehead on her arm leaning against the rough concrete surface.

Cord jogged to her and draped his body over hers. He wrapped his arms around her waist and kissed her ear. He held Hope, terrified to speak. He knew he had hurt her because he knew too well the feeling of being deceived and cheated on by someone. It was never his intention for Hope to experience that feeling.

When Cord sensed that Hope had regained her ability to think clearly, he apologized. "Hope, I'm sorry. I'm so sorry. I lied to you and I hurt you. I didn't mean to."

Hope tucked her hands into her sleeves and wiped her eyes, cheeks and nose. His arms were still wrapped around her waist and he was holding her tightly. Placing her hands on his forearms, she dropped her head back onto his chest. "Cord, you didn't lie to me. You didn't hide anything. You told me you had plans. You weren't as specific as when you are going to the library to meet another girl, but you didn't lie. I'm not angry with you. You have every right to have coffee with anyone you choose or heck hang out with *another* girl every Saturday if you want. I'm angry because I let this upset me so much. This is not who I am." She bent over, covered her face with her hidden hands and released a few more tears.

My God, she does have every reason to be upset with me. I do spend Saturdays with another girl and she did just find me holding hands with my ex. I'm an idiot.

Hope sniffed and said, "You should go back in there. Kendal is waiting for you."

"Hope, babe, turn around. Look at me. I am so sorry. I've been so wrong." Cord pulled on her until she was facing him. She backed up to the wall and he moved forward to keep her in his arms straddling her legs with his. There was no space between them. Hope pressed her face into his chest.

"Hope, look at me." He lifted her chin with his fingers until he could see her sad and scared eyes. "Why'd you tell her you'd heard so much about her? Why'd you tell her we were only church acquaintances? Why would you lie?"

Hope didn't have an answer to the first question, but it was almost time to tell Cord that she, Harmony, *had* heard a lot about Kendal. She answered the second part avoiding the first. "I saw her smiling and kissing your hand. I ran to your table to act like a ridiculous, jealous brat, but I couldn't. She's so beautiful. She sat there like she was made for you and you for her. I was suddenly an intruder in your life. She's older, your age. I'm nothing compared to her. All I could think to do was to try to save face by pretending that we simply go to the same church. She doesn't need to know anything else about me. We should be only looking forward Cord, but you coming here is not just looking backward, it is moving backward. I left my past, but you chose your's over me today. You two have a history and maybe you should try to work her into your future again."

"Hope, I came here to tell her everything about you. She's in there waiting because I want her to know how much I love you. I don't want her calling me anymore. Kendal and I broke up two years ago. My time with her is behind me and that is exactly where I want her to stay. I need her to know that she has absolutely no place in my life. I love *you* Hope. I have nothing but every intention of you being in my future."

Although his statement was deliciously iced with two "I love yous", she still didn't believe him. The entire situation should have never happened. There were so many reasons Hope was angry and she began remembering them all. Seeing fury increasing in her eyes, he held onto her face hoping he could lull her back into his embrace.

"Cord, you know I had a relationship before you, but you don't really know anything about how I felt when it was over. The difference between our situations is that I am not spending every week with another man and responding to calls and texts from the guy I was engaged to. I said goodbye to someone forever. You have not."

Her next words were the most difficult for her to say and for Cord to hear. "And, you know what Cord, I don't think I am ready after all. I thought you were my new light but I was wrong. I need you to stay away from me. You see, you ran back here to Kendal because she is what you know. You care enough about her still to face her and share your feelings with her. I promise, I'm not mad at you about that. I'm mad at myself for not trusting you, and the reason I didn't trust you, is because *I'm* not ready. I just watched another woman, whom you cared deeply for, kiss your hand and look longingly into your eyes. I thought those were my eyes now. I just had to share them with someone else, again. Maybe there's always going to be someone else. I have realized that I am not ready to have to face another forever relationship. I'm still too weak from the last one. I'm going home Cord. Go back and finish your coffee with Kendal. You two looked like you still have a lot to discuss. You probably don't need to tell her that you love me though."

"Hope stop this. Let's work this out right now."

"There's nothing to work out Cord. I'm not ready. This is all too soon. I thought eight months was enough time to recover, but I was wrong. I'm not ready. You know it. You just won't admit it."

"She means nothing to me!"

Hope was getting even more upset. "You are lying! You wouldn't be here if she meant nothing to you. You are still attached to her somehow! It's so evident! I watched her kiss you and you didn't even flinch! She's burned into my brain now. Kendal obviously wants you back. You can't deny that, especially after her cute little double date suggestion. I was humiliated, and you sat there, holding her hand."

"She held mine! Forget Kendal!

"How can I Cord? When I walked up to you two, she was three seconds from sliding your fingers into her mouth... in a freaking coffee shop!"

"Geez Hope! That's disgusting! And that is the opposite of forgetting her. That is shoving her into our situation and making it a thousand times worse!"

"You are the one who did that. Not me." Hope twisted out of his arms. "I'm done Cord. I'm pretty sure I've cried more than my fair share of tears over the past eight months. It's time for me to get myself put back together again. This," she pointed back and forth between them, "this isn't helping me get better."

He stood dumbfounded. *Did she just break up with me?* He watched her walk briskly away from him. "Hope! Stop!" She did. "Do you love me Hope?" His voice cracked, she almost couldn't bear it.

She opened her arms as wide as she could and lifted her chin to the sky. "This much Cord!" She kissed her hand, waved to him and turned.

"Hope! Stop!" Once again she did. "I love you that much too and even though you think you're not ready to be with someone else, you are. We both are. I don't want this to be over. Everything will be okay tomorrow right?"

"Not this time Cord. Don't come over. You can't fix this."

"Hope," he called, she waited, he finally said, "you live the other direction babe." He pointed over his shoulder.

She forced a smile and said, "I'm not about to tuck my tail and walk by that window Cord. I'll go around this entire block, heck that entire mountain if I have to, to keep from having to see her sitting there waiting for you. I'll be fine and so will you."

Hope turned and left for good this time. He watched her wipe her eyes once more and pull her hat down low on her face. She really did remind him of Harmony the way she tucked her hands in her sleeves and was hiding her tears from him. "I love you so much," he whispered to her back.

Chapter 24

That argument was not going to be wasted time. Cord returned to the table and told Kendal the entire truth. He told her he had never regretted anything with her until that very moment. The way he hurt Hope was causing more pain than he thought he could bear and he was only ten minutes into it.

"She sure is young Cord," Kendal snidely concluded.

"Well, fortunately age is no indicator of morality and honesty Kendal."

"Cord, I made a mistake. People make mistakes in marriages all the time."

"Perhaps, but we were never married, nor will we be. If our experiences were a mere glimpse into what I could have expected for a lifetime with you, I don't want any part of it."

"You said you've only been seeing her for a month!"

"She's been more loving with me in that one month than you were in four years."

"Cord, you can't possibly know much about her yet. Are you sure you can trust her?"

"I trust her more than I trust myself these days. Kendal, we're done. I don't care if it takes one year or seventy to get her back, I'd rather wait for her, than always wonder about you. Good luck. You'll find a great guy someday. I wish you only the best." Cord was surprised that he meant all of those final words to her. He didn't wish her any harm or sadness. He realized he didn't wish her anything. He just wanted to figure out how to salvage his relationship with Hope.

Maybe Harmony can help.

Hope took her time walking back home after her embarrassing outburst and verbal flood. She didn't know what she wanted out of all of this anymore. *What was the point? Why did I fall in love with him, just so it could end so quickly? I will figure this out. Evan, are you watching me. How do I do this? You did it all for us. Certainly I learned something. Can I do this?*

The first thing Hope did was fix herself a cup of hot tea. She then went to her bed, placed her book beside her and took her engagement photo with Evan out of her nightstand drawer. Staring at the photo and sipping her tea, she imagined what Evan would say to her.

"Hope, soon, very soon I'll be gone from your thoughts every day. Laugh! Love! Live everyday! You're learning and finding who you are and who you are meant to be with. Accept and face the challenges in your life. Don't sulk. It's wasteful of the gifts you've been given."

"Ugh! Stop talking Evan! You were supposed to cheer me up. Please Evan, please, cheer me up. Come back to me." Her face was swelling from all of the tear collecting she had been experiencing that afternoon. Hope placed the framed picture of her draped over Evan's shoulders, his hands holding her's, their eyes locked, and smiles shared that nothing in this world could ever change, on the pillow beside her. She closed her eyes and prayed for every memory to play in her mind like a movie she could watch again and again. Hope decided she did still need and want Evan and only Evan, so she began talking to him.

* * *

"I was a sophomore in high school, you were a junior. It was September, the first football game of the season. During half-time, I left the field with a few of the other cheerleaders to go to the concession stand. It was so hot. We were buying water and then going to the ladies' room to freshen up our makeup of course. I noticed you getting your hand stamped as you came into our side of the stands. I wished I was one of those girls who was born with the nerve to walk right up to you and tell you that you would never be with anyone other than me for as long as you lived. However, the reality was that I was only fifteen and knew whoever that amazing guy was, with that shaggy, curly, blonde hair, he was never going to know that I existed on this planet. As you were standing with the teacher who was stamping your hand, the sound of your laughter became necessary in my life. I was disappointed that I would have to live without it."

In her thoughts, she heard Evan telling his side of the story. "I was telling the teacher that I came to meet my wife. She said I was way too young to get married. I told her I was there to *meet* my wife, not *marry* my wife. Then, in a childish tone I said to her, 'My mom and dad have very strict rules about sleepovers.' That's why we were laughing. She wished me luck. I told her I didn't need luck. I was never the guy who counted on luck. I was the guy who counted on faith, hope and persistence. I lived to make things happen, not wait for them to happen."

Hope repeated his last sentence in her mind a few more times before continuing her memory.

"When you entered the gate Evan, I was walking through the door into the restroom. I turned my head quickly away from you so wouldn't see me staring. A few minutes later my friends and I emerged feeling a bit more confident and refreshed. I have to be honest with you though, I had forgotten all about you by the time I came out. From the first instant I noticed you, I knew someone like you would never want someone like me."

"Boy, one person couldn't be more wrong about something Hope," he used to reply.

She smiled shaking her head and continued her memory...

"Anyway, as my friends and I were walking back toward the bleachers, you were in our path. You were already smiling at us like you were choosing between delicious options at a buffet. I was terrified that I was going to have to watch you pick one of them to flirt with. There was no way you were going to see me. I wasn't about to stop. I glanced around at the girls in my group and they all had their sights and smiles locked on you. I put my head down preparing to slink by the painful scene. When our group flowed around you like a cool, slow moving mountain stream around a smooth rock, I felt a gentle grip on my bicep. And…" Tears fell as she spoke these words aloud. "And, I felt you pull my arm to your chest. I stopped and looked into your eyes. All of the other girls kept walking. You asked me,"

"What's your name?"

"Hope."

"I'm Evan. So, you're a cheerleader huh?"

"I looked down at my uniform and back at you. I sassed, 'No, I'm an imposter, a wanna be. There's a girl in the bathroom over there lying unconscious in a pile of my clothes. I attacked her and took her uniform hoping no one would notice that I don't actually know any of the cheers.'"

"Hmm… since you attacked someone, you could get into trouble. Maybe you and I should get out of here so you don't get caught."

"What!? No way! It wasn't easy getting this thing off of that poor girl. I'm going out there and making a presentation, a spectacle of myself if you will."

"Alright, suit yourself, but I'm going to be in the first row right in front of you the entire time. One mistake and I'm going to rat you out!"

"Rat me out huh?"

"Yep, it's for your own good."

"How's that for my own good?"

"It's for your own good because the decision you should make is to leave here with me right now and since you've decided not to do that, I'm going to have to teach you a lesson if you mess up."

"Maybe Evan, you should want to see me out there. How will you ever know what I am capable of if you keep me hidden away?"

Evan's smile softened as did his voice. He leaned very close to Hope and said, "I already know everything that you are capable of just by taking one look at you. You can climb the highest mountains or run the longest lengths or swim across the oceans. You can do anything and everything, and I'm going to watch it all. You are my hope in this world. I found you. I can't believe I found you. Will you marry me?"

He bound himself to her soul. He became a part of her forever. She stared into his eyes unable to move. She wasn't even breathing.

He was in charge and he was going to make sure she knew it. "Say yes Hope. Say you'll marry me. Say yes."

She smiled and whispered, "Yes."

"I'm going to kiss you now."

"No you're not. I fought hard for this uniform, I'm not having it taken away because I kissed some complete stranger in front of hundreds of spectators while wearing it." She then admitted, "Besides, I've never been kissed. I don't want to do it wrong in front of all of these witnesses. If I'm going to mess this up, I'd rather no one know about it but you. Hopefully you wouldn't rat me out if I made that mistake."

He leaned even closer and pressed his lips to her ear. Suddenly the excruciating heat and humidity of the September night dissipated. He exhaled a warm whisper, "I won't let you mess it up. I'll be with you the whole time." Softly, almost undetectably, he kissed her ear. He then linked his fingers between hers.

"Hope! Let's go!" A shrill voice screamed from between the bleachers.

They both jumped. Evan added, "Hey, at least I have something to look forward to now Hope since your team is beating the pants off of my team. Go. I'll be right behind you. I'll be cheering for you while you cheer for everyone else. I've got your back."

Evan didn't sit in the center of the front row. He sat off to the side of the student section. He made sure he had a clear view of Hope, but he wanted her to have her moments in the spotlight without worrying about him. He wanted her to shine her light for all of her school mates and bring the same excitement and joy to them that she had brought to him in a matter of minutes.

That night after the game, Evan jumped over the railing and down onto the track that encircled the field. He took Hope's bag from her and held out his hand. She took it and they left the field together. Hope walked Evan directly to her parents for introductions. She gave them her car keys as she informed them that Evan would be bringing her home later. Evan won them over instantly with his natural southern manners. He referred to them politely as "sir" and "ma'am." He shook her dad's hand and hugged her mom. He asked them about her curfew and assured them she'd be home safely and on time. Hope and Evan left the stadium hand in hand and stepped into what she thought would be the rest of their lives together.

Evan drove them to a fast-food restaurant and they ordered a pile of fries and two burgers. He then took her directly to the beach. After parking his car at a tiny remote public access lot, he told Hope to grab the food. Evan jumped out of the car, got a blanket and a small lantern from his trunk, ran to open her door for her, and then escorted his date down the boardwalk. They mutually chose a spot for their picnic halfway between the dunes and the surf.

Evan fluffed the blanket and took the bags and soft drinks from Hope's hands and set them down. He slipped off his shoes and she did the same. He then took her hands and guided her to him. Lowering them both to their knees Evan said to her, "You're not nervous." Hope shook her head. She wasn't nervous at all. "Good, because we belong together." He looked at the blanket and she knew to lie down. Evan stretched out beside her and bracing his head in his right hand, he held her face with his left. Without discussing it or allowing Hope time to prepare, Evan leaned over her and kissed her. He didn't let either of them mess it up.

Hope and Evan stayed at the beach well past her curfew that night. She texted her parents, not wanting them to worry, informing them they were hanging out at the beach and they may stay to watch the sunrise. Surprisingly, her parents didn't worry nor lecture even though she was only fifteen at the time.

Before dozing off listening to the waves, Evan said to her, "A day won't pass between us Hope, I promise, a day won't pass where we don't see each other. I don't care what it takes. We may be too young to actually be married, but we are a part of each other now. Life is too short for me to spend a moment without you." He kissed her once more and returning his gaze to the stars, he squeezed her hand and whispered, "I am so glad today happened."

* * *

Hope opened her eyes from her daydream to once again see his love for her in that photograph. She had one more question for him for the afternoon. She had asked him this question countless times during their four years together because his response to it was always exactly the same. Evan would never change a word or a look when he answered her because he knew her heart needed this story. It gave her strength.

Holding the framed photograph she asked, "Why did you come to our side of the field that day Evan? Tell me again why you were there."

Evan's voice in her head told her one more story. "I came over because I had been talking to my best friend's girlfriend about not being the least bit interested in any of the girls at my school. They were all too proud of themselves. I told her that I wanted a girl who would stop my world with her beauty and humor and I wanted that one girl who would only believe *me* when I tell her how perfect she is. I wanted the girl that no other guys dared approach.

"Our mutual friend told me she had a class with a girl like that. She said the girl is sweet, smart, funny, beautiful, but also sort of shy, and the guys avoid her because of it. She said the girl I was going to marry was over there. I pointed and said 'Over there? The girl of my dreams is over there? Right now?' Nodding and grinning at me, she pointed also to your side of the stadium and told me you'd be easy to spot because you're a cheerleader."

Mid-memory Evan would always pause his story to take a deep breath and kiss Hope.

He'd continue, "I said, 'Well then let's go. Why are we standing here if my wife is over there? Take me to her!' Maryann wouldn't join me though. She said I'd have to find you myself. That way I'd know it was meant to be. I thought about it for two seconds. I knew I wouldn't be allowed back into my side of the stands that night, and I knew I'd have to buy another ticket to get in to your side, but I didn't mind investing six dollars in my future wife. I had to see if Maryann was right."

Before his final words, Evan would steal another kiss. "I saw you right away in the center of all those squeaky girls. You were the calm in the center of the storm. You were the peaceful eye of the hurricane. Unmistakeable." He would then finish his answer every time in a breathy and heart moving tone saying, "God she was right."

Hope turned the picture face down beside her.

Chapter 25

Feeling determined to return to a pre-Cord existence, and needing to accept that Evan wasn't going to be coming back to her, when Hope awakened from her nap, she placed the framed photo on her nightstand and opened her book.

With all of her distractions of late, she had lost track of the plot. She flipped back to the beginning and started skimming the pages for reminders. "Let's see... Young wizard, young princess, the key to banishing the evil queen has been planted literally inside the heart of the princess. The entire kingdom and all its inhabitants will die if the queen isn't defeated. Enter handsome prince, of course, Lord forbid the princess do this on her own. Prince is jealous of young wizard and wants to fight him for the love of the princess instead of save the kingdom, chill out prince, the wizard is probably some old dude anyway. Prince can't kill the wizard because he is the only one who knows the spell to release the key *without* killing the princess. He hasn't used it for fear of losing her once her heart opens. And now my new friends are offering the Queen Lyra earthly sacrifices like gold, diamonds, and fertile land in an attempt to spare the life of Princess Vega. Cygnus is watching over it all and seems to be hiding something crucial to the story but the author won't reveal what he's hiding. Hm. Am I intrigued or frustrated?" Hope settled in and continued her reading.

Hours passed. As she began realizing her legs were locking up and her back was aching, Hope strained every muscle to stand. While stretching, she checked the time. It was six o'clock and she was feeling a mild pang of hunger. After picking up her mug, she shuffled the ten steps from her bed to her kitchen. Since it had been cold Saturday, she had spent the day painting and had skipped her weekly grocery trip. Now there was nothing appealing to eat in her refrigerator.

Even though it was dark and cold, Hope wanted something besides a can of soup or a peanut butter and jelly sandwich. Still dressed in her leggings and sweatshirt, she decided to walk to a nearby pizzeria for dinner.

On her way out her phone buzzed, "I know it's early, but I'm tired and don't know how much longer I'll be awake. I wanted to tell you goodnight babe. I wish you were here. I mean that. I've gotten used to you being next to me at night. Please don't waste too much time being angry. It's just that... a waste of time. Please don't erase me from your thoughts. I love you."

Hope dropped her keys dramatically onto the counter top and almost stomped to her bedroom to put on pajamas, instead, she texted back. "I'm not good enough for you Cord. You deserve so much better. I still cry every night over someone who will never come back to me." Her finger hovered over the send icon. Delete, delete, delete. New message, "You deserve better." Send.

Taking a big risk, Hope exchanged her phone for her keys. Device facing down, keys in hand, out the door she went. "Thank you for the suggestion Cord. I won't waste time being angry or sulking."

Hope skipped every other step as she bound upward and onward from her apartment. An energetic trot to her gate followed and hearing, "Hope!" scared her yet again.

Hope gasped, spun, and slammed her back against the fence.

"Are you okay?"

"Colton, try knocking on my door or calling! What is wrong with you people?"

"I tried calling. I left a really long message about how bad I felt for you and how sorry I was that my brother was ditching you for another girl every weekend and today for his ex-girlfriend this afternoon. I went on and on and told you to call me back, but you didn't."

"I never got that message from you."

"I know. Some guy left me a message and said 'Dude, whoever that message was for needs to dump that BLEEP. If you ever find her, tell her I said that's a BLEEP way to treat someone and she can do better. Oh and dude, good luck.' I guess I typed your number in my phone wrong."

Hope screamed and bent over laughing so hard she forgot to breathe for a few seconds.

"Hope? You okay?"

A huge gasp, another scream of laughter, and she yelled out, "Yes Garrett. I'm fine. I'm good."

"Just checking."

Colton watched her and asked, "Your bodyguard lives above you?"

Another scream from Hope and Garrett replied, "I'm her landlord funny guy." They heard the window slide and lock.

Hope and Colton held each other's wrists as they both cried from laughing so hard. When they finally stood and took a few cleansing breaths, he asked her where she was going.

"I'm off to the PePe's Pizza. Oh wait, no I'm not. No, I am."

"Are you always this indecisive?"

"Apparently. Haven't you noticed?"

Colton held his fingers out like he was pinching the air. She grabbed his hand pushed it down.

"I had pizza for lunch, but I remembered I can get pasta or salad at PePe's, so it's a yes. I'm going there. Wanna join me?"

"That's why I'm here, to join you. I came to hear about your day. I got Cord's version. I'm ready for your's."

"Hmm... Can we eat first and come back here to talk afterward? I'd really like to enjoy a meal without having indigestion before I even sit down to eat."

He huffed at her. "Sorry. Yes. Food first." He took her hand and placed it in the bend of his arm just as he had when he walked her from her car to church. She held tightly with both hands while they laughed and talked nonstop the entire walk.

Not much time passed between her yard and their food being placed in front of them. They both got right to eating.

"Tell me something Harmony," he casually began.

"Yes, what would you like to know?" She looked up and wiped her mouth.

"Why exactly is it that you are spying on my brother by pretending to be someone else?"

She gaped. Her eyes widened. *Oh crap! Did he? He did!*

"Yes I did." His response made it very clear that he had called her Harmony and he could read her mind or at least her expressions.

There was no reason to deny it. She resolved that she had nothing to hide from Colton. "You were supposed to let me *finish* eating before you gave me indigestion. How'd you know?" She swirled her pasta and took a bite trying to casual.

"You look like you are handling it just fine to me." They smiled. Watching her suck in noodles, he continued, "I had to see for myself about this library girl so I waited in the parking lot for Cord to show up and when he did, I asked him what was going on."

Ah, that's why he was late. I sure am glad I street parked around the corner.

"Cord said I should meet this girl *Harmony* that he'd been seeing there on Saturdays. He said you'd be or *she'd* be perfect for me. He didn't really need to sell me on her, I was already going in no matter what. Anyway, he sent me in alone to meet you. I was three steps from the top and saw you sitting in the corner where he said Harmony would be. I turned around trying to avoid possible fireworks because at first, I thought you showed up and sent her away or something. Then I thought he had to be joking. There was no mistaking that Harmony was you. I'd recognize you a mile away.

"Did you tell him?"

"No! I went back outside to him and asked him to describe Harmony. He described the girl sitting in the corner! There was no question that he thought that girl was Harmony. I laughed and told him to have a nice night, but that you were not my type. I walked away stunned that he was so clueless."

Colton laughed and then added, "Harmony? You even told us all that you were named after your dad. You were wearing your dad's team hat. You! Everything was all you Hope!

"I know. I did it all on purpose. He never saw me. I tried Colton. I tried, but he was so desperate for her, that he couldn't see me sitting right in front of him." Hope then told Colton the entire background of how it all started and how it continued to progress.

"I am so sorry Hope. As if you don't have enough to deal with in your life. I do need to know though, are you done messing with him?"

"I am not messing with him. But no, I'm not done meeting him there. I'll be done in four days. He told me he wasn't going back there anymore. Then he told Harmony he'd see her Thursday. This will be the last time."

Colton pressed his face into both of his hands, then slid them down slowly. He chuckled, "Can I watch?"

"No! I'm going to tell him that I won't be there anymore. Then, I'm leaving. Don't make me nervous by showing up and spying on us."

"Oh! Like you're spying on him!"

"I am not spying! I'm gathering intel."

"Isn't that the actual job description of a spy. One who gathers intel."

"This is different because I'm gathering information about myself!"

"God you two are ridiculous. I am so glad you guys are so dysfunctional."

"Why does that make you happy? And we're not dysfunctional anymore. We broke up."

"It makes me happy because maybe you will both realize that this isn't healthy and you'll both find the right person elsewhere. All I ask Hope, is please try not to hurt my mom in all of this."

"Colton, your mother is an adult and she has three sons. Many women will come and go from her life until all of you are married. She'll forget me soon enough."

"I doubt any of us will Hope."

The bill was placed between them and Colton took it from the table. "How much is my half Colton?"

"That depends."

"Depends on what? You know what I ordered and I'm not getting dessert. So how much is my portion?"

"It depends on whether or not you have a coat yet."

"No. I don't, but I'm working on it."

"Then I'm paying. Your amount is… eleven dollars, but put that money in an envelope when you get home and save it for whatever you plan on buying, that you can't seem to get enough to pay for. You must have your eye on one expensive winter jacket. It's almost November, you better hurry and find some cash!"

"Well, I have chosen a nice one. I'll take you to visit it this week if you'd like."

"Visit? The coat you want?"

"Yup. I visit it a couple of times a week."

"Okay Hope. Take me to visit your future coat. Ready?"

"Yep. You'll stay with me for a while after dinner won't you?"

"I planned on it. You still have your side of the story to tell."

Chapter 26

The two held tightly to each other in an attempt to stave off the cold during their walk back to her apartment. Approaching her top step, an automated light was triggered. Mildly startled Colton asked looking toward the beam, "Your bodyguard watching over you again?"

"No. That's a new light with a motion sensor so I don't belly surf down these steps in the dark and end up at the bottom looking like a Hee Haw character."

"Agh! The mental image! I can't erase it!" Colton stopped to laugh for a few moments. "Oh, I can't make it go away Hope."

"It'll pass Colton."

His hysteria continued and they entered Hope's apartment still smiling. Colton's laughed turned to a chuckle as he sauntered to the sofa, barely able to take everything in as he shuffled his way there. Hope went to her room and returned in workout shorts, a clean sweatshirt, and fuzzy, over-the-knee socks. She had taken her hair down from the ponytail it was in and let it fall over her shoulders and around her face. While she was in her room, she brushed her teeth and washed off all of her makeup. The girl who emerged and was now standing in front of Colton, was a completely different person.

"Do you need need anything Colton?"

Yes, but you'd probably throw me out for saying it! "Uh, no. I'm good."

Hope proceeded to the couch and sat next to him. He bent down and scooped her legs up draping them across his lap. She lay back and rested her head at one end and he adjusted, laying his head at the other. Both propped up with each other's feet beside them, they began their conversation about the events of Hope's afternoon.

As she filled Colton in on the details of her arrival and the state of familiarity in which she found Cord and Kendal, Hope found it nearly impossible to speak with maturity and unbiasedness. All of her descriptions were shared with sarcasm and derision.

At one point, in a high pitched, condescending tone Hope said, "Kendal said, 'Let's double date with Hope and Colton baby!' She said that! While holding his hands! I looked like such an idiot."

"Are you sorry you went? I mean, you showing up wasn't random. When Cord finds out, he's going to be mad."

"Mad? At me? Regardless of how I found out about them meeting there, he still went. He sat there while she held his hands. There was no sign of him making any efforts to move away from her until I walked up to their table. And even then, he still sat there not even noticing that Kendal was playing with his fingers. No! I'm not sorry!"

"Do you think you may have reacted before you thought it through?" Colton asked.

She responded, "Seeing him with Kendal and breaking up with him wasn't an impulsive act out of jealous rage. It was more like a veil being lifted. I knew in my heart that I should never have to feel that way in a relationship. Never. In the six years Evan and I were together, never, ever, did he give me any reason not to trust him. I was the only one for him. I never doubted that. With Cord, I know he loves me, but I have been consumed with doubts since the very beginning. I love him Colton, I love him so much. Our feelings are real, but there is a barrier between us, a very thin barrier, so thin we can't see it or even detect it, but it is there."

"Cord isn't going to let you just slip away Hope. He really loves you. His feelings are not disingenuous. He intends on working this out. If you're being honest with yourself, he didn't do anything wrong."

"I know he wants to work it out. He's already texted me. Why are you so concerned anyway?"

"I'm concerned because he's my brother and you are quickly becoming my closest friend. I want you both happy. What did his text say?"

"I don't remember. He said something, I replied something. You can go read it if you'd like. Knowing Cord, I'm sure he replied again."

"You really don't mind if I check your phone?"

"Nope. It's over there on my kitchen counter."

Colton couldn't resist. He went and got the phone. There was an unread message from his brother on the screen. "What do you want me to do?" He walked back over to Hope with the phone in his hand.

"Sit back down. I was comfortable and now I'm not. You were holding me up, and now I'm all slumpy."

"No, Hope, what should I do about the message?"

"Let's put your thumb in there so you can read all of his messages."

Colton returned to his original position with his and Hope's legs entangled. He looked at the phone and asked, "Is Cord's print in here?"

"Heck no!" She reached over and placed her thumb over the scan button. "There, you can find the setting yourself. I don't know where it is."

"If Cord can't get in here, why are you okay with me being able to unlock it?"

"Because you know everything about me and seem to like me despite all of my flaws, craziness and stories. Cord needs the perfect me. He doesn't need to know about all of the baggage I come with."

"Hope, do you listen to anything you say?"

"Of course I listen. I'm saying it!"

"Let me rephrase the question. Do you believe everything you say?"

"Well, I don't lie."

He squinted at her. "You don't lie to me. You didn't lie to Evan. But you sure seem to have a hard time telling Cord the *whole* truth about anything."

Hope processed his statement very carefully and replied, "Are you saying I should be open with Cord and see if he likes me anyway."

Colton was disappointed in her translation. "No Hope, that's not what I meant, but if you think that is what's going to make you feel better, then try it." *Here we go again.*

They eventually fell asleep on her couch with their heads at opposite ends and their legs positioned like they were one big pretzel. Early Monday morning, her phone alarm rang out like an airhorn.

"Colton! Turn it off!" she grouched with a dry voice.

"It's five-thirty," he mumbled fumbling with the screen.

"I know!" She whined with her face buried in the sofa cushion. "I can sleep 'til six. Wake me up then."

He had already pressed snooze so he didn't respond. They both fell back to sleep while the airhorn and snooze combination occurred three more times.

"It's six Hope. Get up."

Hope lifted Colton's legs off of her's, sat up, took her phone from his hand, and went into her room. Even though she was extremely tired, she was ready to read Cord's message. She checked her phone. The message read, "I deserve better what? Better weather? Better gas mileage? Better pay? Don't tell my dad I said that!" One side of Hope's mouth formed a smile. She clicked a watch image and sent it.

His reply, "We'll talk soon." Send.

Hope went about her routine that morning and when she was ready for work, she opened her bedroom door to see Colton was still sawing logs on her couch. She tiptoed to him, knelt down and stroked his messy, dark curly hair. He thought he was dreaming when he felt her breath on his cheek and heard her voice in his ear. "Sleep good. I'm glad you stayed with me. I'm not sure I can do life without you now."

Colton absorbed the feeling of her affection. His hand reached up and touched the side of her face that she had rested on his in a sweet hug. He told her, "I'll come back later if you want."

She whispered, "Please do. Seven." He nodded and smiled. Then, she asked, "Colton, will you be my best friend? I haven't had one in almost a year."

He rolled onto his back and wrapped his arms around her so she had to lie over his chest. He wanted to hold her for his reply. "I think that is why I was born, Hope."

Chapter 27

Cord had decided to give Hope the space and time she requested. He knew where to find her. He was fairly secure in the fact that if she wasn't interested in him, she certainly wasn't interested in anyone else. He was going to give her one week, then he'd move back into her life and insist that she pull herself together. If she didn't want him, truly didn't want him, he would leave her alone. Many prayers would be sent in hopes that she came to her senses on her own. The only problem he had was that it was impossible for him to imagine his life without her.

* * *

Colton became the filler of the void Hope had been living with during her time in Riverton. In a matter of days, they realized they were practically the same person. He knew everything about her because he could read her every expression, tone or movement. Nothing could be hidden from Colton as it pertained to Harmony Hope Hanover.

They figured out right away that they could meet on campus and return to her apartment together each evening. Separating them wasn't a consideration. Colton wasn't getting too far from her just yet. He even slept on her couch after they stayed up talking, laughing, studying, or binge watching zombie flicks. On Wednesday, she took him to visit her dream coat and he didn't mind waiting around while she tried on a bunch of clothes that she wasn't going to be able to buy. They stayed in constant contact. Everything about him made her happy and he had never had someone in his life like her.

When they left the *couture* sporting goods store Wednesday evening empty handed, he teased her about torturing herself there. His arm went around her shoulders as they exited the building and his lips pressed to the side of her head. Hope held onto Colton's waist and they synced their steps to his car. A mild though icy breeze was blowing, and Hope couldn't help but notice Colton shivering. She laughed at him and said, "You brought me one of your coats on Monday so I wouldn't be cold, yet you didn't bring your own tonight?"

"I know. I figured I'd tough it out from door to door. Man, it's gotten cold fast."

Hope made a pouty face to him and teased, "Aw, poor baby."

He laughed.

Colton had unlocked the door remotely, and when he reached for the handle to open it for her, Hope leaned against it. "I think we should stay out here for a while longer. I'm toasty."

"Really? I'm so glad you are enjoying my jacket!"

"Aw, you're right. It is your's. You should enjoy it with me. Come on, get in here with me, but make it fast. You'll let all of my warmth escape if you don't hurry." Hope laughed and opened the coat like birds' wings. Colton smiled and slipped his arms around to her back pressing his entire body against hers.

"Ooo. It is warm in here. I think I want it back now Hope. This is a good one."

"No way. I may keep it." She rested her head on his chest and relaxed in the comfort of him. He placed his cheek on the top of her head and held onto her as well.

Neither wanted to think about the complications of what bonded them in that moment and neither cared. Hope wasn't sure what she wanted but Colton was. He wanted to know if they were meant for more. Firmly, Colton pressed his lips to Hope's hair. He then lifted her face to his. After reading her expression and gaining full confidence in her affection for him, he kissed her. He didn't care about anyone else in the world except her. His kiss started at their mouths and progressed through their hearts, arms and bodies. Neither could let go of the other.

Hope's hands pressed on his lower back. She pulled him. He felt her returning, sharing, his desires.

Hope craved Colton's touch. Deep down though, her heart began realizing its deception. She was feeling Evan, but imagining Cord. Not sure of exactly what she was wanting from him, she knew that regardless of her growing feelings for Colton, she obviously was not ready for this. She pulled back and whispered, "This is too soon Colton."

He didn't hesitate in his response, "You're right. I'm sorry. I'm so sorry."

"Please don't be sorry. You know as well as I do that we're connected somehow. But until we figure out how, this needs to wait. I need to do this right." By this, she meant her next relationship.

With their foreheads pressed together, Colton begged her, "Promise me Hope, promise me this is the one lie you will tell. No one, especially Cord, needs to know this happened."

"I'm not accountable to him Colton."

"Hope, please, promise me you'll lie. This is about us, you and me, no one else."

Thinking that she shouldn't have to tell Cord anything, she agreed. "Alright Colton. He doesn't need to know about this. No one does. We work through us before anyone else is a part of it."

Colton's heart hurt. "Yes. There's still a lot of road ahead."

He opened the door for Hope and she climbed up into his truck. He closed her door and when he sat in his seat, they leaned toward each other right away and she nuzzled into his neck. "You're still my best friend," she told him. He nodded and squeezed her a little tighter.

Colton stayed at her apartment that night as well. Thursday morning, they parted for work and decided to skip classes that evening. Hope was nervous about her upcoming meeting with Cord, and Colton wanted to be there with her every minute until she left. He was hoping he could talk her into not going through with it.

Although Colton brought them a light dinner, neither was able to eat. They sat on her floor in front of the couch and each nibbled or played with their forks. Their conversation was more important to them.

For most of the time that they sat together, each equally shared in avoiding the main topic of the night. Until finally, Hope wanted to know Colton's unique perspective on her state of being. She asked, "Colton, who am I? I came here to be someone different. I came here to put Evan behind me. I spent months alone thinking that any interference in my life would change who I was supposed to become. With Evan, there was no mistaking the fact that he and I were one united being. We were each ourselves, but we were one at the same time. When I lost him, I was broken, completely shattered, and I lost everything about myself too."

"Hope, this is who you are. You are someone who is finding her way through the tough times. You're learning and getting stronger."

She interrupted, "Why, after all these months alone, am I still so afraid? I think I've proven that I can handle life by myself. I can work, go to school, pay bills, save money, cook! I can do this on my own, so why am I afraid now?"

"I think you are afraid of choosing what's next for you. You had Evan, you didn't get to choose him, he claimed you and you gave him your whole heart. You also didn't get to choose to be alone. You were forced to be alone. Then, when you felt ready, you chose Cord. You feel hurt by him, so now you're afraid to choose what's next."

"How do I make the right decision from here?"

"Maybe I can explain some things the way I see them. Maybe it will help."

She listened curiously.

"To Evan, you were the world. You were his planet earth. He could look down from the heavens and see how the big picture of Harmony Hope Hanover works together to create a life giving experience. He could look beneath the clouds to see the glorious oceans and the snow capped mountains, but he could also see the chaos and the pollution. No matter what happened beneath those clouds, Evan still saw the entire experience of you, and that is, your creation is perfect. You were his world."

"And Cord?"

"Cord looks at you and sees the rarest and most precious flower that has ever and will ever grow. He sees the one of kind creation, the tropical flower that grows on the highest mountain peak alone. And he wants it for his own. Nothing else surrounds it or can be above it. He loves it with all of his heart and he wants nothing else. He climbs to it and stares at it trying to decide what role it plays in his world. But, he also knows that once he takes it for himself, it changes, it withers. He doesn't know how to keep it alive and vibrant."

She silently released a tear from each eye. "And you Colton? What am I to you?"

"Hope, you're the universe. You are not just the earth, you are the moon, the stars, the planets. You are infinite. You are discovery, exploration, fire, ice, excitement, curiosity, danger, mystery. You are everything that has ever and will ever exist to me. I can't see my life without you in it."

"So I'm the vacuum that is outer space that sucks the air out of you until you suffocate and die?"

"That's not exactly where I was going with that, but I should have seen it coming. I guess yes, you are also capable of suffocating me. Please don't though."

They laughed and he reached over and wiped her cheeks. "What time are you meeting him Hope?"

"I'll leave here at seven. My book needs to be turned back in anyway. Perhaps, now that I'm single again, I'll have time to pick back up on my reading. This will be my first winter in Riverton. I have a feeling I may be spending a lot of time under my blankets with tea and books. Garrett says I can come upstairs and read by the fire anytime with him. So, I'll go and find some new books to read until Cord shows up."

"I have you to myself for another hour then."

"Yeah."

A tap on the window of her door startled them both. Hope looked at Colton, shrugged, wiped her face herself, and walked to see who was visiting. Even though she saw him, she opened the door immediately without waving or thinking about anything, A simple, inviting step to the side allowed him to enter.

Cord stepped in and fought every nerve, muscle and drive to pick her up and kiss her. "Hey Hope. Thanks for letting me in."

With sincere affection she responded, "Why wouldn't I? You haven't done anything wrong."

Cord didn't reply, he only checked her eyes for proof that she believed that.

Colton kept his place on the floor, wishing he was invisible. Cord didn't know he had been spending all of his spare time with Hope for those five days straight. Even though Cord was focused on Hope, Colton's presence drew his attention. He walked to him with a smile and open arms. "Hey Colton buddy. How's it going? I love you."

Colton got up and returned his big brother's hug. They actually held for a few seconds while Cord pressed his lips to the top of Colton's head.

Colton replied, "I'm great Cord. I love you too." Then he thought, *God I'm the worst. He does love her.*

"Do you mind if I have some time alone with Hope? You two can catch up later. I'd really like to talk to her for a while."

"Sure Cord. No problem." Colton looked to Hope and she clearly was terrified. He nodded to her and she ran over to help him pack up their floor picnic. "I'll take all of this with me Hope so you don't have to worry about it."

"Thanks Colton. I'll walk you to the door."

With all of the boxes placed back in their to-go bags, Hope walked with Colton to the door. He nudged her to step outside with him. She closed the door behind them.

He wasted no time, "What do you want Hope?"

"I want someone who won't give up on me no matter what."

"What are you going to say to him?"

"I don't know. I'm learning. I've never had to say anything. I've never had to fix anything before now."

"That's because love doesn't ever have to be fixed. It's unbreakable. Evan never fixed anything between you two Hope. Did he?"

"No, he didn't."

"Then you shouldn't have to either."

"What Evan taught you was not how to navigate love and repair it, but how to live in it and let it repair you."

Hope wasn't sure exactly what Colton was trying to imply. She could read his statement in two different ways. This time, she was going to listen to Cord and figure out what Colton's advice meant to *her*."

They exchanged a loving hug and Hope returned to find out why Cord had stopped by to see her.

Chapter 28

From where he stood, waiting for Hope to return, Cord could see that she had once again set Evan's photo on her bedside table. Although he wondered what that meant, he wasn't going to let it deter him from following through with every plan he had made and every statement he intended to make that night.

Hope walked back to him and asked him to sit. She placed herself beside him, and in her mind she watched them in each other's arms, desperate to live every second attached.

His voice broke her thoughts. "I planned on giving you this week so you could get back to a normal routine and decide if you still wanted me in your life or not. I figured if you were able to go back to being alone each night, you would be able to make a definite decision about how you feel about my role in your life. You'd either want me, or you want your solitude once again. I see that Colton has been keeping you preoccupied though."

"It's been a long time since I've had a friend, Cord. I sat here alone for months. I forgot what it was like to have someone to just hang out with, shop with, or watch movies with. Colton and I have a lot in common. We like pretty much all of the same things."

"I thought you enjoyed doing all of that with me for the past month."

Hope thought about his statement. How could he not understand that spending evenings with him was completely different than spending them with Colton? "Cord, you and I are nothing like Colton and me. There is no comparison in our relationships."

"Like mine with Harmony?" he asked without raising his voice.

However, her reply did contain emotion, "Cord don't!"

"Does he sleep here?"

His question made her mad but she answered it and then some. "Yes. He sleeps on my couch like a hobo! He makes messes, and he doesn't always clean them up. He's been here every waking moment since Sunday."

Cord puffed out a laugh and felt some relief. He then asked, "You said you weren't ready on Sunday. How do you feel now?"

"I feel like I need a little more time. At this exact moment, you still deserve better than me. That could change soon, but until I feel like I am all you want, neither of us is ready."

"Hm, I think I could say the same thing to you, Hope."

She knew he was referring to Evan and now Colton too, so she had to ask, "Are you planning on seeing Harmony or Kendal again?"

Cord was so calm. Nothing seemed to stir him. "I'm seeing Harmony tonight. I have one more question for her. As for Kendal, I don't want to talk about her anymore."

"Did you say everything you came to say Cord? Did you learn anything new about me that helps or hurts your plans for your life."

No, I came to say I love you and I haven't been able to eat or breathe without you. I came to say, stay with me tonight and every night for the rest of our lives. He looked down at his hands and said, "I don't have anything more to say, and I didn't learn anything that will help me."

God I want to hold him! I want him to stay with me! Stop needing another woman, Cord! "Well, if you have nothing more to say, you can go see Harmony now."

Cord stood and Hope stood beside him. He looked down to her, "Do you still love me?"

"Absolutely."

He left thinking about the photo on her nightstand.

* * *

Their much anticipated magical Thursday meeting arrived. Cord had waited for this since Sunday when Hope left the coffee shop. He was nearly dying to talk to Harmony. It was all he could do to keep from running to the library, up the stairs and to the corner where they met each week, especially after the way he felt from just seeing her.

Upon his entrance through the revolving door, Cord got a sick fear that Harmony may not show up. She could have forgotten or decided that she was too busy. His follow up sickening fear was what she was going to say to him. He was there to get an answer to one question. That's all. He wanted one answer, then he planned on leaving.

Before going to the second floor, Cord pulled a chair out and sat at a table near the front entrance. *What are you doing? Why do you keep coming back here? It's obvious that Harmony is fine and doesn't need you. You should be having these conversations with Hope!* Cord needed to listen to his heart. He sat idle, just staring, his elbow resting on the table and his head being held up by his hand.

The relationship he wanted was with Hope but he had messed that up. Perhaps the reason she wasn't ready was because he hadn't treated her the way she deserved to be treated. She was the one who deserved better. He had been meeting another girl there for six weeks now, and Hope had walked up and caught him holding hands with his ex-girlfriend. It was no wonder she was a wreck. He was aware of all of the things he had done to make her feel insecure.

I'm such an idiot! We supposedly are giving each other space to figure out what the heck we want, but I know what I want.

Cord marched up the stairs to the obscure corner where Harmony may or may not be this evening. He didn't care one way or another if she was there because he was going to talk to Hope again. They had to be open with each other. He looked up and breathed a sigh of relief that she was waiting. Cord's approach became more hurried than ever before because he wanted to get to the point with her.

Cord sat right down. "Hey, Harmony. *Still* reading that book?"

"Yeah. I'm almost done though. You want to read it next?"

"Nah. I'm good. I'm not into the Fantasy novels. I'm more of a sports or history type guy."

"Cool." She shrugged, then added, "So does your girlfriend know you're here tonight?"

"No. I mean yes."

"Which is it?"

"Yes, Hope knows I'm here and no she's not my girlfriend, at least not right now. We broke up Sunday. She's mad at me. I was a jerk. I met with Kendal when I should have stayed right beside her and napped our day away with football playing in the background. I should have... never mind."

"What?"

"Never mind. Private."

"Ah, nuff said." Harmony held out her hand as if to say, *Yes you can stop right there.* She continued, "You sure are chipper and energized for a guy whose girlfriend is mad at him. Why aren't you on the phone ordering her flowers or knocking relentlessly on her door at all hours of the day and night?"

"First, I already did knock on her door. Second, she works and goes to school all day. Therefore, she sleeps at night so she can have the energy to work and go to school all day. She's already ticked off at me. Why would I want her ticked off and tired by knocking all night? Isn't that a lethal combination for women?"

Harmony laughed, "You're so perceptive. You add in a few other things and you've got yourself a weapon more potent than a nuclear bomb." He joined in her laughter but dared not comment. *Smart man*, she thought.

"So Cord, what's your plan? I don't know you well, but what I can derive from you based on our few meetings is that you really like this girl and you haven't been afraid thus far to let her know it."

"I'm going to visit her Friday night when she gets home."

"That's tomorrow."

"Wow! I guess tomorrow night then. I'm going in and demanding that she give us another chance. She may need time to forgive me, but she's worth the wait. What have I got to lose?"

"So you're going to rush in and slay the dragon?"

"If I have to. If that's what it takes to make her see that I'm not temporary."

"She knows that, but Cord, what if she has plans and isn't home?"

"Then I'll wait. There's no reason for her not to forgive me."

Harmony's voice became serious, "Cord, perhaps it's not forgiveness you need from her. Has it occurred to you that she's running?"

"Do you think she's running from me?" Cord was shocked by Harmony's word choice.

Harmony remained focused though. "Yeah. I believe she is. I don't really know why though. Maybe it's guilt. Maybe she doesn't think you can forgive her for something or look past something in her life. Maybe she's afraid if you know the truth about her, you won't want her anymore. She's just beating you to the inevitable by breaking up with you first. These are all possibilities."

Cord asked a direct question, "Do you think she loves someone else? Anyone else? The guy in the photo? Someone new?"

Her heart pumped. Harmony was not answering that question. He was going to have to find that out for himself. "She might, but only you can get that out of her. Why don't you try to learn something real about her? You are always asking me question after question, Cord. Talk to Hope!"

"We talk about a lot of things."

"Well, I'm sure whatever you discuss are all great topics, but after a month of those conversations, perhaps it's time for you two to be open on a deeper level about who you are. You were with another woman for four years. How can a twenty-one year old, who just met you, compete with an experienced, twenty-five year old woman who has known you for years? How can she compete with a stranger you spend hours with each week?"

"There's no competition, Harmony! None!"

"Sure there is. If relationships were races, Kendal would have a four year head-start on Hope, and this goes both ways. Don't you want to know more about her past? Once we start dating, who we are becoming for our spouses is defined by all of our previous relationship experiences. All of them, romantic, sibling, friendships, parental. Every relationship will define who you are and how you will function in a marriage. Find out what you're getting into."

Their conversation was very deep. Cord was feeling uncomfortable. He began to think of how Hope would feel if she were a fly on the wall. He decided to level with Harmony. "Harmony, I appreciate all of your advice, but I need to tell you something and I don't want you to get offended."

"I won't."

"I don't want to sit here with you anymore. I want Hope to tell me how she feels. I don't want a stranger, who I couldn't even pick out of a line up, telling me how my girlfriend might or might not feel."

"So she's still your girlfriend in your mind?"

"She's everything in my mind."

"I don't want to sit with you anymore either, Cord." She paused then asked, "You said you have one more question for me. What is it? What's the last question you want to ask me?"

Cord thought for a minute. "I never said I had one more question."

"Yes you did."

"No Harmony, I didn't."

Oh shoot! Did he say that to me at my apartment a little while ago? Remain calm. "Well, maybe you didn't say that. Are you done then? Can we get on with our lives and end this?"

Cord shifted and seemed agitated. He looked at her with a serious countenance, his eyes were suspicious. He said, "Harmony, you haven't told me yet what you would have done if Evan called and said he wanted to see you again."

"I haven't told you yet, because you haven't asked."

"Well, I'm asking. This is the last thing I want to know from you." He waited.

She took an eternity to answer, then said, "We're not in the same position, Cord. However, if Evan called me and said he wanted to see me again, I'd grab ahold of him and never let go. I would *never* let him go." Cord was stunned. Her voice reverberated. "Then, when he faded away again, because he would, I would beg him to stay. And when he was still leaving me anyway, I'd tell him thank you for leaving me and for taking care of me. You see, Evan sent me my new boyfriend, and this man makes every single day brighter for me." She burst into tears. Cord raised on his knees to comfort her. "Stop there. Do not come near me. You asked me a question, you got your answer."

"I don't understand you Harmony. How can you beg a guy to stay with you, then thank him for leaving you at the same time?"

She replied in such a hushed tone, he barely heard her, "Evan died nine months ago while I lay across him listening to him take his last breaths. I felt his spirit hold mine. Then, I felt him leave me. Now you know too much and not enough. I won't be here anymore. Good luck with your girlfriend."

Harmony shoved her book in her backpack, got up and walked past him with her hands tucked in her sleeves wiping away tears.

"Harmony?" he called to her.

She stopped but didn't turn to look at him. "Yeah?" she whispered.

"You're in his clothes again. That means you didn't have a good week with your new guy."

"You're very perceptive. Use that talent with Hope, not with me."

"Also, Harmony, I'll miss this time with you."

"Same," she replied with a sniffle. As she walked away, he studied everything about her.

Hope left knowing that she was going to have to face this situation with Cord very soon. *He does deserve better than me. Colton was right, in a way, I am lying to him. How can I be angry with him, when I am far from perfect?*

Chapter 29

The vagabond was reclined on her sofa when she returned home from the library. A look of curiosity was sent her direction, but Hope held out a hand and retreated to the privacy of her bedroom.

Then next morning, Colton planned to leave before Hope emerged for her coffee. He tapped lightly on her door, knowing she was awake and listening. He gently said, "I'll see you around six. No more moping, life's too short. Today is a new day." She listened. He left.

Upon her return that evening, a boisterous, "Ready to dance the night away? We are going out and not coming home until dawn!" rang through her ears as it echoed up her concrete stairwell.

"Home? So you do live here now huh?" Hope replied smiling.

"I think so. Is that okay with you?"

A direct answer was difficult, so she chuckled at him rolling her eyes.

Colton had been waiting outside her door just as Cord had done many times. He took her bags as they entered. Once inside, he followed her to her room and flopped onto his back across her bed. Feeling more lively this evening than the previous, not one argument was conjured. Hope proceeded directly to her closet in search of her next outfit for the day. This would be her third since she had changed from work clothes to workout clothes for classes.

"How's this for my first night out downtown?" She laid an outfit out beside Colton and dropped a pair of shoes on the floor to tie the ensemble together.

"Crap, Hope!" He shook his head back and forth again and again. "I don't know about that. You leaving your hair up or taking it down?"

"Oh down and curled of course. Hey, what's wrong with this outfit?"

"Babe! Everyone is going to wonder what the heck you're doing out with a guy like me. You're going to make me look bad." He thought, *The girl wearing that would be out with my brother.* "Wear it! I can't wait to show up with you. I may take you to every bar downtown just to be seen with you. Get dressed. I'm hungry."

Colton left her room and closed the door behind him. When Hope had her clothes changed and her makeup reapplied for a night club look, she emerged in her skin tight, low-waisted jeans, high-heeled boots, and her fitted, knit, black, turtleneck that was cropped to just below her bra-line. She had fluffed and re-curled a few strands of her dark blonde hair and her makeup was heavy with darker, shinier lipgloss than Colton had ever seen on her.

"Back! Go back in there!"

"No!"

"Yes! Give me a minute. Oh, and warn me before you come back out again."

Hope laughed, shaking her head at his inappropriate innuendo. There was no way she was returning to her room. Instead, she walked very slowly to Colton and held her hand out. His eyes screamed uncertainty and excitement. When he took it, she pulled him to his feet and he placed his hands right on her waist. With her heels on, she was nearly eye to eye with him. Her arms draped loosely on his shoulders, while her hands clasped behind his neck.

"Colton?"

"Hm?"

"You should get used to seeing me look like this. We're going to be together all night, and you are going to need to be able to control yourself. This, right now, is a lesson in self-control. Learn it!"

Allowing his hands to transfer the way her skin felt beneath them to his brain was quite enjoyable. "This might be too tough of a lesson for me Hope," he said looking into her eyes envisioning what he wanted and not hating himself for it.

She whispered in his ear, "Okay. Let me help you." Hope pulled her phone out of her pocket and backed away from him pressing the screen. A song came on and she started dancing around like a monkey on drugs.

"Oh! No! Hope don't do that. You're ruining it for me. You look ridiculous!"

She kept dancing and laughing until he grabbed her and said, "Okay, fine, seeing that certainly helps me with my self-control."

"Good. Remember that look every time your brain or whatever else you think with wants to cross any of my boundary lines."

"Agh!" Colton turned away in embarrassment. "You're a good teacher."

With Colton's coat snuggled around her, they went about their evening. They met Colton's roommates and their dates out for dinner and Hope had more fun than she had had in a long time. After dinner, they all headed to a bar to dance. Never being one to drink, Hope planned all along to be the driver.

The music was blaring and her cohorts were all tipsy. Everyone was having the time of their lives. Colton was glad all of his friends had brought dates, that way he wouldn't have to share time dancing with Hope. He had her all to himself. They flirted and held onto one another in some way for every song. The only times Colton left Hope, were when he went to the bar for a refill or to get her water. In those instances, she danced with the friends who were still on the floor. Colton was very proud because it was a fairly small bar and each time he went to get a drink, some guy would ask him about his date, fishing for information about her availability.

Out of breath and thirsty, Colton left Hope again. A guy at the bar said, "Hey man, that girl you've been dancing with, is she with you? Mind if I ask her to dance?"

"Dude, that girl is with me and not one soul in here stands a chance with her. She is one hundred percent taken."

With Colton still facing the bartender, the guy looked back to the dance floor. "Huh, you sure about that man?"

"Yeah. Why?"

"'Cause she's with someone else right now. Check her out."

"Colton turned around to find Hope in Cord's arms. The music had changed to a slow song, and they were locked and focused."

"What do you think now, Romeo?" the man asked sarcastically.

Colton was saving face. "That's my brother moron. That's who I was referring to when I said she's taken."

"Oh! Sucks to be you, Dude! Too bad she's not yours. I think it would be worse to have to watch my brother hold onto her than some stranger." The guy held up his drink to Colton and said, "You're a bigger man than me. Good luck to you." He walked away.

When the first note of a slow song played through the speakers, Cord appeared at Hope's side. She hadn't seen him in the bar the entire night and was shocked by his presence. He stood next to her like a dream holding his hand out, asking for a dance. Hope gaped, took his hand, and placed her cheek on his shoulder. He rested his cheek on hers. They swayed. His hands covered the exposed, soft skin of her back. Her mind began memorizing the feeling of his fingers caressing her. She could feel him inhaling, taking in the aroma of her hair. His palms pulled her closer to every part of him. Their thighs offset and brushed gently together to ensure they were truly as close as they could get to one another. Their moment wasn't going to be wasted.

Hope looked up to Cord, smiled and said, "I'm sweaty. Sorry."

"I'm not sweaty or sorry."

They giggled.

"Why are you here Cord? Who are you with?"

"I'm with some guys. A friend from high school is getting married tomorrow, so a bunch of us decided to come down here for a while tonight. It's sort of a reunion, so there are more people than usual in our Friday night group. We haven't all been together in a long time. They're all over there drunk."

"I've been here all night and didn't notice y'all."

"We're bar hopping. We just got here. As soon as we walked in, one those yahoo's spotted a girl dancing and made a colorful comment. It got my attention. Imagine my shock when I saw it was you he was referring to. I slapped him on the chest and told him to settle down. That one is spoken for. Well darned if my brother didn't appear and slide all over you. They, of course, all know Colton so they were pretty darn proud of him." Cord rolled his eyes and smiled. "It took a while, but I convinced them you two are just friends. They believed me after he left you out here to go get a drink."

He pulled back slightly and asked, "Can I kiss you, Hope?"

"Do you think that would be awkward for Colton at this particular moment? I don't want to embarrass him. We have been here together all night."

Cord looked to the bar and spotted Colton staring at them. Cord waved. Colton waved back. "He does look rather puppy doggish right now."

"Cord, I've grown very attached to Colton very quickly. He's important to me."

"The kiss can wait then. Will you tell me *how* important he is to you though?"

Hope lowered her head onto Cord's shoulder again and added some pressure to their hold. He replaced his lips to her forehead while he worried about her reply. She finally said without moving from her position, "I can't see my future without him."

"And where does that leave me?"

Hope wasn't sure what Cord was willing to give up for her. She felt confident that Harmony was out of his life. She just needed to know if Kendal was too. "Before I answer Cord, where's Kendal in this conversation?"

"Nowhere." He paused and Hope waited. He continued, "Hope, she'll be at the wedding tomorrow. I've told you our paths will cross. You are going to have to trust me."

Looking to him again, she said, "I will trust you. I promise. I will trust you with all of my heart, but I get to decide when I'm ready to do that."

"Do you still love me?" he asked.

Her reply, "Do you still want me?"

"Yes. You are all I want."

"Okay then."

Cord moved them to a far corner of the dance floor near a wall and turned his back to the crowd so Hope was nearly invisible. His hands slid well below her back pockets as he pulled her into a deep kiss. Maneuvering her against the wall, he made sure there would be no misunderstanding about how serious his feelings were for her.

In the midst of her elation, she thought of the vision of him and Kendal together only six days prior. Then, she remembered all of her own deceptions, including the kiss she and Colton had shared that week. Within a mere second, those memories completely vanished and all she could imagine was them together in her bed or his. She let the kiss run its course.

As the song concluded and the next began, they released one another, and though they didn't need to, feeling guilty for their own indiscretion, they both looked around for prying eyes. Hope noticed that they both had an identical reaction to their kiss. "Tell me we have nothing to hide from Cord."

"We don't. I don't know why I did that. I love you."

"There you two are. Can I have my date back now, Cord?"

"Of course you may. How does it feel to be the luckiest guy in the room, Colton?"

He replied, "You would know."

"Yeah buddy. I do know. I think for the first time ever, I'm jealous of you."

"Ah! You should be!" Colton patted Cord on the back and took Hope's hand from his. "We'll see you later, Brother." He asked Hope, "Few more dances or are you worn out?"

She replied, "One or two more! I'm having fun!"

Cord hugged them both and returned to his friends across the room. Hope and Colton continued their night with their friends for a few more songs. When her feet and his equilibrium couldn't take another minute, they went to the bar for water and to retrieve their coats.

Waiting, holding hands, chatting, laughing, they were greeted, "Hope! Colton! I knew you'd make a great couple!" Kendal threw her arms around them both.

"Hey, Kendal. What are you doing here?" Colton asked.

Even though Cord had been very clear with Kendal about his relationship with Hope, she couldn't resist trying to wedge herself between them and prove that she clearly had the upper hand. Kendal replied flirtatiously, "Cord and I are out with a bunch of our friends from high school. We're partying! I told Hope Sunday when we met that Cord and I would be out tonight."

Did he really show up here in the same group with her and not tell me after I asked him point blank? "Oh, that's right. Sounds fun." Hope nodded trying desperately to keep a smile on her face.

Colton wasn't going to let another second of that continue. He grabbed their coats from the bartender and said, "It was good to see you, Kendal." He hugged her since they had known each other for many years. He then turned to his date, "You ready to go home, Sweets? It's been a long night, and I'm ready to sleep this off."

"*Home*? She's a keeper, Colton. I can tell." Kendal winked at Hope and droned in a sultry tone, "You two have a nice ni-ight."

Colton put his arms around Hope as they watched Kendal return to their group. She went straight to Cord, hung her wrists on his shoulder, and obviously began to tell him that Colton and Hope were on their way home *together*.

Hope saw Cord exhibit a mild panic as she and Colton exited the bar.

Colton managed to shoot a glare to Cord that clearly expressed, *Unbelievable,* before the door closed behind them.

Chapter 30

Hope never expected Cord to chase her down that night. She had learned that Cord is not impulsive. He thinks through every decision, every word, every action. He did not chase her when she first met him and she said she didn't want to see him the rest of the week. He didn't chase her when she broke up with him at the coffee shop. And, he did not chase her this time when she left a bar with his brother after seeing him with Kendal again. She had learned that was the difference between a man who is twenty-one and a man who is twenty-five. One thinks before he acts and the other thinks after.

Late Saturday morning, Hope finally poked Colton until he woke up. "You need to bathe and brush your teeth. You are contaminating my house with your stale, alcohol scented, after-shave and body lotion."

Colton laughed and groggily said, "And you still love me anyway?"

"Of course I do. Somehow we turned into the same person this past week. Well, except I smell way better than you do."

"You got that right. I'm jealous."

"Don't be. There's a shower within your current line of sight. It's calling you."

"Okay. I'm going. Is coffee ready though?"

"Yes coffee is ready but I will dump it all down the drain before I'll let you drink any of it if you haven't bathed! Go!"

Hope heard the squeak of the handle turn and the spray hitting the walls and floor of the tub. While she was pouring another cup of coffee, there was a light tap on her door. She looked to her right out the window and Cord stood there waving with a somber expression. She knew he thought she was mad about the Kendal issue from the night before, and he was correct.

"Hey, Cord. What's up?"

"I'm here to clear up last night. You didn't even come to me so I could explain."

"Oh, sorry. That's because your *baby* was hanging on your shoulders. I didn't want to risk sticking around and having to witness another one of your signature kisses. I wanted to escape the night with the vision of only one of those in my mind."

"Hope! Stop it! I've about had enough of your jealousy!" He looked up and around. "What's that sound?"

"I don't know. Is it my shower running that you hear?"

"Yeah. Why's your shower on?"

"Because Colton is in it."

"Why the heck is he in your shower?"

"Cord, I told you Thursday when you were over here that he is literally a hobo! He moved in. I made him shower because

300

he was stinking up my sweet little apartment. Can't you smell him from there!?"

Colton, dang him! He didn't tell me he was over here that much. I'll kill him. "Hope, We'll talk when my youngest brother is not naked in the next room!"

She calmly replied, "He's not naked. He showers in his swimsuit."

"What!? Are you serious? And how would you know?"

"No, I'm not serious. I'm sure he's probably naked in there. And I wouldn't know! Look who's jealous now!"

"We are getting nowhere right now. I'll call you later."

"Have fun at the wedding tonight, Cord."

He cut his eyes at her as he closed the door.

Hope didn't tell Colton that Cord had stopped by. She let them go through their day as if nothing had happened. The few times her attention was away from Colton, it was only because she was revisiting the sensation of Cord's hands, body and lips on her.

* * *

After a rowdy night out, the two, who were quickly becoming one, went to the library. Hope had finished Cygnus Enduring and wanted to check out more books. With Cord stopping by her house on Thursday before visiting Harmony, Hope had forgotten all about needing to return her books.

They arrived and went in different directions. Hope dropped her books in the receptacle and headed to the Witches, Wizards and Wanderers section. Colton headed to the graphic novels and comic books. She was studying covers, scanning summaries and finding nothing interesting.

"Psst... Hope! Come over here."

Hope jerked her head around, took a few steps down the row where she was looking for a book and saw Colton waving for her join him. He was sitting in the same corner where she had sat week after week talking with Cord.

"Come on Hope," he whispered. She walked to him. "Let's read this one together. I bet we can finish it in an hour. When's the last time you read out loud for fun? We'll do crazy voices and stuff!"

Hope raised her eyebrows and said, "Alright, sounds like fun. What are we reading about?"

Colton gave her the back ground of the zombie graphic novel he had chosen, and the two got to reading right away. Very soon, their performances became too loud, and they began laughing so hard they cried. It wasn't long before they were bothering the few people who were in their vicinity.

Unbeknownst to them, Cord had arrived and sat on the floor a few rows away listening to their playful time together. He stayed there until they finished, and as they left, he watched them walk to the steps with Colton's arm tight around her shoulders and hers holding his waist. They said they were going home.

He loves her too. He definitely loves her too. The first time I saw her, I was afraid I'd scare her away and I have. I'm not sure how to handle this though. Seeing her with another guy was my greatest fear, until I saw her with my brother.

Chapter 31

Hope shooed Colton away after they returned to her apartment. She had not been alone that entire week and she really needed her home to herself. It was still early when they arrived so she didn't even let Colton in the door. He didn't mind, he wanted to go out with his friends again that night anyway. He told Hope he didn't plan on going to church the next morning since he knew he'd probably be out late.

Hope closed her door and said a prayer of gratitude for the silence. After brewing a pot of coffee, she sipped, read, and nibbled on her favorite cookies. With no new books checked out that night, she skimmed through some fashion magazines while listening to her playlist.

Around eleven, she turned off all of her lights and got ready for bed. The coffee was beginning to seem like a mistake. Hope was wide awake as she lay in bed. *Now what am I going to do? I've read everything in my apartment, and I am NOT going to study.*

When she turned the lamp on, she rested her head looking at her photo of Evan. *Were you real? How can anyone as perfect as you ever have been real?*

Instead of crying, Hope opened her nightstand drawer and took out her Bible. *I haven't read this in a while.* Not sure where to start, she turned to a marked page and slipped the bookmark out. The highlighted verses were about grape vines being pruned. Placing her opened Bible on her chest, she wondered what the message was for her at that time. She looked over at the photo again, and the bookmark caught her eye. There was writing on it. "Don't waste your life. Don't waste your time. You were created to bear much fruit. Trust God when he prunes what holds you back from fulfilling His purpose for you." *I love you, Evan.*

Love and gratitude abounded in her.

"Evan, you were a single root in my life that was nourished. Then you grew, and as you grew, your influence on who I am grew. We strengthened together and we became beautiful, until one day, the gardener pruned you. Your vine was cut so mine could flourish and bear fruit. I promise I won't let your life be a waste and I promise I won't let my life be a waste. I am who I am because you were a part of me and will always be a part of me. I'll try not to disappoint you. All I have now is because you loved me enough to send me out to the world. I would have never left you. So thank you for making sure I continued my path forward."

Hope was tired. She finally slept.

* * *

Sunday morning, Cord sat in the same place at church where he had been sitting since the day he met Hope: center row, right side, aisle seat. Every few minutes he watched over his shoulder for her to enter, until he gave up. He focused his eyes forward, though his attention was elsewhere.

Just prior to the commencement of the service, someone bumped his hip and shoulder simultaneously as they took their seat. He looked immediately to his bold neighbor and was shocked to see Kendal sitting there with the sweetest smile he'd ever seen from her.

She whispered in his ear, "Cord, let's try this again and let's start it right here today." His reply was a simple nod accompanied by a half smile.

After the week and weekend Hope had with and without Cord, she was ready to face him and repair the damage she had done to their relationship. She was confident he'd be at church that morning.

Although it had snowed a few times already, the sidewalks were clear so Hope decided to wear a long fitted sweater with leggings, and as usual, one of her many pairs of high-heeled boots. Once she was dressed, she readied herself to face a new beginning. Before she left for church, Hope stopped at the photo beside her bed. She picked it up and said, "Evan, I hope I make you proud. I hope my life counts. I hope the part of you that I carry forever makes your life count. You are the *only* reason I ever found him. Thank you." She blew a kiss to the sky, kissed the picture, then placed it back in her dresser drawer away from her bed.

When Hope arrived, she walked confidently into church with her head held high and her back straight. She saw him and paused in the middle of the aisle. For some reason, from the first night he spoke to her, she couldn't help but think, *There it is, the back of his head. I'm going to marry that man someday.* Then she thought, *Keep moving Hope, you're almost there.* With a small pep talk and the knowledge in her heart that this was right, she slowly walked down the aisle.

The worship leader called the congregation to their feet and the band began playing. Watchful and optimistic, Hope continued her careful stride to Cord. When only a few remaining feet separated them, a woman slipped her arm through his and rested her head on his shoulder. His left hand moved from its hold on the pew in front of him, to the back of her hand. Hope slowly pivoted, retreated, and slid herself quickly into the back row, far left side of the church. With a lump in her throat and humility consuming her soul, she stared at the man she had just lost.

He took her back. He took her back. I am such an idiot to think he would want me. God, Evan, why did you let me think he was the one you chose for me?

Unable to truly focus on the sermon and equally unable to stand at the moment, Hope sat through the service not even aware of anything that was happening around her. Her body tried to wait patiently for the closing hymn to begin, but it was no use. Wanting to be the first one out of the building that day, she listened to her heart.

"Get up and face every day even if it's just to see what's going to happen next. Hope, it's time to get up," he would say to her.

She nodded imagining Evan's 'you're going to be okay' facial expression.

"I see your future and it's beautiful, Hope," he would say next, pulling a rogue strand of hair from her face so he could see her eyes and force her to smile.

"Yes, it is," she whispered.

Hope labored an upright stance. Then, much like a zombie, she turned, exited the sanctuary and proceeded through the narthex hearing only a high, piercing, ringing in her ears. With her head down, she walked somberly through the doors and out into a few inches of freshly accumulated snow.

The brisk air lifted her chin and awakened her to reality. Hope was alive. She was feeling pain. She was feeling cold. She was feeling sadness. And... she was feeling scared. That morning, not wearing Colton's coat had been an oversight, not checking the weather app had been a mistake, and not wearing more sensible shoes had just become her biggest regret.

The snow was coming down in such masses that it was blinding and already collecting on her black garment. With a hurt heart, a cold body, and a terror of injury eating away at her, before proceeding, Hope mumbled, "This is the first day of the rest of your life Harmony Hope Hanover. You promised you'd make it count. He'd give anything to be here with you. He dreamed of the snow. He begged and prayed for snow. Be grateful. And as for Cord, well you are no worse off right now than you were an hour ago. He's going to have an amazing life. Keep going Harmony Hope. Go find your path."

Hope tightened her legs in preparation for the slippery descent down the fifteen concrete, un-shoveled, snow covered steps. She reached for the railing with her left hand and a man's hand clasped her waist and right elbow in the exact same instant.

"I've got you. I'm here."

Startled and gaping, Hope looked to her right.

Cord added, "I'm sorry he's gone, but I'm here. And Hope, I plan on *us* having an amazing life."

Nothing existed in the world apart from his crystal, clear, blue eyes and his voice. After a moment, Hope released the railing and pressed her left hand to his chest. She looked up to him and with no remorse, she asked, "Where's your girlfriend, Cord?"

He replied with an almost goofy grin, "She's in my arms."

"But I saw you sitting with her; you took her hand."

"You didn't watch quite long enough. I took her hand so I could remove it from my arm. Only two women are allowed to touch me like that, you and my mother."

Speechless and elated, Hope nodded and jumped into his embrace. Cord held her with his face nuzzled to her neck. He inhaled her sweet, mild perfume and squeezed her tightly.

When he placed her onto her feet he said, "I'd like to take you home with me miss, but I think it would be best if you told me what I am actually supposed to be calling you. What *is* your name?"

Hope's expression was one of joy, but also of guilt. She replied, "My name is Harmony Hope Hanover."

"Okay. I like it. What do I call you?"

"Hope."

"What did Evan call you?"

"Hope," she replied with confidence and relief. Then she asked, "Are you angry with me Cord?"

"Well, I have a lot of questions, all of which you better answer, but I'm not angry. I just have a lot of catching up to do. You already know everything about me because you've been posing as a double agent for months. Now it's my turn to get everything out of you. I'll play fair though and you better too from here on out."

"I promise. I'll tell you anything and everything you want to know."

Cord kissed her.

When they finally separated, he took one step down and said, "Hop on. I have a feeling carrying you will be easier than guiding you when those turn into ice skates. I also don't want to risk you taking me down with you when you do slip in those shoes."

Once again Hope had a view of the back of Cord's head. She paused before jumping onto his back and kissed his dark brown hair.

"What'd you do that for?" he asked laughing.

"I'll tell you someday," she answered.

Cord jerked his head straining to look at Hope over his shoulder and he said, "Oh no! You promised you'd answer my questions, Hope."

"Ugh! Fine! I kissed the back of your head because the very first time I saw it here at church, I said to myself, 'I should marry this guy some day.' Satisfied?"

"You decided you wanted to marry me two months ago because you liked the back of my head?"

"Yes. Don't make fun. You forced me to tell you."

"Are you some sort of a freak?"

"Sometimes. Definitely sometimes."

"Good! Normal is boring."

Reaching the sidewalk, Cord lowered Hope to her feet. When he turned to offer her his arm, he noticed she was being covered with flakes and she was shivering. "Still no coat, Babe?"

"Almost."

"It's November in Idaho, Hope. You need to stop messing around and get a coat."

"I see that now. I guess I'll go shopping and settle for a different one."

"*We'll* get you one." Cord took his jacket off and held it for her to slip onto her petite body. It was warm inside so she cuddled it. He loved watching her every move as he walked her to her car.

"I'll meet you at your house."

When he closed the door, she drove away.

Once her car was safely back in her driveway, Hope didn't go inside to change. She didn't want to miss a single second of time with her boyfriend. She shuffled from her car to his and was grateful her seat was already warmed as she sat.

"To my house?"

"Definitely," she replied.

Their fingers locked.

Inside his garage, before they got out he said to her, "Hope, second question." She nodded in approval. He continued, "Can you do me a favor?"

"Of course, anything."

Cord looked serious so Hope knew his next statement was going to be in reference to her not telling him she was Harmony. She waited while he seemed to be compiling his words into a concise and gentle statement. She watched with nervous anticipation.

He finally said, "Hope, please don't ever pretend to be someone else with me again." He paused and before she could offer a reply, he added, "And please don't ever expect me to be someone else."

Hope could see how deeply she had hurt Cord by not being honest and forthcoming with him from the start. The sadness in his eyes caused more pain than she had felt in a long time. She leaned her head onto his shoulder while she gripped his upper arm with both of her hands. She knew she was beyond blessed that this man was willing to not only forgive her, but also accept her and still love her.

Cord stroked her long soft hair as he whispered, "I don't want you to speak or apologize or try to explain yourself. Just know, I want us to have a fresh start." She nodded while his lips rested beside her ear.

When Hope was able to pull herself together, with a small weight of her guilt lifted, the two stepped out of his car and walked hand in hand into his house. As soon as Cord closed the door behind them, he released her and went straight to his bedroom. Hope thought it a bit odd since he left the room so hurriedly, but she stood in place awaiting his return.

A few seconds later, Cord emerged with his hands hidden awkwardly behind his back. Expressionless, he stepped close to Hope and kissed her very gently. He then moved his arms between them and handed her a gift. Inside was the winter coat she had been visiting.

"How'd you know?" she asked excitedly.

"Colton took me to visit your coat too? I went straight to the store when I left your apartment yesterday morning and bought it." She slid his jacket down her arms, and he held her new one out for her to try on for the hundredth time. "You chose a good one Hope. The royal blue looks great on you. I have one more thing in the bag for you too."

Hope had been so excited about the first gift she didn't notice another. She reached in and pulled out an old sweatshirt.

"What's this?" she laughed.

Very lovingly he explained, "I'd prefer it if you'd wear my baggy clothes from now on. Will you agree to that?"

Maintaining a serious countenance, Hope took the bag and shirt from Cord. While backing away from him, she took off her coat. Dramatically, she dropped everything on the ground leaving him confused and concerned. When she bent slightly at her waist, he thought she would retrieve them but instead, she unzipped her boots and slipped them off of her feet.

A smile appeared on her face as she reached for his hand. He lifted his and let her take ahold. Hope stepped on the sweatshirt and walked Cord to his bedroom. Happily following, he struggled to seem overly anxious. Once Hope had him positioned beside his bed, she pushed him onto his back and crawled teasingly over him and to his side. An expression of pure elation could not be contained by either of them. Cord curiously allowed Hope to continue. Their eyes remained locked as she slid her foot along the outside of his leg until her knee was bent and draped over his waist. He held her hip, then lower. She helped him find every place that she wanted him to enjoy. Pulling her closer and closer, he marveled at how much he enjoyed her comfort in the privacy of their relationship.

Hope's hands controlled him, and with their lips just barely touching and teases for more not stopping, she said, "Are you sure you want me in your baggy clothes?"

Cord didn't speak. He smiled and wisely shook his head.

She released a breathy moan.

As she continued caressing his outer thigh with her foot, she offered, "Good, I didn't think you had given that much thought." Next she asked, "Do you want to ask me questions?" Again he smiled and wisely shook his head. Her soft and sultry reply, "Good, I didn't think you really felt like talking right now."

Hope had completely drawn him back to her. Lost in love, actual, deep, love, Cord gently rolled onto her. "I love you, *all* of you, Hope."

"I love all of you too, and I'm ready when you are for us to erase the last line."

"Very soon," he whispered.

Knowing she was now all his and no other gift would ever be more important or more valuable to him, Cord pressed a kiss to her and secured his place as the only man in her life. He became her forever and she became his.

Chapter 32

The man she was going to spend her life with was an organizer, a planner. Not one stitch of clothing was removed because he had already told his parents that they would be meeting for lunch at their house.

Lying across his bed, neither wanting to leave their place together, Hope asked him, "Cord, what do you want for us? What do you see?" The response she received was unexpected.

From his position on his back next to her, Cord turned onto his side and braced his head in his hand so he could see her face. Hope looked at him. He said, "I want to wake up to the sound of my baby crying with my wife next to me. I want my son on my shoulders. I want my little girl running around with pig tails in a pink dress. I want my boy's sticky lollipop drool on my hands. I want my daughter's gum in my hair. I want slobbery kisses. I want all of these things, and I want them with you and only you."

Absolutely no words formed, only images of everything he had just said to her. Hope had never imagined her life with children of her own in it. Never. Her dreams always ended with her simply in someone's arms. Her mind reviewed his shared visions for their life, not lives, but life. She smiled, grinned, was thrilled. She asked, "You think my kisses are slobbery?"

Cord dropped onto his back, closed his eyes and roared out a deep laugh. "Oh my gawd! And that is why I want every single memory from two months ago to eternity to have you in it!" When he was able to answer her, he said, "I like your kisses just the way they are. The only thing I'd change is the amount. I definitely need way more."

"Thanks for showing me a future with hope," she said softly.

"Yeah. We have both of those." Cord lay there quietly and then asked, "Will you tell me either your beginning or your end? Can you do that?"

Knowing he was ready to know everything about Evan, and knowing beyond any doubt that Cord was her forever, Hope would never withhold anything from him again. "Sure Cord. How about if I tell you our beginning?"

"Okay. Then we'll go see my family." He looked at her, "Will you tell me another story tonight?"

"Yep. If you want me to."

"Yes. I want to know him, so I can know you too." Cord was actually excited to hear all about her past. He couldn't wait to know everything there possibly was to know about Harmony Hope Hanover.

* * *

Mr. and Mrs. Cooley, Cal and Catherine, as it turned out, drew Hope in and made her part of their lives too. Cord's parents didn't even know that they had had a rough start to their relationship. They also had no idea that Colton had been in the middle of everything they were going through almost from the very beginning.

Sunday lunch at their house was filled with joy and it reminded Hope of what is was like to be a part of a family again. She had missed spending every single Sunday of her life with a big group of relatives at Grandma's house. Someday soon, this was going to be where her children played and spent Sundays with their Grandma. That thought would have never crossed her mind if Cord hadn't planted it there.

Colton had showed up looking grungy, though Hope was proud that his hair was frozen. That meant he had bathed and washed all of the booze from his pores. They all were helping his mom clear the table when Colton casually mentioned, "Hope, I need your key to the apartment."

She heard his verbiage and retorted, "You really think I am just going to hand you the key to *my* apartment?"

He whispered, "It's our apartment." Cord heard and shook his head while rolling his eyes. Then louder Colton said, "and no, I don't. I'm just waiting to see if I'm going to have to pull it out of my eye, ear, nose, or jugular." Their parents found the request odd but stayed out of it.

Hope scolded, "Colton, it better be clean when I get home in a little while. Pick up all of your crap and either take it home or hang it in the closet."

"I'll hang it. I'm sure I'll need it there."

"Hope! Are you listening to your conversation with him?" Cord finally intervened.

She wasn't insecure nor worried. "Yes! I am. He has a mess to clean up and he better do it before he goes anywhere today."

Although Cord knew he had nothing to worry about with those two, he leaned down to Hope, and speaking at a level so Colton could hear him too, he pointed back and forth between them and said, "I think it's time to reconsider your living arrangements."

They both mostly ignored him and Colton repeated his request. "Hope, I'm ready. The key?"

She looked around and saw a printer nearby. "Cal, may I have a piece of paper?"

"Of course." Mr. Cooley tried to look like he was minding his own business in this exchange between the two.

Hope walked over, took a piece of paper from the printer and wadded her entire keychain up in it. *It needs weight*, she thought. "Outside Colton. If you can catch it, you can keep it."

"Ooo! The car too?"

"No!" she snapped.

They all went out the front door to the snowy front yard. Colton knew Hope so well, he knew to put a distance between them. While they were spacing themselves, she bent down and packed a bit of snow around the paper ball.

"That's no fair! That's gonna hurt!"

"Then say goodbye to three pairs of your favorite stinky

318

shoes and all of your favorite shirts and jeans because if they aren't picked up when I get home, I am burning them!"

"Never mind. I can take it. I'm ready." Colton squatted like a catcher and held is hands in front of him.

Everyone laughed at the two best buddies.

Hope turned her right shoulder to him, prepped and threw the snowball covered keys as hard and direct as she could. Terrified of her arm, Colton jumped out of the way landing on his side in the snow while the bullet pounded right into Cord's driver's side door.

"Hope! What the hell!?" Cord yelled as he ran to check on his car.

She screamed and Colton laughed. Cal and Catherine gaped, though seriously suppressing laughter themselves.

Cord wiped and polished, wiped and polished, searching desperately for any signs of damage. Hope ran to him, draped over his back and shoulders and begged for forgiveness, though laughing through every gasp.

"I'm so sorry!" she kept repeating.

"Yeah, you sound sorry, Babe!" He giggled at her. "You're lucky it's okay or we were going to take that coat back and use the money to fix my car door."

"What? No way! That was a gift. It's mine. You can't have it back."

Cord rolled his eyes and held her in his arms. "You're right. I wouldn't do that. Maybe this is practice for handling those kids we're going to have someday."

While they were settling their minor disagreement, Colton had run over, grabbed and unwrapped the keys. He jingled them at Hope once he was free and clear of her reach, and he called out to her, "Your dad would be so proud to know that you inherited his wicked left pitching arm."

"He knows, Colton, but there's not much need for a woman in the majors yet."

"Back inside, Babe, it's cold out here." Cord hugged her shoulders.

"Bye, Colton. Do some dishes too and maybe scrub the tub and toilet. There's no freeloading in my house!"

"Our house, Hope!" Colton said shuffling through the snow to his car.

"Hope, love of my life, you are not living with my brother in that tiny apartment."

"I know. I'd kill him. He can have it. Garrett already loves him. Also, I think he's my brother too right?"

Cord nodded and he knew what she meant by that statement. He already had a plan in the works, and he was thrilled that she was ready to start moving every day of their present toward their future.

* * *

The apartment was spotless when Hope and Cord arrived to pack some of her things for the night. Colton had left a note that read: "You keep storing your stuff in my apartment and I'm going to have to charge you rent. No freeloading!"

"Truth time."

"Okay," she agreed.

"How close did y'all get this past week without me in between you?"

"Promise me Hope, promise me this is the one lie you will tell. No one, especially Cord, needs to know this happened." Colton's pleading pierced her thoughts.

Instead of answering him, she asked, "When did you realize that I am Harmony?"

"I think I knew it a bit sooner, but I was absolutely certain when you showed up at the table next to me in the coffee shop. I knew you had been testing me all along. I knew your name had come from your dad. I knew you always tuck your hands in your sleeves when you cry. I knew you were trying to tell me about Evan without upsetting me. And I knew you were trying to get information about Kendal without looking jealous. I recognized the backpack. I had a pretty strong feeling it was you when Colton came right back out of the library without even talking to you. Finally, the dead give away was your obsession with the book. How'd it end by the way?"

Hope thought for a quick moment and said, "Well, Princess Vega's young wizard love interest was really her childhood best friend. Deneb wasn't an old man all along. He had cast a spell on Vega to make her forget him because Cygnus had told him he had a different plan for her. Deneb's purpose was to propel her into the life she was meant to have with the prince. The key that needed to be released in the princess's heart was her attachment to the young wizard, and the reason only Deneb could release it was because he alone brewed the spell and owned the anecdote. He kept refusing to use it throughout the book because he hoped that he himself could keep Princess Vega, but they had to be separated to work together for the good of the world. Deneb knew he was always meant to simply be the light behind her that made her shine brightly. Her impenetrable light was what killed the evil Queen Lyra, the queen of all fears and darkness. In the end, the young wizard stood behind Princess Vega giving her the light that drew the prince to her side. Prince Alastair realized he never needed to be jealous of the wizard. He was grateful to the wizard for sending her forth and loving her enough to deliver her to him. The prince and princess were the ones meant to conquer the world together and try to help fulfill the ultimate plans Cygnus had for all of the people of his realm. There are heroes and there are those who support the heroes. One isn't independent of the other. All have the single goal of defeating the villains who reign with fear and darkness."

"Huh? So you were actually reading a book that whole time?"

"Yes! Did you think I was faking it?"

"A little bit, yes," he replied honestly before asking, "Now, my brother?"

Hope didn't hesitate this time, "We kissed one time and I could only imagine it was you. We vowed to lie to you for the rest of our lives about it."

Cord nodded feeling surprised that nothing in him cared or was concerned. She had been his all along and he knew it would never happen again. He picked up her frilly over-night bag. "Let's go home."

They walked from her room toward the door and her painting caught his attention. "You chose the ocean, huh? Why's that?"

"I chose the ocean because from the moment I met you, my heart told me to plan my life here in the mountains. If I am going to live here, I wanted a bit of home to look at every day."

"It's perfect." Cord lifted it off of the easel. "Will you cover it? I don't want anything to happen to it. It's coming home with us."

Chapter 33

"Every decision is permanent now."

Each touch, kiss, look, and movement was different this time. Cord's only intention was to make sure Hope was prepared for what they were about to do. She compared the other times they were together to this one and she knew that even though they had thoroughly explored every part of one another, he had kept a distance. This time, as she lay there with him, she knew he had one goal, to make this as perfect for her as it could possibly be.

His whispers told her what he wanted, what he was going to do, and how much he loved her. His caresses guided her, instructed her, seduced her, and placed every part of her in positions that would ensure she was comfortable, ready and wanting. When Cord was certain Hope would never regret this and would only remember it as treasured, one more deep kiss was given from him and she became his, just as he also became hers.

Cord opened Hope's heart, mind and body to a new relationship, a unique one that was only between the two of them. They became, together, what is meant to be between two people so deeply in love.

In his arms, she lay quietly listening to his heart beat beneath his skin. "Are you okay?" he asked lovingly.

"Why wouldn't I be?"

"I just wanted to be certain you weren't having any regrets."

"None," she said softly.

"What are you thinking?" he asked as his finger tips continued rubbing her bare back from her neck to her waist.

"I'm wondering if there will ever be anything in my life again that I love more than feeling like this with you."

"There will be."

"You think?" She sounded naive and disappointed.

"Yes. I know, because this never ends. It continues to get better and better."

"That sounds great, but this one is special to me."

He suddenly realized that he wasn't thinking anymore about how important this one was to both of them. "I take it back. You're right. This will always be the best."

"So it is downhill from here?" She smiled but kept her face on his chest so he couldn't see it.

"I know you're smiling, Hope. I can feel every one of your muscles move."

Hope rested her chin on the back of her hand that was placed on him and she grinned. "I have a question?"

He raised his eyebrows letting her know he was attentive.

"Does life just go on from here? The world doesn't change?"

"My world changed. Your's didn't?"

"Well yes, but I mean, do I still have to go to work tomorrow?"

He laughed and his torso bounced so that she had to move off of him. He finally answered, "You do still have to go to work tomorrow, but we can do this whenever we want from now on. Well… except when we are at work!"

"You're right. We can't do this at work. It definitely took more than six minutes."

"I'm glad you noticed," he replied proudly placing himself gently on top of her again.

She pulled him to her for more kisses. "Do you want more yet, Cord?"

"Do you!?" His shock was evident.

"I do."

Out of the seven billion people on the planet, this is what it feels like to be the luckiest man in the world.

* * *

Hope never slept in her tiny apartment again and she never missed it. Cord waited until her parents visited at Thanksgiving to ask her to marry him. He had already reserved the church weeks earlier on the Sunday morning that she met his mom and dad.

During the week long holiday, Hope, her mom, and Catherine shopped for her honeymoon wardrobe. The wedding dress shopping was going to wait until they were all back in

North Carolina at Christmas. Hope wanted her Grandmas, her bridesmaids and Evan's mom with her for the dress selection.

Their wedding was planned for late April (after tax season) in Riverton at their home church, and a big reception was planned for the same week in her hometown. Everyone was happy with the arrangements, especially Cord, who had a lot of input in all of the details.

Christmas and New Year's came and went. Spring semester began. Cord was working twelve or more hours a day and Hope maintained her twelve hour a day schedule. They were living, sleeping, *not* sleeping very often, and waiting for their wedding date to arrive.

Valentine's Day, Hope and Cord cleared their schedules to be with one another; after all, this was their first Valentine's together. When she left work at three, he did the same. He got home just ahead of her and sat at the kitchen table decompressing and reading mindless garble online.

Hope walked in through the kitchen from the garage and went straight to Cord for an enticing kiss.

"Mmm…" He was enjoying her already and wanting to get started right then and there on the evening's activities.

She smiled and with her hands on his shoulders and her lips nibbling his in between each word, she said, "Remember a while back when you asked for some pamphlets from my office?"

The vision that appeared in his mind of the medical posters took him aback just a bit, but he let his body keep him focused on his soon to be wife. "Yeah babe. Why?"

More kisses… "I finally brought you some."

Deciding to turn the creepy images into flirting he asked, "Why? Are you not satisfied with the way I've navigated the territory? I'll gladly practice more if you think it'll help."

Hope laughed but stayed in contact for a few more moments. "Oh no, your skills have been spot on, Babe. All I can ask for is more." She stood up. "But in case you need more information, here." Hope tossed the brochures onto the table next to Cord's tablet and walked away.

He was not done with her, but he was going to play along. "Oh boy! I can't wait to read these." He joked as he picked one up. "This ought to be fun."

He opened the top one. Pause. Then he opened the next one. Longer pause. Then the third. Deep brow scrunch as he looked at Hope for clarification, unsure of what expression he should wear.

She grinned as she said, "You're having a baby, Cord. Don't grow your hair out, lollipops and gum will be much easier to remove if you keep it short."

"What? What! What do you mean? Are you okay? How do you feel?" He scooted his chair back and stepped to her grabbing her upper arms while offering a smile, then a worried expression, and that combination went on and on.

"I feel happy that my dress will still fit in two months at our wedding. If you wouldn't have already booked the church a few months ago, we'd be in a pickle."

"What do we do now?" he asked nervously.

She shrugged, "I'd like food and then, I guess we'll figure everything else out as we go. I'm just glad we get to learn how to do all of this together."

"But Hope, we're not married yet. Are you upset that we didn't do this right?"

"Well Cord, according to the test, we certainly didn't do it wrong." He smiled as she added, "Nothing we have done is wrong."

"Hope, we get to share our life with someone else."

"Yeah, and hopefully someone else after this one and at least one more someone else after that one."

"Three?" he asked with a grin.

"If not more. You know I always want *more*."

Her seductive eyes and tone left them with no time to relocate. The kitchen worked just fine for them.

www.ingramcontent.com/pod-product-compliance
Lightning Source LLC
Chambersburg PA
CBHW022027260626
47156CB00017B/423